CW01432315

HELLO HELLO
BY MANDIE
BEDSITT

Chapter 1

Gosh it was a hot day, thought Sarah, as she sank back into the deckchair. The sun was glowing bright overhead, casting no shadows on the beach. She could see her two young boys playing just by the water's edge a few feet away from her. They were intent in showing another boy their new Action Man toy boat. Ah, to be that age again, thought Sarah idly. No worries or fears or guilt, just totally fulfilled with playing.

She smiled indulgently. It really was a beautiful day, and she felt so lucky to be living on this little island in the English Channel, with it's golden sandy beaches just a few miles from her home in Seaview.

Sarah closed her eyes for a second, luxuriating in the heat of the sun, and then quickly opened them again, worried for a second that she would drop off to sleep. She then noticed that the water was coming a little nearer than she would like. The tide had obviously turned and was now coming in with gusto. She should move further back towards the cliffs before she got her toes wet. She sighed and got up, picked up the deckchair and walked back up the beach towards the bottom of the cliffs. She went back to collect the towels and bags, gathering everything up into her arms, and made the same journey again. She put the deckchair back up, and shook out the towels. Then she glanced up, checking where the boys were.

Where were the boys? She ran her eyes quickly over the water's edge. They had been there, right in front of her.

No wait, they were no longer there. Sarah's stomach lurched. Where were they? She quickly scanned the beach. No, she couldn't see them. Panic started to rise in her stomach.

She looked along the cliff edge. Maybe they had climbed the steps back to the car park and were playing a game over there, but no a quick scan didn't show any small boys. Her heart was in her mouth, and she started to feel sick.

Suddenly a cry came up and a woman ran to the water's edge. She was shouting and waving. Sarah ran to the woman, and cast her gaze to where she was pointing, about a hundred yards off shore, the other side of the breakwater. She could see three little shapes in a bright yellow dingy, rapidly being taken away from them, further out to sea.

The shapes were waving and shouting. "MUM!" "MUM!" "MUMMY!" Sarah made an attempt to run into the water, but the tide was too strong and it sucked at her, trying to pull her under. She could see dark water where the rip tide was running. She pulled herself back to the shore. It was no use: she would be sucked under.

The other woman, presumably the other boy's mother, also ran into the shallows, intent on swimming out to the disappearing dingy. "NO!" cried Sarah, trying to hold her back, "The tide is too strong." She cast her eye widely around, hoping to see a life buoy or something that might help her, but she could see nothing.

A man came running up to them. "What's happening?" he demanded. Both women pointed out to the disappearing shapes in the dinghy. He kicked off his flip flops and started to enter the water.

"NO!" cried Sarah, trying to pull him back as well, "There's a rip tide. You'll never reach them."

Another man came running up. He had been coming down the cliff steps from the car park when the woman had screamed out. "I've called the Coastguard," he said, "they're sending out the Air Sea Rescue. They won't be long. Don't worry." That's easy for you to say, thought Sarah, as she watched the dingy bounce around in the strong differing currents. She felt so helpless.

"SIT DOWN!" she shouted as she saw one of the figures try to stand up. "STAY THERE!" The mother of the other boy was sobbing next to her. Sarah reached out and put an arm around her shoulders. "It's OK," she soothed, although the last thing she felt was OK.

"Do you know whose boat it is?" she asked the gathering crowd.

"Yes it's ours," sobbed the woman, "I told Bobby, don't you dare go off in the boat on your own. I don't understand. He knows he's not allowed to take the boat into the water on his own."

The man who had called the Coastguard answered. "I don't think they deliberately took the boat out," he said, "I saw them playing in the boat but it was on the water's edge. I think the tide came in too quickly and they probably didn't notice until it was too late. The tide here is very strong and it comes in very quickly. I've been campaigning for notices to be put up, but the Council aren't interested."

He was interrupted further by the sound of screeching police cars from the top of the cliffs, and then the sound of shouting as a couple of policemen ran down the steps and across the beach to them.

"It's OK," shouted the first policeman, "Air Sea Rescue are on their way: they're just off of Portland. They'll be a couple of minutes. And the Inshore Lifeboat has been launched and should be here soon too. Where are the boys?" He scanned the sea, "Oh yes, well at least you can still see them. The tides here are vicious - I've known it to take seconds for dinghies to be swept right round the corner of the headland and on to the rocks."

Sarah heard the other boy's mother catch a sob. "That's helpful," she muttered in the direction of the policeman.

A small crowd had gathered now, and they all watched the dinghy getting smaller and smaller, all of them feeling helpless.

"Here's the lifeboat!" called out one of the policeman, pointing out to sea. And at the same time the sound of a helicopter could be heard, and seconds later its big red and white bulk was seen hovering over the now tiny dinghy.

Sarah and the crowd on the beach watched in awe as the boys were winched to safety, and the lifeboat hauled the dinghy on board. Sarah's boys looked so tiny dangling from the thin rescue wire, and Sarah held her hands together praying for their safety. Her heart was in her mouth, seeing the little figures disappearing into the open mouth of the helicopter.

And then it was over as quickly as it had begun. The policeman's radio crackled next to her. "They're safe," he said, "The helicopter is going to land on top of the cliffs so I'll give you a hand taking your stuff up to the car park, and then I'll need to ask a few questions."

Once up on the cliff tops Sarah held her breath again as the helicopter landed and three little figures came running out of it. "MUM! MUM!" called out Tom, her eldest, "We rode on the helichopper." He hugged her tightly.

"I know Sweetheart," she murmured hugging him back, and then welcomed her younger son, Alfie, into her arms.

"Come here, darling," she said giving him a big squeeze and picking him up. She pulled his little legs around her and propped him on her waist. She pushed his salted wind swept hair back, and wiped his tear stained face. She planted a kiss on his cheek. It tasted of salt. "Are you OK?" she asked him. He nodded and choked back a sob.

"He didn't like the chopper or the winch," Tom told her matter-of-factly. "I expect he didn't like the whole experience," said Sarah, "I can't think why you were in the dinghy."

"We were just playing," said Tom. Sarah decided this was not the time or place for remonstrations. She gathered the two boys to her and went to walk off.

"Just a minute," said the policeman who had helped her carry her things up the cliff steps. He had been talking to his colleague. "Have you been drinking?"

"What?" asked Sarah incredulously. Had she just heard him right? "Have you been drinking?" he repeated, his notepad and pen poised. "NO!" she snapped at him, and went to move away.

"I'm sorry," he said, "But I have to ask. Someone has reported that they saw you drinking wine on the beach." He saw her flushed face. "I know it's not illegal to drink on the beach, and you are over 18, but it's not wise to ….."

He tailed off as she angrily brushed passed him, and putting Alfie down, gathered up her bags and deckchair, dropping half of the contents of her picnic bag. "I. Have. Not. Been. Drinking." She said between gritted teeth. She stood up and faced the policeman. He was looking at his notepad uncomfortably. "Who said that? Tell me, who the hell said that?"

The policeman glanced up at her, and then unconsciously glanced over at the two ladies stood talking to another man with a notepad and a camera around his neck.

"Oh really?" Sarah said. "I haven't been drinking. I am a Primary School teacher. Do you think I would be that stupid?" She saw the two ladies and the man with the notepad look over at her, and then down on the ground in front of her. The ladies started nudging the man. He was scribbling furiously.

The policeman bent down and picked up an opened bottle of wine that had rolled out of her bag. It was nearly empty. He could see another bottle peeking out of the picnic bag. "It's elderflower cordial," explained Sarah, opening the bottle and thrusting it at the policeman. "Here, taste it," she said. "My mother makes it and thinks it's hilarious to put it in wine bottles." He sniffed and satisfied gave her back the bottle.

"Thanks," he said. "I have to check it out, you know, because they said you were giving it to the boys." "Well I was," said Sarah, "because it was cordial. Now if you have done I'd like to get the boys back home and settled. Alfie is a bit upset as you can imagine."

"Yes, yes of course," said the policeman, "but I will need to ask you a few more questions, so I'll call round later if that's OK."

He reached into his shirt breast pocket and brought out a calling card. "PC Ben Lewis. I have some paperwork to complete." He looked at her. She looked drained, he thought. "It won't take long but it's got to be done. What time is it now?" he looked at his wristwatch, "3pm, I'll call in about 5.30 if that's OK?"

Sarah sighed and nodded, taking his card. "If it needs to be done," she said, "So can I go now?" "Yes, just give me your address." He noted it down and smiled kindly at her. She scowled back at him.

Sarah walked over to her car just as the man with the notepad came over to her. "Hello," he said to Tom, "Wow that was an experience riding in that helicopter. Now what's your name sonny?"

"Er excuse me," said Sarah, standing between Tom and the man, "And exactly who are you?"

"I'm Nick Bell, reporter at the County Press," he pulled out a card from his pocket, "Just want some details for my report."

"Well you won't be getting any from my son," said Sarah, looking him in the eye, "Or me. Now if you'll excuse us I'd like to get my sons home."

"Just a couple of questions," persisted Nick, "Just to complete my report. The old ladies said you were drinking. Were you drunk on the beach in charge of your boys?" He looked at her expectantly.

"No I flipping well wasn't," said Sarah angrily, "How dare you! And if you print that I will take you to court." She opened the car boot and threw the beach things inside, then slammed the boot hard to emphasise her point.

The reporter backed away. "Just doing my job," he said.

"Well go and do it somewhere else," said Sarah, as she got the boys into the car.

"Is it true you're a teacher?" continued Nick. Sarah just glared at him as she got into the driver's seat, and slammed the door shut. As she drove away she saw that Nick was taking photos. Bloody cheek, she thought.

CHAPTER 2

As soon as Sarah got into her flat, she ran a bath for the boys, and then telephoned her best friend, Kate. They had known each other since school, and despite Kate living away from the Island whilst at university and then her subsequent first marriage, they had kept very close. Sarah was so glad that her friend was now back on the island with her new partner.

"Oh God it's been a terrible day," she burst out as soon as Kate answered the call and without waiting for an answer she quickly told her of the events. "God, hang on," said Kate, "I'm on my way." Kate lived not far away and was there in ten minutes.

It was nearly 5.30pm by the time Sarah and Kate had got the boys settled into their pyjamas and sat at the dining table with plates of chips and pizzas. Sarah heard the sound of a cork popping out of a bottle and the chink of glasses coming from the small kitchen.

"What are you doing?" she asked as Kate walked into the room with a glass of white wine in each hand. "That policeman's coming in a minute and he thinks I'm an alcoholic as it is."

"Well if you don't need it I certainly do," said Kate. "Anyway it's good for the shock." "I think that's tea," said Sarah, taking a glass from her friend and putting on to the table.

Just then there was a knock on the door, and through the big bay window Sarah could see a police car parked opposite the house. Oh great, she thought, Mrs Nosey downstairs will be having a field day. Kate had beaten her to the front door, and she showed the policeman into the living room. She had one of his cards in her hand.

"PC Benjamin Lewis," she announced, "Police Constable, Hampshire and Isle of Wight Constabulary," she read from the card. "Ben," Ben said, "Please call me Ben."

"Ben," repeated Kate with a bemused smile on her face. Sarah read the warnings and took the card from Kate with a look which said don't start. "Please sit down," she hesitated, "er... Ben."

Behind his back Kate was pulling faces at Sarah. He's cute, she was mouthing at her. Sarah mouthed 'fuck off' back and then realised Ben was watching her. "Sorry, Kate has to leave now. Would you like a cup of tea or .." she saw his eyes glance at the glass of wine on the coffee table, "or something else. Er coffee?"

Ben looked up at her. "No, thank you. I just want to run through this and go. You must be shattered. I don't want to hold you up for long."

He turned round to look at the boys. "How you doing boys?" he called across to them. "Mmm yeah," Tom shouted back, waving a fork full of chips at him, "We went in a chopper," he said. "Yes I know," said Ben.

"I'm going to drive a chopper when I'm 16," continued Tom, "and I'm going to swing down on that rope like that man did."

Sarah shushed him. "Eat your dinner," she said. Kate picked up her car keys with a loud jingle. "Well I'm just going to er leave you to it," she said looking pointedly at Ben.

"Yes, bye," said Sarah, waving over to her, "Thanks for coming. And thanks for the wine," she added as an after thought.

"Kate brought some wine," she explained to Ben with a wry smile after Kate had gone, "Thought I might need it, haha, said it's good for shock, but I said that's tea." She stopped. She realised she was gabbling. She sat on the settee opposite him.

Ben smiled at her kindly, and opened the file he was carrying. "Just some forms," he said, "all just routine." And he quickly, and as gently as he could, took her through them.

Fifteen minutes later he was finished. "Thank you for your co-operation," he said, "I think that's all for now, but there might be some follow up over the next week, but we have your details." He smiled at her and stood up.

"Right then boys, I bet you'll sleep well tonight. But try not to have nightmares." He noticed that little Alfie, at only 6 years old, was struggling to keep his eyes open. Sarah noticed too and went over to her son. "Come on my lovely," she said taking his hand and pulling him off the chair.

"Say goodbye to the policeman and let's get you into bed. I'll read you a story. Thank you PC, er Ben. I think I shall take Alfie straight to bed." "Sure," said Ben heading for the door, "No need to see me out, and thank you again."

Sarah heard the front door slam shut after the policeman as she tucked her little son into his bed. She had barely reached for his favourite Thomas the Tank Engine story before she could hear his gentle snores. She smiled to herself and planted a kiss on his cheek before quietly tip-toeing out.

"Right then Tom," she said as she entered the living room, expecting to see her other son still sat at the dining table, probably finishing off his brother's chips. But he was curled up on one of the settees, also gently snoring. She picked him up and carried him into the bedroom next to Alfie's and tucked him in, planting a kiss on his forehead.

Well, she thought as she entered the living room. That was easy. Normally the boys put up resistance going to bed, but it was still only 6pm, what should she do with the rest of her evening? She took a huge gulp out of the wine glass she had placed on the coffee table and then sat back into the settee. Within minutes she too was fast asleep.

CHAPTER 3

Ben clicked the send icon and shut the lid to his laptop. He had sent his reports for the day, including the one reporting the three boys in the dinghy rescue. He rubbed his eyes and picked up the glass beside him and put it to his lips. To his surprise it was empty. He stared at it for a minute, wondering where the alcohol had gone, then reached across his tiny kitchen and grabbed the brandy bottle. He poured a few millilitres into the glass, and looked at the amber liquid, and before he put the bottle back down he poured himself a decent amount. It would help him sleep if nothing else, he thought to himself.

It was a lovely night, so Ben headed for his tiny garden at the front of the cottage. From his position sat on the garden wall he could look up at the stars. The summer sun had set a couple of hours before and the sky was peppered with tiny lights twinkling away. He could hear his neighbours clanking and twittering, the sounds carrying on the night air, whirling all around him. They were comforting and he felt very fortunate.

Ben loved his little cottage. It was a couple of hundred years old, although no one was really sure of its age exactly. It was once part of a row of Fishermen's cottages, standing on the foreshore in the bay, surrounded by beach and countryside, but over the years the town had grown up around the three tiny cottages and they now found themselves at the back of a row of Victorian houses, totally hidden from the road, and only accessible through a path between the imposing town houses.

Ben took a sip of brandy and thought about the day's events. He had been investigating a burglary that morning, and then the rescue of the three boys in the afternoon. He took another sip and the image of the boys' mother came into view. He thought of her soft long blond hair and crystal clear blue eyes. She had looked drained, even when he saw her at her flat afterwards. He could understand her worry. That was a tricky piece of coastline, and he always wondered why kids were allowed to have dinghies. Actually why did anyone have dinghies? They were unpredictable and dangerous things. It was always a shame, he thought, that he always met the good-looking ones when he was on duty and they were in a scrape.

Ben thought that he had been single too long. He hadn't been very lucky in the love stakes. When he had first left home to go to Police College he had hitched up with a fellow police cadet. Donna had been forceful and domineering but he had admired her determination and drive. He felt she had what it took to become a first rate officer and he secretly hoped some of it would rub off on him. They had been together for over 5 years, but in the end she had ruined it. Apparently her willingness to do anything it took to be the best included shagging the Commissioner, in the men's toilets, as he had found out one day when he had walked in on them. He could not accept any excuses which was just as well as she offered none. It was over and Ben asked for a transfer to another division.

He was offered Diplomatic Protection, with the Met Police in London. It was a bit of a cushy number – he spent most of his time politely smoothing ruffled feathers when foreign diplomats in the UK did some misdemeanour, like parking in a disabled bay or stealing a few cigarettes. Occasionally he was invited to diplomatic receptions, and it was on an occasion like this that he had met Jennifer Fortescue Farqhar.

OK her name wasn't really Jennifer Fortescue Farqhar but it wasn't far off. Why did Foreign Office staff always have double barrelled names? Her friends told him she had been plain old Jenny Smith when she joined the Foreign Office as a secretary, but promotion and a transfer into the Diplomatic Service, particularly into Protocol Department, transformed her into Jennifer Pattison-Smythe – the Pattison being her mother's maiden name. They had been together for four years. He had thought the relationship had been going well. So they hadn't exactly talked of marriage, or even of the future, but he had imagined a continued life together. He knew she was looking for a foreign posting, and he had been quietly investigating police attaché positions at UK embassies overseas. Either that or he could take leave and become a househusband for a few years – he knew other policemen who had done this to follow their wives' careers.

Then one day he had come home from a five-day course to find the flat empty. That is empty of Jennifer's things. Everything was gone, not even a stray Tampax. Everything except for her liquor stash. That was decent of her to leave that. He had tried to phone her mobile but it went straight to voicemail. He had called her best friend. There had been a stilted and very awkward conversation in which her best friend explained that Jennifer had left on a posting – to Kazakhstan of all places. Ben was exceedingly hurt. He had been thinking of proposing to her, he had even spotted the perfect ring. Why had she left without saying anything?

"I don't know," said her friend, "I don't know what to say. I'm sorry." "Yep," said Ben, "so am I," and hung up. He immediately deleted Jennifer's number and her friend's, in fact all the numbers of all the friends they had known together. And then he made inroads into the left liquor.

It was after this he decided to return to the island. Declining to live with his mother he had found this little cottage and at first rented it before eventually persuading the owner to sell it to him. It was his mother's idea to hitch up with her friend's daughter. She was also back on the island after a failed marriage. A lucky escape she called it, before they were stupid enough to have kids. Egged on by his mum, he had invited her out for a drink, and they had spent a very pleasant evening telling each other their histories since leaving school. They had laughed and acknowledged they enjoyed each other's company.

They had sex on their second date. After the sex, wrapped together in the duvet, Sadie had made it very clear what she wanted from the relationship. She enjoyed his company, but she didn't want love. She wanted sex, easy going no strings attached sex. That is until either of them met someone else. They both wanted it, they both needed it, so why shouldn't they have it. She was very free in bed, willing to try new things and encouraging him to suggest some. He enjoyed their love-making, oh hang on, not love-making. She wouldn't want him to think of it as love-making. It was sex, and he enjoyed it. But he did feel on occasions he would like a little more. She admonished him when he had once suggested that love or affection came into the equation. "Don't start", she had said, scandalised at his voiced thoughts. "Don't ruin it." So he had never mentioned it again.

He thought of the beautiful woman on the beach with the long blonde hair and the sadness in her eyes. He had felt a strong urge to wipe her tears away, to gently cup her face in his hands and kiss the dry salty lips.

He threw the dregs of brandy across the lawn, and turned to go inside the house. I'll have to give Sadie a ring, he thought.

CHAPTER 4

It was a couple of days later, and the incident almost forgotten, except for Tom who now was in no doubt that he was going to fly a helicopter when he was 16, when the doorbell rang. It was early evening, teatime, and Sarah was clearing away the mess the boys had made from making home made burgers. Who is that? thought Sarah, mildly annoyed at the interruption. She heard a commotion from the dining table and realised that Alfie was about to make a beeline for the front door to open it. Sarah grabbed a tea towel to wipe her hands and made a dash to beat him.

"ALFIE!" she shouted as she tried to run in front of him, "I've told you before not to open the door on your own!" "It's a lady," said Alfie, seeing a shape through the stippled glass of the outer communal front door.

"Yes, right, now go and sit down, please, and finish your tea," Sarah commanded as she opened the door.

"Hello?" she asked when the door revealed a smiling, yet worn out looking lady in an aqua suit holding a file. Another file, thought Sarah, this was not good.

"Hello," smiled the lady holding out an ID card, "I'm Yasmine Collander, from the Social Services."

"Yes," Sarah politely smiled back but inside she could feel her heart pounding. As a single mum she dreaded Social Services. When her husband had literally run screaming from Alfie's delivery to his nubile nymph in Thailand with whom he had been having an affair, she had desperately tried to keep going. The boys had only been very small, Tom just 2, and with the help of her parents she had bravely carried on, working and providing a small but rain proof (and paid for) roof over their heads. Her husband did not and had not contributed a penny to their wellbeing, and she was past caring. The boys were hers, and this could not be good.

"Can I help you?" she asked the lady in the aqua suit.

"Are you Sarah Blake? Mrs Sarah Blake, and you have two little boys, Tom and Alfie?" asked Yasmine Collander, pleasantly. "Yes I am," said Sarah, she was nervous now. Yasmine smiled a reassuring smile at her.

"Good, may I come in?" She bent down to pick up a large bag bursting with more files, and behind her Sarah got a glimpse of Mrs Nosey's backside sticking out of the shrubbery, no doubt trying to catch every word, especially the words 'Social Services'.

"Yes, please come in," said Sarah, "Can I help carry your bag?" She took the heavy bag from Yasmine. "That's very kind," said Yasmine following her into the hallway.

"Hello young men," Yasmine addressed the boys as she entered the living room. Alfie was now sat back at the dining table, his half eaten hamburger being greedily eyed up by his brother, who was eagerly waiting for the moment Alfie would push it away. Sarah laughingly called Tom her Gannet, swooping in on any uneaten food, often before Alfie had the chance to declare himself full.

"Hello," the two boys chorused.

"What's that you two are eating?" asked Yasmine cheerily, peering at their plates. "Burger," stated Tom, "we made them ourselves," he continued proudly.

"You made them yourselves?" repeated Yasmine, with a slight question in her voice.

"Yes," confirmed Tom. Alfie vigorously nodded in agreement, "We have a plastic thing and we press the meat into it and it makes it all round and squidges out the side, and then Mummy cooks it. Today we added mushrooms and tomato ketchup to the meat." "Well that sounds absolutely delicious," said Yasmine appreciatively.

Mentally she made a note to herself to leave as soon as she was able. She had been sent to check up on a neglective mother who had been seen quaffing wine whilst her children played dangerously on a dinghy in a rip tide. Homemade burgers were not what she was expecting. She glanced at her watch and thought if she wrapped up the interview quickly she could get to the ironmongers in town before they closed. She had been after a washer for the kitchen tap for ages and now it was getting crucial.

She turned to Sarah and smiled at her. "So, I am here in response to the dinghy incident the other day. Just a routine check." "Oh," said Sarah tightly.

"Yes," continued Yasmine as she perched herself on the edge of one of the settees, "it was reported that you had been seen drinking, and with the fact that the children are so young we needed to check out your home situation. Now, the police took some details and I can see that you are living alone, and your husband no longer lives in the UK, or has any involvement with the boys." She looked at Sarah questioningly, her notes in her hand.

"For God's sake, I wasn't drinking alcohol," said Sarah exasperated. "It was elderflower cordial. As I explained to that policeman, my mother makes it herself and thinks putting it in wine bottles is a bit of a laugh. I showed it to him and he sniffed it and was satisfied." She went into the kitchen to pick up an offending bottle. "Look, you can taste it yourself."

Sarah picked up a spare glass from the kitchen unit, poured some of the liquid and proffered it to Yasmine. Yasmine took a sip. "My, that is lovely," she said, smacking her lips, "Your mother is good at this. So refreshing."

"Here, take the bottle," said Sarah, putting the cork back in, "Mum makes plenty for the summer."

"Thank you, I will if you don't mind," said Yasmine, taking the bottle and putting it into the side of her bulging bag.

"As I said, this is just a routine check. The reports are automatically passed over from the police to Social Services and we have to respond."

"Yes I understand," said Sarah politely but inside she was seething. It was that policeman and those interfering buggers on the beach that caused this visit. How dare they? She was proud of how she had been providing for the children. She was an attentive mother, always putting their needs first. This was a waste of everyone's time.

Yasmine obviously thought so too. She smiled at Sarah and closed her file, shoving it as far in to her bag as she could. "Well boys," she said addressing Tom and Alfie, "You are making me so hungry I am going home to find something for my tea. But I don't think it will be as good as your burgers."

She turned to address Sarah. "Thank you for your co-operation, Mrs Blake, it is much appreciated," she picked up her bag, "and thank your mum for the cordial. I shall enjoy that. Sorry to have bothered you. Have a lovely evening." She turned and headed for the door.

Outside Mrs Nosey was still in the shrubbery, with scissors in hand appearing to be pruning, but Sarah was aware that she had sprung quickly back from the bushes under Sarah's open bay window when they had opened the front door. A little too quickly, she thought. Had she been listening? Obviously she had because as soon as Yasmine had driven away Mrs Nosey was quizzing her.

"Did she say she was from Social Services?" she called out to Sarah before she had a chance to close the front door, "I thought I heard her say you had been drinking."

"No," called back Sarah, "You're mistaken. She wasn't from Social Services," she laughed dismissively, "I don't know where you got that from." And she shut the door firmly.

Clearing up the boy's tea things from the dining table she was really angry. It was that policeman. Oh he was Mr Charming to her face, yes I understand, oh your silly mother, no everything is ok. He hadn't meant any of it. As soon as he had got back to the office he had obviously reported her to the Social Services. Well she hoped she never saw him again. Cute indeed. He was a wolf in sheep's clothing, a snake in the grass. To think she had liked his kindly face and, for a few moments, just a very few, had imagined running her fingers through his dark hair. She mentally pulled herself up. Get a grip woman.

Taking the tea things into the kitchen she caught sight of PC Lewis's calling card stuck to the fridge door. She took it down, read it and then ripped it into tiny pieces. Feeling a little bit better she threw the bits into the kitchen bin, grabbed a wine glass, opened the fridge door and took out the bottle of wine Kate had opened the other night. Defiantly she poured herself a large glass and went to tell the boys it was nearly bath time.

CHAPTER 5

The next morning Sarah was sat at the dining table with her usual morning coffee, studying the Visitor Guide to Events. She wanted to do something with the boys that didn't involve water, or money. It was nearly the end of the summer holiday, there were only a couple of weeks left until the start of the new term and she was running out of ideas of how to keep the boys amused. At that moment she could hear them squealing from Alfie's bedroom. She suspected they might be having a pillow fight and she was in two minds whether she should go in and break it up before it ended in tears.

Just as she was about to get up to go into them, her mobile rang.

"Hello Headmistress," she said, noticing that the number was from her school.

"Hello Sarah," said the voice of Mrs Gilmore, Sarah's Boss, "If you are not doing anything this morning I would be grateful if you could spare me five minutes?"

"Well, yes," said Sarah hesitantly, and slightly puzzled, "I've got the boys so I shall just need to see if my mum can watch them." "Oh that's OK, Sarah," said Mrs Gilmore, "Bring them along with you. They can play in the library. What I have to say will only take a few minutes."

"Oh," said Sarah. She was feeling uneasy. "Is something wrong?" she asked.

"Nothing that can't be cleared up I'm sure," said the headmistress in her breezy dismissive tone, "I'll see you around 10." Oh dear, thought Sarah, that doesn't sound good. It was one thing being sent to the Headmistress's Office for smoking when you were 15, it was quite another matter when you were 37 and she was your boss. Sarah still felt that tingle of apprehension in the pit of her stomach.

On arriving at the school, Sarah left the boys playing happily in the Library, rolling around on the Quiet Play Area mat with their cars, making crashing noises. She walked the short distance to the Headmistress's Office. The door was open.

"Hello," she called out hesitantly, knocking the door slightly. Mrs Gilmore looked up from her work and smiled at Sarah. "Ah, Sarah. Thank you for coming in," she put her pen down and motioned to the chair in front of her desk. "Please sit down. Boys alright?"

"Yes thank you," said Sarah sitting down in the chair indicated, "They're playing cars in the Library." "Good, good," said Mrs Gilmore, smiling, "And none too worse for wear after their little escapade?" she asked.

"No, they seem fine. No nightmares or even mentioning it. Tom was fascinated by the helicopter and is now intent on being a pilot for Air Sea Rescue," Sarah laughed. "Oh bless him," said Mrs Gilmore.

"Now Sarah, I have to speak to you about this incident. I've had a rather alarming telephone call from one of our Governors." She picked up a piece of paper in front of her on which there was writing. "It seems there is a rumour going round that you were drunk on that beach whilst in charge of the children." She looked sternly over her reading spectacles at Sarah. She put the paper down and took them off.

"Oh for God's sake," muttered Sarah, "I wasn't drinking, Mrs Gilmore," said Sarah, a little exasperated. "Do you know I'm fed up with this. I've had the Social Services around too questioning me about this." Mrs Gilmore blanched. "Social Services," she repeated faintly.

"Oh nothing to worry about," said Sarah quickly, "Apparently they received a report from the Police that they have to check up on but she was satisfied I am a competent mother and my boys are well cared for."

"Well, yes, quite," said Mrs Gilmore, "But you know dear, you were seen drinking alcohol and I understand appearing quite drunk, and we just can't have that."

"I was not drinking alcohol," said Sarah emphatically, "Did you get that from the Police?" That bloody policeman again, she thought. He was intent on causing trouble. How many times does she have to deny it? "You know my mum makes Elderflower cordial," she explained.

"Oh yes my dear," said Mrs Gilmore, "and very nice it is too." She smiled at the memory of receiving a bottle of her own.

"Well, she puts it in wine bottles, doesn't she?" Sarah continued. Mrs Gilmore nodded. "Oh yes I seem to recall mine was in a wine bottle," she agreed.

"Well, that was what I was drinking. And I have no idea why anyone would say I appeared drunk. That just isn't true."

Mrs Gilmore smiled. "I knew there was a satisfactory explanation," she said, "I told the Governor myself that it was untrue. He heard it from a reporter who was at the scene. He was asked to comment. I told him you are one of our best teachers. Of course there would be no impropriety. You take the children's welfare very seriously." Sarah nodded but she was close to tears. But that bloody policeman. He must've passed her details to that reporter too. Ooh she could kill him!

The Headmistress got up and came round to the front of the desk. She bent down and put her arm around Sarah's shoulders and gave her a squeeze. "Now don't you worry about this," she reassured Sarah, "I shall telephone this reporter myself and give him a terse talking to. How dare he cast doubt on the respectability of my teachers. Tch, tch. Now you run along, my girl, and make sure you and the boys have some fun with the rest of your holiday."

Sarah stood up and the Headmistress touched her arm. "You know I'm not one for sentimentalities," she said, looking at Sarah, "But I would like to say how much I admire your strength and how well you are doing bringing up those boys on your own. They are a credit to you. And let's hope we can all forget this little incident."

Sarah smiled and brushed away a little tear that had escaped. She sniffed. "Thank you Mrs Gilmore," she said quietly, "I appreciate it."

"Right," said Mrs Gilmore, moving towards the door and signalling for Sarah to leave, "Away with you and see you in two weeks time." Sarah started to leave. "Oh, just one last thing," said the Headmistress, "It will feature in tomorrow's local rag so just be aware."

Sarah was not surprised. There was little enough news worthy that went on on the island anyway that even a sneeze was reported, so she had expected it. She nodded. "Thank you," she said and left.

CHAPTER 6

"Well, well you made the front page," said Sarah's father, gleefully waving the newspaper in his hand as he entered through the front door the next day.

"Oh George, be a bit more sensitive," said Sarah's mother, pushing him into the living room, "I'm sure Sarah just wants to forget about it now."

"Too right, Mum," said Sarah, giving both her mum and dad a quick peck on their cheeks.

"TOM! ALFIE!" called George, going to seek out his grandsons excitedly, "Look at your photos in the paper."

"Oh God," exclaimed Sarah, "Really, a photo? I bet I look awful."

"You are talking to that nice Policeman," said Maureen.

"He's not nice," said Sarah quickly, "Why does everyone keep saying he's nice? He shopped me to Social Services. I'm a file on their computer now." She pulled a face at her mother. "Every time anything happens they will pull up the file and know what an incompetent mother I am."

"Shush now dear, I'm sure that's not the case," said Maureen, going into the kitchen to put the kettle on.

"Look Mum," screamed Tom, crashing into the living room, "I'm in the photo." He showed his mother the front page of the local paper. And there was a photo of Sarah looking drawn and close to tears, with Alfie clinging on tightly to her and Tom stood talking to that policeman. THAT POLICEMAN. She could barely look at him.

"Very nice," she said non-committedly. She wondered what the report had said about her. "I suppose it says in there I was rolling around the beach drunk?" she asked her mother, following her into the kitchen.

"No dear," said her mother lining the teacups up on the work surface and spooning sugar into one of them, "Actually it hardly mentions you."

Well that was a relief, thought Sarah. So Mrs Gilmore's ticking off seemed to have worked. Knowing Mrs Gilmore, the reporter probably turned out to be an old pupil of hers.

"Can I have the picture, Granddad?" Tom asked. "Of course you can, Sunshine," said George, "Let's cut it out and you can keep it. I know, we can get a special book from Smiths and you can stick it in, and then you can keep all the photos of you from the newspaper as you get older." He beamed proudly at Tom.

"Can I Granddad?" said Tom beaming back.

"Well I'm sincerely hoping there won't be anymore incidences like that, Dad," said Sarah bringing him out a steaming mug of tea. George shrugged and smiled indulgently at his grandson.

CHAPTER 7

THAT POLICEMAN was also looking at the front page of the newspaper. His mate slapped him on the back and put down a steaming mug of coffee right on top of the photo.

"Stop gazing over that photo," he said, "You're either admiring your own profile or mooning over that woman," he laughed. Ben removed the cup of coffee from the paper, and placed it on the desk. He gave the photo one last look and then folded the paper up.

PC Paul Dorey grabbed the paper and shook it out. "She is a mighty fine piece," he said, pointing at Sarah, "even looking like she's been washed up." "Is she?" asked Ben trying to appear casual, "I never noticed."

Paul laughed. "No of course you didn't," he said, "Are you going to ask her out?" "I don't have her number," said Ben. "Oh doh," said Paul, getting up, "That's what records are for."

Ben looked at him aghast. "I can't use that to phone and ask her for a date." "No but you can phone her and ask her to meet you for some follow up questions," said Paul, grabbing the paper, "Mind if I borrow it?"

"If you're going where I think you are I don't want it back," said Ben, also getting up, "Now I've got to get round to that burglary. They've got some explaining to do. The insurance company said this is their third theft in eighteen months and they are thinking it might be an inside job. See you later."

All the way to the location of the burglary report Ben mulled over in his head the prospect of calling Sarah. But what would he say to her? He knew he had told her there might be more paperwork for the incident, but now that a few days had gone past he didn't want to dredge up what was after all an upsetting episode in her boys' lives. And he couldn't just come out and ask her for a date. For one that would be a gross misuse of personal data, and he could be reprimanded for it.

And then he thought, why bother? She probably wasn't interested in him anyway. He would probably just remind her of the incident. He should leave well alone.

Later that night, Ben was laid in Sadie's bed, after what had been a very energetic sex session. He was in a reflective mood, and Sadie noticed it.

 "What's wrong with you?" she asked him as she went in to her ensuite, "You've been strange all night."

"I've just been thinking," he said.

"Thinking?" commented Sadie, "That doesn't sound good. What have you been thinking about?" She came back into the room, wrapping a robe around her naked body and began picking up their clothes that were strewn over the floor.

"I was thinking we should get married," Ben said, pulling the covers back across his body, and snuggling under the duvet.

"We? Get married?" echoed Sadie, "Oh no Sunbeam, you're not pulling that one on me." She picked up Ben's underpants and threw them at him. "Get dressed and get out," she was cross with him, "We agreed. Fun sex, no strings, and certainly no marriage." She threw one of his shoes at him, and when he didn't move, its partner also came hurling across the bedroom towards him still lying in the bed.

"What?" he said, ducking further under the duvet away from the flying shoes, "I only said I think we should get married, I didn't say we had to."

"No, no you didn't but you mentioned the M word. Next you'll be talking about babies."

"Well now you mention it we're not getting any younger," Ben said.

"Oh boy are you so out of here," said Sadie, marching across the bedroom and pulling the duvet off of him. "If you weren't so adorable I could be really cross with you," she laughed and softened her tone, "but you really do have to go." He got up and put on his underpants and reached for his trousers that Sadie had thrown on to the bed.

"I thought I could stay?" Ben tried to pull a cute face with big eyes and curled down lip. Sadie laughed. "Not working," she said, "I have to get to Southampton early tomorrow and I don't want you under my feet when I'm trying to get ready. Now go." She was virtually pushing him out of the room.

"I feel like I'm being used as a sex toy," Ben moaned as Sadie escorted him down the stairs, still doing up his shirt buttons.

"You are," Sadie confirmed, "But you love it, so stop complaining." She opened the front door. "Geeze any man your age would be begging to get what you get. On tap, almost when you want it, no strings, certainly no marriage proposals or pregnancies. Oh and a free meal every now and again. No mate you can't have any complaints."

She pecked him on his cheek and pushed him out the front door. "Now go, I need my beauty sleep." And the next thing he found himself standing in the street with the door firmly closed behind him.

CHAPTER 8

It was a few weeks later, and the golden days of the summer holidays were firmly behind them when Sarah found herself standing in front of the mirror, pinning her hair up into a messy bun. She was wearing her favourite going-out dress, a now faded black velour dress which clung to her shapely body in such a way that it seemed to iron out all the bumpy bits. Sarah knew that it was really on its way out – some of the hem was beginning to fray, but she loved it so much she was loathe to bin it. It was now relegated to casual night out wear, and she usually teamed it with a faded demin jacket and pumps.

Although it was September it was still a warm evening, and Sarah had the big bay window open so a slight breeze could blow through the flat. She did wonder if the dress was a little too warm, she was feeling quite clammy, but she didn't want to change now.

As she applied her lipstick she burped. Eugh! There it was again, that slightly sickly feeling. She had been burping all afternoon, after she had eaten the seafood lasagne from the school canteen. And now she thought about it, her tummy was making churning noises. Oh please don't be ill now, she thought. She had been looking forward to the evening all week.

Kate's divorce had come through, and the girls had decided to celebrate. Kate deserved all the happiness she could get, and now the divorce had come through Sarah really hoped Kate and her boyfriend, Steve, could get on with the rest of their lives.

Sarah heard a car pull up outside. Running to the window she saw it was Steve and Kate. Steve was dropping them off in town, but he was then on duty as a bouncer at one of the night clubs over in Southampton and he had to get to Cowes for the late ferry service to take him there. It wasn't an ideal solution but they needed the money – divorce was a messy, and expensive business, and neither he nor Kate had come into the relationship with much money, so Steve took what jobs he could, working at a local leisure centre during the week, and at the clubs at the weekend. But they were blissfully happy, and Sarah was really pleased for them.

Sarah closed the window and went around switching off all the lights and securing the flat. The boys were staying the night at their Grandparents, which they often did at the weekend so Sarah could at least enjoy a bit of life, so she didn't have to worry about getting home for them tonight.

As she got into the back of the car, she leaned through the gap between the two front seats and grabbed Steve's head awkwardly, giving him a big juicy kiss on his cheek. "Congratulations!" she said.

Steve laughed and looked in the mirror to rub off the big red lipstick smudge he had on the side of his face. "Thank you," he said.

Kate was excited. "Steve and I are getting married," she said turning round to Sarah, "Will you be my Maid of Honour?"

"Oh you don't want an old hag like me," said Sarah, smoothing down her dress. " Yes I do, and so does Steve," Kate poked her boyfriend who was now concentrating on the road.

"What? Oh yes of course we do," he said. Sarah laughed, "OK then I would love to. When is it?" "Well we thought we might have it in the late Spring," said Kate, "but we haven't set a date yet."

She looked round at Sarah. "Are you OK?" she asked, suddenly concerned. Sarah had turned very pale, and Kate could see beads of sweat on her forehead. "Oh I think I may have a touch of food poisoning," Sarah answered, squirming a little in her seat, "I've got a bit of a tummy ache."

"Are you sure you're OK to come out?" asked Kate, now feeling concerned. "Oh God yes," said Sarah emphatically, "I've been looking forward to this all week. It's probably a dodgy prawn, it will pass I'm sure." She burped softly. "There," she said, "that feels better already."

By the time they got to the pub where they were meeting their other friends who were also celebrating Kate's divorce, Sarah was feeling quite ill, but she didn't want to spoil Kate's evening, so she didn't say anything. But Kate noticed.

"You are looking very green," she said to Sarah as they entered the pub, "Are you sure you want to go in?"

"Oh stop worrying about me," said Sarah opening the door, "And come on. I just need a drink." She marched into the pub and over to the girls who were already there.

The girls called out 'hello's' to Sarah and Kate, and then offered them each a glass of Prosecco. By now Sarah was feeling quite queasy but she still took the wine and managed a sip. She thought she felt a little better.

About an hour later it was clear that Sarah was not feeling any better. In fact she was most definitely feeling worse, but she really didn't want Kate to know. She had pains tearing across her stomach and she really wanted to be sick. The glass of wine she had drunk had not calmed her tummy in anyway, and in fact had made her feel worse. She felt faint as a pain ripped through her and the urge to retch was more than she could bear.

Kate caught sight of her friend just as Sarah toppled over, being sick at the same time. Unfortunately the involuntary retch sent the vomit projecting across the room, and over a group of lads standing next to them. In the next instant the pub was in total uproar, with the men shouting at Sarah, and her friends who were now trying to get Sarah to stand up and get to the toilet. Sarah could hear people shouting, but the sound came as if from far away. She was aware of people trying to make her stand up, but her legs didn't want to take her weight, and all she wanted to do was to be sick again. She also wanted to poo. Please don't let me poo here, was all she could think, as another uncontrollable spasm of vomiting took hold of her.

"GET HER OUT OF HERE!" the lads were shouting. "WE'RE TRYING TO!" Sarah's friends were shouting back at them. "SHE'S DRUNK!" others were shouting. "She's only had one," Kate kept saying, over and over again as she tried to get her friend to stand up.

The Manager came over. "I've called the police," he said.

"What have you done that for?" asked Kate, trying to get her arms under Sarah's to support her, "She needs an ambulance."

"She's paralytic," said the Manager, "You shouldn't let your friend get into that state. Now get out of my pub." "She's ill," emphasised Kate, "she's only had one drink." "Yeah yeah," said the Manager, "I've heard it all before."

Sarah managed to stand up, supported by Kate. "Isht OK," she said, "I can walk out." She held her head up and lurched forward. "God I feel awful," she said, pronouncing each word slowly and carefully. For some reason her words were slurred and the act of speaking was difficult.

Blue lights could be seen through the pub windows, announcing the arrival of the police. An officer walked in and the Manager went over to him. "Drunk as a skunk," he said, pointing out Sarah. Although Sarah had now stopped vomiting there was still mayhem with the lads still complaining about the sick everywhere and the girls trying to clear up the mess with paper towels from the toilet.

"For Chrissake," said Kate, "How many times do I have to say, she's ill." She looked imploringly at the officer. He seemed familiar but Kate was too distressed to make any connections at that moment. "I need to get her home."

The officer recognised Sarah immediately, and Sarah, through the fog of pain, recognised him. "Thwat policeman," she said quietly, "Shit."

She stood up straight and pushed Kate away, intending to walk unaided from the pub, but the moment she tried to take one step she started to keel over. Ben caught her and putting her arms over his shoulder, and motioning to Kate to do the same on Sarah's other side, between the two of them they carried her to the door.

The manager followed them. "I shall be wanting to press charges," he said, "so make sure you take her details. Someone has to pay for this mess. I'll have to get professional cleaners in." "Yeah, yeah," said Kate, "now if you don't mind I need to get my friend home."

"You need to get her some professional help," continued the Manager, "Getting drunk like that so early in the evening, it's disgusting. I wouldn't have served her had I known the state she was in."

Kate glared at him over her shoulder. "She's ill," she said again through gritted teeth. "She sure is," agreed the Manager.

Between the two of them they carried Sarah to the police car parked outside and deposited her onto the back seat. Kate walked around the car and got into it from the other side.

Ben turned to the Manager. "I'll deal with her and then I'll come back for a statement," he said.

"OK, well, we're pretty busy at the moment," said the Manager, "I'll get this cleaned up. But tell her she's barred." He nodded over to the occupants in the back seat, "And her friend too."

Ben nodded, and got into the driver's seat of the police car. "Can we hurry please," Kate begged, leaning over her friend who was once again doubled over in pain. "I think she needs to get home." "Sure," said Ben, starting up the engine and pulling off.

They hadn't got very far when Kate was screaming "PULL OVER! PULL OVER!" Ben obliged, pulling into the kerb. Sarah opened the back door and was violently sick into the gully. "Oh, pleethe, jusht take me home," she begged when the spasm has passed. She was aware that her tongue had swollen, making it difficult to speak.

Luckily it didn't take long to get to Sarah's house, as it was only a couple of miles from the town. Ben helped Kate get Sarah out of the car, and then he picked her up into his arms and carried her into the flat. Kate indicated Sarah's room, and he laid her gently on the bed. She looked terrible.

"I'm not drunk," she mumbled. "No I know," said Ben, wanting to reach down and brush back the sweat sodden wisps of hair from her face. Kate came in with a bowl of warm water, and a flannel and towel and started to wash Sarah's face. She had also brought in a bucket in case there were any more vomiting episodes.

"It's food poisoning," Kate explained, now recognising Ben, "she shouldn't have gone out, but then Sarah does of lot of things she shouldn't do." She laughed softly. "She can be very stubborn," she said.

"I am getting that impression," said Ben.

Sarah sat up as another spasm tore through her but this time she didn't feel sick. "I need a poo," she mumbled as she stumbled off to the bathroom.

"Do you want me to come with you?" asked Kate as Sarah closed the door. "No," they could just about hear Sarah's muffled voice.

"OK, but don't lock the door in case you feel faint, and give me a shout if you need anything," Kate called back through the closed door.

"Do you need me for anything else?" asked Ben as he and Kate made their way into the living room. "No, thank you," said Kate, "It seems like the food poisoning is passing through now. I think she's over the worst of it."

"OK," he reached into the inside breast pocket of his jacket. "Here's my card. If you need anything, anything at all, call me. Doesn't matter what time," he gave Kate the card.

"I hope she's feeling better tomorrow," he said turning to the door, "I'll go and sort out the Manager of the pub. I'll explain everything, he has insurance for this type of thing." "Thank you," said Kate opening the door for him, "You are very kind." And she meant it. He has lovely eyes, she thought as she said goodnight to him and closed the door.

Sarah stumbled out from the bathroom. She felt a little bit better now. The pains weren't so bad, just an ache, and she didn't feel so sickly. "Let's get you undressed," said Kate, "and then I think you had better try and get some sleep."

"He thinks I'm dwunk," moaned Sarah as Kate helped her pull off her dress. "No he doesn't," said Kate, "he knows you're sick. He's going to talk to the Manager."

"Humph, fat lot that will do," Sarah mumbled, "I heard the Manager shaying we were banned." She gave a wry smile. "Another tick in the box."

Kate smiled too. "Yep never been banned before," she said, pulling back the sheets for Sarah. "Hop in Lovely, and get some rest. I'll give my mum and your mum a ring and let them know I'm staying tonight. If you need anything just give me a shout.' She wrapped the duvet around her best friend and gave her a peck on the forehead. "Night night Sleeping Beauty," she said softly because Sarah was already snoring gently.

CHAPTER be

The next morning Sarah was laid on one of the settees, wrapped in a duvet and being administered to with strange concoctions by her mother, Maureen, who was convinced that drinking honey and lime juice and sucking on mints were good remedies for food poisoning. Sarah felt absolutely washed out. Her sleep had been punctuated with bouts of tummy ache, although she hadn't been sick again.

Her Mum had arrived first thing in the morning, leaving George at home to look after the boys. By this time Sarah had moved to the living room and was laid on the settee wrapped in a duvet. "Ben was really nice," Kate said to Sarah, "He left his card." "Yes, he's good at leaving his card," muttered Sarah, pulling a wry face.

"He said to call him if you needed help. He needn't have bothered," reminded Kate, "He could've just charged you with being drunk."

"But I wasn't drunk," said Sarah, "To be honest I didn't feel well from about the middle of the afternoon."

"You shouldn't have gone out," admonished Kate. "Well I know that now," said Sarah.

"Oh well, glad you are feeling a bit better. I'm going now. Steve will be getting back from work. You'll be well looked after by Mo," Kate smiled at Maureen and gave Sarah a peck on the cheek as she got up to go.

Sarah slept for a bit. She really was exhausted. When she awoke she found a steaming mug of mint tea in front of her on the coffee table. She felt a little sick at the sight of it. "Oooh Mum I don't think I can stomach any more mint tea," she said to Maureen when she came into the room to check on her daughter, "Even my farts smell like mint now."

"Well you are feeling better if you're making jokes," said Maureen, "Now get it down you and stop complaining. You know I have cancelled my hairdressing appointment for you, and you know how difficult it is to get an appointment there."

"I am very grateful for everything you do for me," said Sarah sipping the tea and wondering if she could somehow tip the remaining liquid into a plant pot without her mother noticing.

Just then there was a knock at the front door. "It's OK, I'll get it," said Maureen, striding towards the front door. Sarah laid back on her sick bed and pretended to be asleep. She didn't feel like seeing anyone, but luckily her mother was determined not to let anyone in to the house.

"Hello Officer," she could hear her mother through the open living room door. Oh God, no, not him, thought Sarah. He was really the last person she wanted to see. "Yes she is feeling much better, but she is sleeping now, so I don't really want to disturb her."

"No I understand," Ben said, "I was just calling round to see how she was and to let her know that I've spoken to the Manager of the bar. Sarah's friends had cleared up most of the debris, and the rest was taken care of by the cleaner this morning. In fact I think if the Manager is honest the place looks better than it did before. Maybe Mrs Blake did him a favour," he smiled, and then saw Maureen's stern face, "OK, perhaps not. Anyway he accepts that she was genuinely ill, and there are no charges, and I've no evidence that she was drunk: her friend said she'd only had one glass. So that's it."

"Well, there could no be other action," said Maureen, "My daughter wasn't drunk, in fact she actually hardly drinks alcohol." Sarah, still listening from her place on the settee, winced at this fib. She wasn't an alcoholic but she couldn't be described as hardly drinking.

Ben smiled, "Well, please pass the message on Mrs er erm Blake?" he asked questioningly.

"No," explained Maureen, "Blake is Sarah's EX husband's name," she emphasised the 'ex', causing Sarah to wince once again. This also was a fib as they weren't actually divorced. "Her maiden name is Dryer, and funny enough my maiden name was Dryer too."

"Oh yes, it's a big island name," said Ben, "Actually my mother's maiden name was Dryer also. From West Wight."

"Yes, my family came from West Wight originally." Maureen smiled, and then called out "HELLO! HOW ARE YOU?" She waved at a figure behind Ben, and turning round Ben could see Mrs Nosey from the other day peering out from behind a hedge, cutters in hand. "I wonder there is any hedge left to trim the amount of times I see that woman lurking in it," muttered Maureen to Ben.

"LOVELY DAY!" she called, smiling and waving to her.

"Well I best be off. Thank you Mrs Dryer," said Ben turning around. "Bye then," said Maureen, and turned and closed the door.

"What a lovely lad," she commented as she entered the living room. Sarah pulled a face.

"Yes, got nice eyes," she said sarcastically.

"He needn't have helped you," admonished Maureen, "You've been let off again." "What do you mean, again?" asked Sarah, "You make it sound like the dinghy incident was my fault."

"I'm just saying, he seems a nice lad," said Maureen again.

"Because his mother comes from West Wight?" asked Sarah scornfully. Maureen rolled her eyes at her daughter. "More mint tea?" she asked noticing Sarah's empty cup. "NO! Thank you mother. I think I am about done with mint tea." Sarah got up and followed her mother into the kitchen and put her arms around her in a hug. "I do fancy some tomato soup though," she said pecking Maureen on the cheek. Maureen laughed and squeezed her daughter back. "With some of that crusty bread?" Sarah asked hopefully.

"You are feeling better," Maureen said, getting a tin of soup out of the cupboard. "But he is a nice lad," she continued her thread, "And you could do worse."

"MUM!" warned Sarah, "Don't start. I'm not dating anyone. And I'm certainly not going to date that policeman so just leave it."

"Well, alright, but I'm just saying."

"Well don't. I'm going to have a shower." And Sarah hurried away quickly before her mother could continue her line of thought.

In the shower Sarah mulled over what her mother had said. He did have nice eyes, and he was cute and he had been very kind. To anyone else he was probably dating material, but not to her. She wasn't interested. She had had enough of men. She had only had a couple of one-night dates since her husband's departure six years ago. She was too busy with work and the bringing up of her sons, and men just complicated things. And then they left you. No, she wasn't interested. And that was final.

CHAPTER 10

Ben was cooking roast lamb in his tiny kitchen. He really enjoyed cooking but felt he didn't have much occasion to do it. But tonight he had invited Sadie round for dinner, so he was cooking roast lamb with all the trimmings, and he had made a Three Chocolate Mousse. He knew that Sadie loved chocolate.

He took the lamb out of the oven just as Sadie came in through the front porch. "Hello Love," she called as she took off her shoes and came through to the kitchen. She gave him a peck on the cheek as she deposited a bottle of cheap Champagne on to the worktop and put the other one into the fridge.

"Ooh that looks delicious," she said eyeing the lamb appreciatively, "I'm starving." One of the things Ben liked about Sadie was her love of food. She was one of those women who didn't really watch what they ate. Sadie would tuck into a plate full of strawberries and cream, followed by a few glasses of wine and not make any comment about diets or the need to go to the gym. But then she never put on any weight. He guessed she was just lucky.

"Need any help," she asked as she popped open the Champagne and grabbed a wine glass from the tiny two-man kitchen table that Ben had laid up ready for the meal. "No thanks," Ben said, "Just sit yourself down. It'll be ready in a minute. I'm just waiting for the Yorkshires to rise."

"And Yorkshire Puddings?" asked Sadie, "Wow you really do spoil me." Ben smiled at her as he started to carve up the lamb joint.

The meal was delicious. There was no doubt Ben could cook. "You will make someone a fine husband one day," commented Sadie, as she finished off the last of the chocolate mousse. Ben smiled. Just not you, he thought sadly.

Sadie poured the last of the champagne from the first bottle into her glass and went to get the other bottle from out of the fridge. "You remember I went to Southampton?" she asked Ben. He nodded. She popped open the Champagne and sat down.

"Well I got a job." "Well done," Ben said, raising his glass and chinking it against hers. "Yes," said Sadie. Ben's heart beat a bit faster. It was the way she had said yes and was now hesitating. Ben looked at her questioningly. He felt this was not altogether good news.

"It's a good job. It's working on a fleet of luxury cruise ships," she continued. Sadie loved travelling and in the past had had various positions on cruise ships. "It's the role of Customer Service, looking after the administrative needs of the passengers – you know – organising special requirements, getting help when they're sick – you know the type of thing. I'm really excited about it."

She took a sip of Champagne. Ben waited; he could feel there was more coming. "The only thing…. the only thing….," she hesitated for an instant, "is it's working out of Florida as it's an American company." Ben watched her without daring to breath. This was it. This was the Dear John moment. It was fun while it lasted but now it's over. "So I'm moving to Florida."

She reached across the table and took his hand. "I'm sorry," she said, looking at his sad face, "I'm really sorry. I don't do long distance relationships. And anyway I don't think that would be fair on either of us."

"So you're dumping me," Ben managed to croak, trying to make it sound like a joke. Suddenly his throat had tightened up.

"I wouldn't call it dumping," Sadie said, stroking his hand, "More taking our relationship down a peg. I'd like to keep in touch. I will be back from time to time. And you can come over and stay. I shan't be gone forever."

Ben tried to smile as he got up. He turned his back on her as he opened the tiny dishwasher and started loading it up with dirty plates and cutlery. He took a deep breath and then turned back to Sadie. "You'll send me postcards?" he asked her.

"Sure," said Sadie, drinking the last of the Champagne and coming over to him. "Leave that," she said, putting her arms around his shoulder and pulling him to her. He nestled his face against her soft neck and breathed in her fragrance. She smelt of sandalwood and cinnamon. He gently kissed her neck and he felt her shudder. Then he gently kissed her lips. She pulled away, and took his hand and without a word led him upstairs.

CHAPTER 11

"So that's it. It's over. I'm a single man again." Ben was in the pub with his mate, PC Paul Dorey, and he was recounting the night before. He raised his beer glass and downed the amber liquid. "Another?" he asked Paul, and motioned to the barman to refill their glasses. "And she said I would make someone a lovely husband, just not her."

Paul snorted. "Typical bloody woman," he said, "You're better off without them." "Why do I always meet the non marrying kind?" bemoaned Ben. "I mean there was Donna. Ambitious Donna." He took a sip of the refilled glass.

"Bit too ambitious though, wasn't she, old Donna?" commented Paul, "I mean shagging the Commissioner was taking ambition a bit too far." Ben nodded sadly.

"And that snotty cow, Pudgy-Smith, I mean was that your posh totty phase, mate?" Paul also took a glug of beer.

"At least she left me her liquor cabinet," commented Ben. Paul raised his glass. "Here's to Pudgy-Smith," he said before taking another large gulp.

"No I'm done with women," said Ben, staring into his beer. "I'm better off single," he said.

"You see I have a theory," said Paul, "the thing is, by the time you reach our age the best women are all married and knee deep in babies. All you're left with are the rejects."

"Exactly," agreed Ben.

"Mind you," continued Paul, "you couldn't describe that blond bit as a reject." Ben looked at him through blurred eyes.

"What blond bit?" he asked, although he had a good idea who Paul meant.

"That blond bit on the beach in the summer, with the two boys, Air Sea Rescue, that one."

"Oh her," said Ben, pretending he had only just realised who Paul meant.

"Yeah she was decent looking, but issues mate, big issues there." Paul nodded sagely, "Yeah probably right mate. We're better off single. 'Nother pint?"

Chapter 12

It was November already. Christmas was approaching fast and Sarah didn't feel prepared. To be fair though, it didn't matter if Sarah had started buying Christmas presents in August she still never felt prepared for the Christmas onslaught. And this year it was starting earlier than usual.

This was why Sarah found herself in the cheap clothes shop in town, searching through tacky Christmas jumpers. One of the girls in her gang had decided they should have an early Christmas party, and that the mode of dress would be Christmas jumpers: as cheap and tacky as they could find.

Sarah had managed to find an hour spare while the boys were out at the BMX circuit with Kate's boys. They loved their BMX-ing and every Saturday morning either Kate, Steve, Sarah or George took them to the track in the woods. To Sarah it was organised chaos but the boys loved it, coming back splattered with mud. And Sarah sometimes helped out at events, as she was a qualified Advanced First Aider.

But this Saturday she had managed to beg off a couple of hours and she was looking through cheap jumpers for the most tackiest she could find. She picked up one with bells on. Mmm, she thought it looked a bit tame, even though there was some tinsel running through the pattern's border. She put her bag down on the floor by the rail and held the jumper up to herself in front of the mirror. Mmmm. No. Wait. In the mirror's reflection she could see another rail behind her, and there was the most awful reindeer head with a bright red bobble nose. The jumper was pink. Pink? For a Christmas jumper? God that was awful. She turned around, putting the bell jumper randomly on a rail and picking up the reindeer jumper.

As she turned to hold it in front of the mirror, she felt someone rush past her, and then she realised that her bag was gone. WHAT THE FUCK? She turned to see someone legging it out of the shop, WITH HER BAG.

Sarah didn't think. Rage boiled up inside her and she ran. She ran after that bastard. She had her credit cards in that bag. And the little papier mache key ring that Alfie had made her at school. They weren't getting that. She shot out of the shop, and then stopped suddenly. The figure had dropped her bag just outside the shop and was now nowhere to be seen, lost in the throng of shoppers in the precinct. She picked up her bag, thankful that everything was still in it.

As she went to turn to go back into the shop she felt a hand on her shoulder. "Right madam, come this way please," said a stern voice, and she turned to stare into the chest of a security guard.

"What?" Sarah was confused. Couldn't the man see what had just happened? "That man, woman, person, just tried to pinch my bag," she stuttered.

"Yes, yes we saw what happened," said the Security Guard, "Now madam if you wouldn't mind coming this way we can discuss it in the office." He was calm but insistent as he coaxed her back into the shop.

"Bloody shoplifters," said the Manageress coming up to them as they entered the shop, "We prosecute," she said loudly to no one in general. A couple of the customers in the shop were staring at them and tutting.

"I'm not a shoplifter," said Sarah indignantly, "Didn't you see? Someone tried to pinch my bag."

"Yes, yes well you can tell that to the police," said the Manageress unlocking the door to the office, "I've called them and they're on their way."

Sarah sighed and rolled her eyes. "I'm not a shoplifter," she re-iterated, "There's a mistake. I was running after the thief who pinched my bag."

"With one of my jumpers in your hand," observed the Manageress, "and another hooked to the back of your jumper." She turned Sarah round and unhooked a jumper on a clothes hanger that was hanging from Sarah's back.

Sarah stared at the jumper in confusion, and then she looked down at the jumper she was still holding in her hand. "I wasn't pinching it," she said, "I was running after the person who pinched my bag. I just forgot to let it go. And I have no idea how that jumper got hooked up. Must have been when I was running passed the rail."

She handed the reindeer jumper over. "Not sure it's my colour anyway," she said trying to make a weak smile. The Manageress glared at her. Sarah turned to go, but the Security Guard was blocking the door. "Now if you'll excuse me I have to get home for my boys. I only had an hour to come out."

The Security Guard stood his ground. "Sorry madam but you're not going anywhere," he said.

"Sit down," commanded the Manageress, "I need your details. We have a policy of prosecuting shoplifters you know. The company is very keen on it."

"I wasn't shoplifting," repeated Sarah indignantly, "It was a genuine mistake that I ran out of the shop with the jumper. I was trying to get my bag back." She looked at the television screen on the desk and realised the shop had security cameras. "Just look on the CCTV," she said, "That will show that I had no intention of shop lifting. I had my bag pinched. And I was on my way back into the shop when Jungle Jim here stopped me."

"It could've been staged," said the Manageress, "I've seen it before. An accomplice steals the bag and then runs out of the shop, closely followed by the shoplifter who happens to have some clothing in their hands which they conveniently forget to drop."

"But I don't know who that person was," said Sarah, still perplexed.

Just then there was a knock on the door and an assistant showed in a police officer. Sarah turned and then stared. Her stomach did both a leap and a dive when she realised who it was. She rolled her eyes. "Oh God, not you," she muttered.

Ben stared at Sarah, slightly surprised, and then he turned to the Manageress. "We had a report of a shoplifter?" he asked her questioningly.

"Yes," confirmed the Manageress, "This woman was caught trying to steal two of our Christmas jumpers." She picked up the two jumpers that were now lying on the table in front of them.

Ben looked at Sarah. "We really have to stop meeting like this," he said with a wry smile. Sarah glared at him.

"It was a mistake," she started to explain, "As I keep saying, someone pinched my bag and I ran after them. I didn't realise I was still holding a jumper. Now can we clear this up please as I have to be somewhere?"

"Did you catch them?" asked Ben, concerned for her.

"No but they dropped my bag outside the shop," said Sarah. Ben nodded.

"You were going to buy one of these?" he asked Sarah, wrinkling his nose and nodding to the jumpers. Sarah laughed and made a wry face. "I know, awful aren't they?" she said, "but we've got a tacky Christmas jumper party coming up."

"Excuse me," said the Manageress haughtily, "When you two have quite finished, we have a shoplifter to process."

Ben motioned to the Manageress to come round to the other side of the table, and half turned his back on Sarah. "Are you sure you want to prosecute?" he asked the Manageress, "You see this one is well known to have a mental illness. It might get messy – you know – Social Services reports, medical assessments and the like. For this jumper? It might be better just to give her a warning." The Manageress looked at him, unsure.

"Well," she said, "The Company does normally prosecute straight away. It discourages others."

Ben nodded. "I know," he said, "Most of the larger companies do. But I'm just thinking, it's near Christmas, your busiest time. Do you really want your time clogged up with an investigation? Because as I said, with her mental record there will have to be a proper investigation. CCTV analysis, etc."

Sarah stared at Ben incredulously. "My what?" she spluttered. Ben turned his head to her and gave it a slight shake, as if warning her not to say any more. She understood and instantly shut her mouth.

"Oh I see what you mean," said the Manageress, "No I don't have time for any of that. What do you suggest Officer?"

"Well, I would suggest she apologises to you and she leaves with a verbal warning, and we let the matter rest there," said Ben, "She won't give you any more trouble, will you?" he looked at Sarah and again gave his head a slight shake as if he was signalling to her.

Although Sarah was indignant she caught on that this was her quickest way out. "Yes Officer, you are right," said Sarah in a monotone, "I'm really sorry to have caused you trouble and I'll never do it again. There can I go now?"

The Manageress still seemed a little unsure, but she thought about it and then decided it would be more trouble that it was worth to report the incident, so she acquiesced. "OK, you can go," she said, ripping up the report she had started to complete, "But you're banned, OK?"

"Like I'd ever come back into this tacky shop," Sarah muttered, and then saw Ben's warning look. "Yes I quite understand thank you very much" she said in a gush, "Now can I go?"

Outside the shop Sarah was seething. "How come I was robbed and yet I am blamed for this?" she turned on Ben.

"Life is unfair sometimes," he replied, "And you weren't robbed – you got your bag back. Would you like a lift somewhere? You said you were in a hurry."

"No, no thank you. My car is in the car park." Sarah turned to go, and then turned back. "And I'm not sure Mrs Nosey downstairs could stand me turning up in a police car yet again. Her heart might give out. And anyway how come whenever I'm in trouble you always turn up?" she asked Ben.

Ben smiled. "Just lucky I guess," he said.

"For who?" asked Sarah. Ben gave her a cheeky wink. For a moment Sarah forgot she was angry and she almost smiled, and then she remembered she was supposed to be indignant.

"Well thank you Officer Lewis," she said haughtily. She pushed her bag on to her shoulder. "Goodbye." She turned and walked off in the direction of the car park.

CHAPTER 13

For once Sarah had really enjoyed the festive period. It was lovely having her best friend, Kate, back on the island. The Christmas before Kate's life had been going through a traumatic time and Sarah had felt very sorry for her, but now Kate was looking forward to a Spring wedding and all seemed right with the world.

Christmas was always a difficult time for Sarah financially and she was continually reminded that she couldn't afford all the expensive games and toys that were advertised, but luckily for her the boys never seemed to care about the most up-to-date X-Box. However, this year her parents had chipped in, and between them they had given the boys their first PlayStation. It was second-hand, but the boys hadn't seemed to notice, and they had spent the Christmas holidays happily playing games, sometimes with their friends visiting but more often on their own.

Now everyone was back at work or school and Christmas was 300 odd days away again, and January was dragging. The weather was particularly cold, with northerly winds blowing keenly across the Downs and flurries of icy rain settling in the valleys and never seeming to melt.

But Sarah had an idea. She wanted to take the older children on a field trip, somewhere they had never been before, and it was all part of their Crime and Punishment project Sarah had started with them in the Autumn.

So this explained why she was now sat next to her Headmistress in the waiting room of the Magistrates Court in Newport, the county town of the island where they lived.

Sarah's idea had been for the children to spend a day at the court, and to enact a trial for themselves, to see how it worked, and to give them a taste of responsibility. The Headmistress had heartily agreed, and with a word to one of her contacts they were now meeting the Court Administrator to discuss the practicalities of the experience.

Sarah looked around the waiting room. It was sombre, filled with official looking notices and self help leaflets. People were speaking in whispers, it had that effect, and men in suits were lolling on hard looking seats. Sarah was disappointed not to see anyone walking around in capes and fancy wigs but it had been explained to her that this didn't happen in Magistrate Courts. She knew the children would be disappointed.

The door swung open and two policemen walked in. They were talking loudly and laughing, obviously comfortable with their surroundings. Sarah wondered if they were there for a case, as they looked smart in their uniforms.

One of the policemen cast his eye quickly around the waiting room, and then alighted on her. Sarah's heart gave an involuntary little jump. It couldn't be, but it was. Sarah tried to turn away but he had recognised her.

"Hello," said Ben. He nodded to Mrs Gilmore, "So what are you here for? The drunk and disorderly charge or the shoplifting?" Sarah blanched. No one except Kate and Maureen knew about the shoplifting incident, and Mrs Gilmore knew about neither. Mrs Gilmore looked questioningly at Sarah.

"He's joking," Sarah said quickly. Ben saw the look the Headmistress had given Sarah and apologised.

"Sorry, I am joking," he confirmed. Sarah introduced him. "Mrs Gilmore, this is the police officer who helped me and the boys in the summer on the beach. PC Lewis, this is my headmistress."

"Pleased to meet you," said Ben pleasantly. Ben's companion came over. "This is PC Paul Dorey," said Ben, indicating the officer, "We've got a burglary case this morning."

"Oh are you giving evidence?" asked Sarah, genuinely interested. "Yes," said Ben, "We should be called in a minute."

"We're here to meet the Administrator," explained Mrs Gilmore, "Sarah thought it might be interesting for the older children to spend a day in the court as part of their Crime and Punishment Project."

"That's a really good idea," Ben agreed, "Here's my card," he passed his calling card over to the Headmistress, "Give me a call. If you're interested we should be able to set up a day at the police station, or we could come and give the children a presentation. We've done it before for other schools."

"Oh that would be super," said Mrs Gilmore, taking the card and putting it in her bag, "Thank you."

Just then the Administrator came into the waiting room, and ushered Sarah and Mrs Gilmore into his room. "You didn't tell me that policeman was so good looking," whispered Mrs Gilmore to Sarah as they followed the Administrator, "He has lovely eyes."

Sarah groaned, "Don't you start," she said.

CHAPTER 14

Sarah and Kate were walking along the shoreline at Appley Beach, the four boys playing in front of them, kicking a ball across the wet sand. It was a beautiful beach, a huge bay stretching from Ryde almost to Seaview and facing The Solent. Kate and Sarah often came here with the boys. Sarah only lived five minutes away from it anyway so it was handy.

Kate loved this beach, and often ran its length with her boyfriend, but Sarah wasn't into too much exercise. For one thing she didn't have much spare time – as a teacher and a mother she spent most of her day trying to catch up with herself, and even if she had the urge to exercise she definitely didn't have the energy. Anyway exercise made you hot and sweaty, and she couldn't be bothered with that. A bit like sex, she had decided, and she couldn't be bothered with that either. It wasn't that she didn't want or like sex, but since her husband left she was too exhausted.

As the boys ran in front of them calling to each other, Kate and Sarah were chatting about this very subject.

"I'm not frigid," Sarah was saying, defensively, "I'm just so tired all the time, and I've just not met the right guy."

"I never said you were frigid. But you're never going to meet the right guy if you never go out," said Kate, slightly exasperated. "I do go out," said Sarah. "Yes, with us girls," said Kate.

Sarah sighed. She didn't want to get into a fight with her best mate, but she could see this was where this was going. "You know why I don't want to get involved. Men only hurt you in the end," she said. Kate stopped walking and put her hand on her friend's arm. "Not always," she said soothingly.

This annoyed Sarah even more. "You have a short memory," she stared at her friend, "It wasn't long ago I seem to remember it was a different tune you were singing." She saw the look of pain flash through Kate's eyes and stopped. Kate had been through a difficult time, and Sarah was immediately sorry for reminding her. "I'm sorry," she said, "I don't mean to hurt you. You've been through it too, but you were lucky and found Steve. I went through a bad time when my husband left. I've got myself together now and I don't want to be hurt again."

"I do understand that," said Kate. She laughed to lighten the mood, "But I'm only suggesting a dinner date."

"I just feel you're trying to set me up," said Sarah.

Kate pulled a guilty face. "OK, you got me," she said, "I was. We were. It was Steve's idea too." She looked sheepish, and then motioned over to the café on the Esplanade. "Can I buy you a coffee to make up for it?" she asked. She looked at Sarah, "And we can discuss this further?" Sarah made out to hit her friend but Kate was too fast for her and went running up the beach, calling out to the boys as she ran towards the café.

Five minutes later they were sat on the café terrace with steaming mugs of coffee in front of them. The boys had abandoned their drinks of juice and packets of crisps and had gone back down to the sand to carry on playing their football match. It was only February, but at last the weather had decided to give Spring a go, and it was a lovely still day, with a watery sun peeking through the trees. Nevertheless, Sarah and Kate hunched over their hot coffees.

"Look, I'll come to dinner, but please don't make it look like a blind date," Sarah was saying to Kate, "I'm sure Steve's mate is very nice and all that, but it has to be clear that I'm not going just to get a man."

"No, I know," said Kate but from the look on her face Sarah knew her friend was thinking the opposite.

"Is there someone else?" Kate probed. "What?" asked Sarah.

"Well, you know, if someone else is occupying your thoughts that's why you are so adamant about not seeing someone else?" Kate looked at her over her coffee cup.

"Don't be so silly," said Sarah, but she could feel herself blushing. "That policeman?" suggested Kate.

Sarah gave her coffee a vigorous stir, slopping some of it accidentally. She started delving into her bag for a paper tissue. "Which policeman?" she tried prevaricating.

"Oh which policeman?" said Kate mockingly, "You know full well which policeman." Sarah found a tissue and took it out, wiping spilt coffee from the table.

"I haven't thought about him in ages," Sarah said dismissively, "Well, actually not at all." She continued to wipe the rest of the table around her mug, and didn't look up. Kate gave a sort of humphing noise, and drained the dregs of her coffee.

It wasn't true of course. Sarah knew that she was fibbing, but she wasn't going to tell Kate the truth. She was not going to admit that she often awoke in the night and thought about the dark haired police constable with the lovely eyes. He didn't feature in her daily thoughts, but every now and again she had dreams in which he was slowly and sensually making love to her. She would wake up and then lay there and imagine him in her bed, cuddling up to her, laughing with her, sharing his life with her. Then she would shake herself and tell herself it was just her hormones. Life wasn't like that. She was lonely, she realised that, and she missed the company of someone else to share special moments with. But she had now spent so long on her own she didn't know if she could stand living with someone else, and anyway, she really couldn't take the chance that she wouldn't be hurt again. Kate had been lucky. Steve had come along at the right time and had shown her what it was like to be loved. But Sarah wasn't sure that there could be a 'Steve' out there for her, and she wasn't willing to take the chance.

Kate looked at her watch. "Well I think I'd better get back home now," she said, "I've got the boys' uniforms to iron for school tomorrow, and we're supposed to be going over Mum and Dad's for our tea." Sarah nodded and drank the last of her coffee. "Look, about the dinner." Kate continued, "I promise we won't set you up, but Steve's sister and her boyfriend are coming to stay, and we thought it would be nice to invite you and Steve's mate from work. He's only just come to the Island so Steve feels he wants to look after him. And you're my best mate," she smiled at Sarah, "And I need someone to help me with the cooking," she added cheekily.

"Oh cheers, " laughed Sarah, "You need me to make you something." "Exactly," agreed Kate, "You got it mate."

Kate called to the boys and waved them to come back. "OK," said Sarah, "I'll come. What do you want me to do?"

"Actually I was hoping you would make a pud," Kate winked at her, "Your famous Caribbean trifle, with extra Malibu," she said, "Please?" Sarah smiled at her friend. "OK," she agreed, "I'll see you Friday."

CHAPTER 15

Sarah dressed very carefully for Kate's dinner. She wanted to look nice, but not desperate, which she wasn't. In the end she chose some slacks and a floaty top in a beautiful blue that suited her and accentuated her blue eyes. She had washed her hair and added some products that made her long blond hair shine, and she finished the look off with a pair of soft mules.

She arrived at Kate's with the trifle, one of her signature dishes, mainly for the amount of Malibu that she always poured into it. Sitting in the living room were Natasha, Steve's sister, who Sarah had met before, her boyfriend William, and Mark, Steve's friend from the leisure centre. Sarah suddenly found herself looking into the most handsome face she had seen for a while, and she felt herself blush. "H..Hello," she stammered, feeling very girly and foolish. She beat a hasty exit into the kitchen, knocking into the settee and nearly dropping the trifle. God, get a grip woman, she told herself.

Kate was in the kitchen. Sarah made sure the kitchen door had swung shut before she gushed "God, where did you get young Pierce Brosnan from?"

"I know," giggled Kate, taking the trifle from Sarah and putting it in the fridge to keep cool, "Isn't he gorgeous?" "And he's a friend of Steve's?" Sarah asked incredulously.

"Oh, yes," confirmed Kate, "Works at the leisure centre. He's just started." "Wow," said Sarah, "I may just join."

Kate laughed. "Mm, gym instructor…. I may have already beaten you to that one," she laughed, remembering how she met Steve, "We could have a double wedding with an arch of weights and hoola hoops to walk under."

Sarah guffawed. "You're OK," she said, "I'll let you have that one."

Kate gave Sarah a plate of tiny canapés. "Here, take these out there for me, will you. Oh and get yourself a drink." Sarah took the plate, took a deep breath and walked back through the kitchen swing door.

The dinner went well, and by the time they got to the trifle the conversation was flowing easily, with much laughter. Pierce, eh hem, Mark told them funny stories about his escapades and had them in stitches. He had spent a couple of years in Australia, backpacking and he recounted meeting with kangaroos and getting lost in the Outback. He was, apparently, an expert bungee jumper, and had jumped off a fair few high bridges in exotic places around the world. Sarah thought that bungee jumping was a few notches madder than jumping out of a plane, and she had no ambition to do either.

After the meal was cleared away, and they had moved to the settee and chairs Sarah looked at her watch. It was gone midnight. "Oh gosh," she said, "I'm sorry but I really have to go." She stood up. "I've got an early morning meeting with my Headmistress, and I guess Mum will be wondering where I am."

Mark stood up too. "I have to go as well," he said, "Has anyone got a number for a cab?"

"Where are you going?" asked Sarah, "I'm going to Seaview. If you're on my way I can drop you off."

"Well, it's Nettlestone," said Mark, "I'm in a holiday flat there for now. It was the only place I could find."

"Oh Nettlestone is almost on my way," said Sarah, "It's not far so come on." She gave everyone hugs and kisses and put on her jacket, wrapping her scarf around her tightly against the cold, and led Mark to the car parked outside.

Mark carried on the easy conversation they had started around the dinner table. He was funny and Sarah was almost wishing their journey was longer, because all too quickly Mark was directing her to pull over outside his flat. "Fancy a night cap?" he asked casually. Sarah was half tempted, but reluctantly declined. She didn't know why, but he made her feel daring.

"I would love to," she said, equally casually, "but I've got to get home. But thanks for the offer."

"So how about dinner then?" he asked. Sarah was slightly taken aback. "Oh, no I don't think so," she said quickly.

"Why not?" Mark asked, perplexed. Sarah guessed he wasn't used to girls turning him down. Sarah hesitated for a moment.

How could she explain she wasn't the dating type, that she wasn't after a relationship, that he was very nice, and probably a date would be good fun, but she wasn't into fun? Oh God, that made her sound like a hermit. "I…just…," she didn't know what to say.

"OK," he could see she was uncomfortable with the idea of a date on her own with him, but he wasn't put off that easily, "What if we go on a foursome with Steve and Kate?"

Sarah smiled, relieved and nodded. "Yes that would be nice," she said. She felt that was a better idea, more casual, otherwise she could hear Kate and Maureen going into overdrive if they knew she had a DATE.

They swapped numbers, and very casually Mark gave her a peck on the cheek as he got out of the car.

CHAPTER 16

It was a few weeks after the dinner, and Mark hadn't called, and no one had made any plans for a foursome, so Sarah was beginning to think he had been all talk. She didn't mind, and she certainly hadn't been sat by the phone waiting for him to call. She had been super busy at work, planning the Magistrates Court activities for the older children, as well as coping with problems of her day to day life. Tom had been ill with Chicken Pox, and she was waiting for little Alfie to start developing symptoms, although two weeks after Tom's first spots had appeared Alfie was still right as rain.

"He may not develop it," Maureen kept telling her, "Not all children do. Some have natural immunity."

"If he's going to get it I just wish he would hurry up," said Sarah, "They're all catching it at school."

"In my day if a kid got Chicken Pox all the mothers used to send their kids round to see them so they all got it over and done with," smiled Maureen, "Same with German Measles, though they don't get that these days."

The last couple of weeks had meant that Sarah was confined to Barracks at the weekend as Tom wasn't well enough to go to his favourite BMX meetings. But now he was back at school, and George was taking the two boys out for the meeting, leaving Sarah free to amuse herself.

So this morning she was in East Cowes, doing a little bit of shopping in the supermarket and then calling in at her friend's Vintage Emporium and Tea Rooms just around the corner. Sam, another of the gang, had opened a vintage shop not long ago with a 1940s themed Tea Room attached. She had also gone through a rough patch in her life, and Sarah was keen to support her as much as she could. She tried to call in as often as she could, but East Cowes was the opposite side of the island, and not on the way to anywhere, other than the car ferry to the mainland, so she didn't get the chance as much as she would have liked.

Sarah had just finished putting the shopping into the boot of her car, and was crossing the car park on her way to Sam's tearooms when she heard a commotion. To her right, in front of the supermarket, perched an old man. He was sitting on the ground on an old sack, and next to him was a little dog. Both looked tired. There was a begging bowl in front of them with a few coins in it, and the man had been playing on an old tin whistle. Sarah had seen the old man before. He busked in various places around the Island and she always tried to put a couple of pound in his bowl if she had change.

There were a couple of lads shouting at the old man, and this was causing his dog to bark and growl. One of the lads tried to kick the dog, but missed, and the other lad grabbed the old man's begging bowl and turned it upside down, scattering the few coins. The lads were still shouting and calling the old man names. Sarah heard a yelp and realised one of the lads' foot had now connected with the dog. The other lad started hitting the old man. People were standing around, clearly wondering what to do.

Sarah did not wonder. She was incensed. She could feel a red mist descend over her and in her rage she ran over to the youths.

"WHAT THE HELL DO YOU THINK YOU ARE DOING?" she shouted at them.

"Go away slag," they taunted, continuing to aim kicks and punches at the old man and his dog. She stood right in front of the lad that was hitting the old man.

"Pick on someone your own size," she said to him. He tried to push her aside. "Get out of way," he demanded.

"Go on," she goaded, "You want to hit someone you can hit me." She pushed him away from the old man. The lad hesitated.

"What's the matter? Scared now are you?" She continued to push him backwards. "Can't hit a girl but can hit a dog and an old man?" The youth went to hit her but she made a nifty block with her arm. "Judo champion," Sarah said, feigning what she hoped looked like a Judo move. "Not quite so brave now are you?"

The lad went to hit her again, and this time it connected with her arm, it hurt but it just enraged her even more. She grabbed hold of the lad by his collar, did a swift pirouette and pulled him over her shoulder on to the ground. Then she quickly rolled him over on to his front, pulled his arms up his back and sat on him. The crowd that had gathered cheered. She looked round and saw that someone had apprehended the other lad, and he was now pinned against the supermarket wall. The old man and the dog were being given tea and sandwiches by the supermarket staff.

"Police are on their way," someone confirmed. "Hey well done you," someone else said, and there was a murmur of appreciation all round. Sarah was suddenly very tired but she was determined not to let this lad go.

"Get this bitch off me," he cried. "Shut up," said a man stood beside Sarah. "She assaulted me," the youth tried again. "Save it for the police," said someone else.

Sarah sat on the lad for another five minutes before the police arrived, screeching around the corner with their sirens and blue lights going. A police van turned up as well as a police car, and out got PC Ben Lewis. He looked down at Sarah sat astride the lad, and for a moment Sarah wished she had a camera to capture the look of surprise on his face.

"Hello, hello, what do we have here then?" he asked, looking down at her amazed, "I didn't have you down as a Wonder Woman. Did you strike him with one of your lightening bolts?"

"Oh ha ha," said Sarah, getting off the youth. Her arm was sore, and she noticed her knees were bruised where she had bashed them on the ground as she fell across the youth. Ben helped Sarah up as another policeman grabbed the youth. He was still shouting obscenities at Sarah as he was led into the police van.

"I am disappointed you're not wearing your red corset and blue pants, you know the ones with the little stars on," he said supporting her whilst she brushed herself down. "I have it underneath," said Sarah, "I didn't have time to change." She tried to rub the dirt off her knees but they hurt.

Ben shouted over to the other policemen, one of whom was talking to the crowd that had gathered round and another was comforting the old man. "Are you guys OK here?" he asked,

"I'm going to take this lady over to the café and get a statement. I think she needs a large cup of tea."

"I need a large something," Sarah said bravely. She realised she was shaking and she felt close to tears.

Ben took her arm, but she winced with pain, and as she walked she realised she was limping. Ben gently led her to Sam's café. Sam fussed around them, especially when she heard what had happened, and sat them down with a large pot of tea, on the house she said.

"What were you playing at?" asked Ben annoyed at her, "You could've been seriously hurt."

"I don't know," said Sarah, "I heard these lads shouting at the old man and I just saw red. I mean, I've seen that guy before. He's no harm to anyone, and they starting kicking him and the dog. I was absolutely furious."

Ben smiled, "Cor don't let me get on the wrong side of you," he said, "Did someone say you did a few Judo moves? Where did you learn them?" Sarah smiled self consciously. "Telly," she admitted.

Ben poured them both a cup of tea each, put some sugar in one and made Sarah drink it. "OK, I need to type up the statement and you will need to come down the station and read it through and sign it," he said, getting out his notebook and writing some things down.

"I can't come now," Sarah said, glancing up at the clock on the wall, "The kids will be back soon. I have to get back."

"That's OK," said Ben, "It'll take me a couple of days to get it typed up. Come down the station when you can. If it goes to court you will need to attend." He looked at her questioningly, "Is that alright?" he asked.

Sarah laughed, "It'll be a good case for the children to attend," she said, "We're wanting a child friendly case for them to investigate." Ben agreed. "Although it might not go to court," said Ben, "It'll depend on what the old man wants to do." Sarah nodded.

"Are you OK to drive?" Ben asked concerned, "Would you like a lift anywhere?" "No, thanks," said Sarah, "I think I have stopped shaking now." She finished her tea and stood up.

Ben stood up too, and hesitated. "Can I see you again?" he asked. Sarah looked at him surprised, then a shadow fell across her face. Ben felt he had overstepped his mark.

"You'll see me when I come in to sign the statement," she said, trying to keep the lightness in her voice.

"Sure, sure," agreed Ben, "Sorry, I didn't mean... I just wondered...yes, see you then." He grabbed his hat from the table and stood looking at her for a second. "Right, well, if you're OK I'd better go and see what's happening."

"Yes and I better get home," said Sarah moving round the table and reaching for the door.

"Sorry Sam," she called out to her friend, "I'll have to call in another time." Sam came over and gave her a peck on the cheek. "Yes and next time make sure you don't get into any fights."

"I always said East Cowes is a rough place," laughed Sarah.

"Only when you're here," retorted Sam good-naturedly. She hugged Sarah, "Mind how you go Lovey," she said opening the door for them both.

Sarah walked across the road to the car park, trying hard not to limp. There was a reporter for the local newspaper still questioning the passers-by. The old man had gone, the police had called for an ambulance to take him to the hospital to get him checked out, and a neighbour was caring for his dog. Sarah kept her head down and headed for her car.

The reporter called over to her. "Hey, do you know anything about this incident?" he called out. "Nope nothing," she called back, unlocking her car and getting in.

CHAPTER 17

Sarah kept her head down under the radar of the Press. She heard a report of the incident on the radio as she drove home. They were calling out for the heroic woman who had single-handedly captured the rampaging youths. Sarah hoped no one had recognised her. She felt she had already had her fifteen minutes of fame with the Air Sea Rescue incident in the summer. And could you imagine what Mrs Gilmore, her Headmistress, would say? So she didn't tell anyone, not her mother, not even Kate. And luckily enough her superficial injuries healed very quickly.

A few days later, on her way home from work, she called into the Police Station to sign the statement. To her disappointment (although this was another thing she wouldn't admit to anyone) PC Ben Lewis wasn't there, apparently he was on leave, so it was another officer who read the statement to her and ensured that she was happy with its content. She was reassured that her name wouldn't be released to the Press at this stage, although she was aware that if the case went to court then everyone would then know who she was. She would face that when it happened, she decided.

A couple of weeks went past, and then Kate rang to ask her if she wanted to go out for a meal with them. Pierce, er Mark, (they really must stop referring to him as Pierce, she would end up calling him that to his face) would be joining them. Sarah was pleased because she had been having some rather racy dreams about PC Plod and she thought that maybe dinner with a real man might put the policeman with the lovely eyes out of her mind.

Maybe Kate was right and she did need a man, she thought. Not a permanent one, like marriage or anything. God knows she had ticked that box, but would it hurt to have a bit of company for a change? As long as it didn't hurt the boys she couldn't give herself any reason why a casual boyfriend was not out of the question. She knew she was changing her tune a bit, but seeing Kate so happy with Steve made her realise she was still young, and lonely.

She carefully chose her clothes for the evening. Dressed down, but still a little sexy. She had a shapely figure so she went for tight jeans teamed with a close fitting sparkly t-shirt, and a pair of high heels. She pulled her long hair back into a messy bun held in place with a single pin, with wisps of escaped hair framing her pretty face. A light application of eye shadow, mascara and lipstick and she was done. She stood back and admired what she could see of herself in the hallway mirror. Yes, she'd do.

She met everyone at the restaurant, her father, George, dropping her off so she could have a drink, and as the boys were staying at their grandparents' place - it being a Friday night – there was no curfew.

Mark smiled appreciatively at her, and kissed her on the cheek in welcome. He seemed genuinely pleased to see her. Kate and Steve also kissed her hello and the boys went off to the bar to get the drinks whilst the girls waited for their table to become vacant.

"Wow, you've made an effort," teased Kate, "For someone?" She winked at Sarah.

"Oh give over," said Sarah, "I always scrub up this well when I put my mind to it."

"Yes, but high heels, Sarah, I don't think I've seen you in those since Alfie's Christening, which must be, what, six years ago." Sarah smiled.

"Yeah you're probably right." She rested one foot against another, "Now I know why," she said, "Oooh these are pinching. I hope we're not waiting long."

As the men brought their drinks the waiter came over and said their table was ready. They all followed him to the table, and then had a debate over who should sit where. Would it be men on one side and the women on the other, or couples together? Kate said she wanted to be next to Steve so it was finally decided. Sarah sat down, and surreptitiously slipped off her shoes under the table.

The food was perfect, and the wine slipped down easily. The friends chatted and laughed and were having a lovely meal. Sarah found Mark very easy to talk to. He recounted more of his Australian stories which had them in fits of giggles and Steve told them tales of when he was in the Army, something that Sarah had never heard about.

Eventually Sarah put her napkin on to her empty plate and slipped her shoes back on. "I need the ...." she waved vaguely but everyone understood what she meant. Steve ordered another bottle of wine, and Kate nodded distractedly, entranced in something that Mark was telling her.

Sarah walked through the restaurant to the toilets at the back. She noticed that there was only one door indicating the toilets.

On opening this door she found there were two more doors, one for men and one for women. She was just about to go through the women's door when someone coming out of the men's collided with her. "Oomph, sorry," the man said, and then he looked at her. "We must stop bumping into each other like this," he said pleasantly.

Sarah turned round, and found herself staring at the chest of PC Ben Lewis. She looked up at his face, and for a moment didn't know what to say. Her heart did a little jiggle and her body was on high alert. She hastily stepped away from him.

"Oh, hello," she said, quite perplexed. He was the last person she had expected to bump into. She looked at him. He was lightly tanned and looked relaxed. And he was sporting a beard, which made her heart beat even faster. "Sorry," she said, "It's just that I don't think I've ever seen you in real clothes." Ben thought for an instant. "I guess you're right," he agreed.

"I like the.." "Out with your…" They both spoke at once, and then laughed. "Sorry," said Sarah. "You go first," said Ben.

"I was just going to say," said Sarah, rubbing her face with her hand, "Like the facial hair. It suits you."

Ben smiled and rubbed his face. "Yeah I've been on leave. Couldn't be bothered to shave, but then I picked up a bit of a tan and now I've got to wait for it to fade until I can shave it back off." Sarah laughed at the thought of his face with a beard shaped white patch on it. "I'm not good at forward planning," he said.

"Did you go somewhere nice?" asked Sarah. "Florida," said Ben, "A friend of mine has just moved out there and invited me out." "Very nice," said Sarah.

"Is that your friend I met at the flat and brought you home that night?" asked Ben motioning over to Kate. "Yes," confirmed Sarah. There was silence. She didn't know what to say. "Well I'd better go … you know…" she motioned to the toilet door. "Yes," agreed Ben, "See you again." "Yes," said Sarah turning to go through the toilet door.

Ben sat back down at his table in the corner of the restaurant. From this position he could see Sarah's table. He had thought it was her when she walked in but he hadn't been sure. He had noticed the good looking guy she sat next to, and had noticed how she had laughed at something he had said, touching his arm carelessly. He now watched closely when she returned from the toilets and saw how the man poured her wine and they entwined their arms and tried to drink from the glasses, their noses almost touching, all the time laughing. And Ben was jealous.

"For God's sake, what has got into you?" asked Paul Dorey exasperatedly, "You're like a bear with a sore head. I wish I hadn't said I would come out with you now. I could've been in the King Lud chatting up that lusty bar maid." He followed Ben's gaze over to Sarah's table. "Isn't she the blond bit on the beach?" he asked. Ben didn't say anything but turned his gaze away from Sarah to stare at his food. "Looks like she's found someone else, mate," Paul commented unhelpfully.

"I don't want to talk about it," said Ben cutting up his steak and taking a bite, although he didn't really feel very hungry now.

"Stop mooning over her," advised Paul, "You either go over there and demand she goes out with you, or you forget about her. And anyway haven't you just spent a week in a Florida apartment with the delightful Sadie?"

Ben didn't say anything. He knew that Paul was right. He had spent a lovely week relaxing with Sadie in Florida. Sadie's invitation for him to join her for a week had been a surprise considering as she had all but chucked him when she left. But he was owed some leave, and he thought a few days in the sun, and, of course, sex would do him the power of good, although he wouldn't admit to Paul that the whole time he had been wishing it had been Sarah in the bed.

Returning to her table, Sarah couldn't help feeling that she was being watched. She knew Ben was in the restaurant somewhere but she hadn't seen where his table was. The combination of wine and knowing he was watching her spurred her on to overact. Mark's jokes seemed funnier and she felt the need to touch him. She knew she was playing up to the audience but she couldn't help herself. Trying to drink with their arms entwined was hilarious and the closeness of his face was intoxicating.

Soon it was time to leave. The men paid the bill, brushing away Sarah's insistence at contributing, and they went outside to wait for the taxis they had ordered. Sarah cast a quick eye around the restaurant for Ben but couldn't see him.

It was agreed that Kate and Steve would have one taxi, and Mark's would drop Sarah off on its way to Nettlestone. In the taxi Mark put his arm around Sarah and pulled her into a deep kiss. She succumbed, enjoying the feeling of his strong arms around her, and his masculine scent engulfing her.

The taxi pulled up outside her flat. It was in darkness and Sarah suddenly didn't want to go in there alone. She hesitated for a moment as she opened the taxi door, deciding if what she was going to suggest next was the right thing to do. But the feeling of loneliness almost overwhelmed her for a second, and she made up her mind. "Would you like to come in for a drink?" she asked Mark.

He nodded and paid the taxi driver. She walked up the steps to the front door and unlocked it, switching on the lights as she entered the dark rooms. She poured them both a glass of wine and sat on the settee next to Mark. He took the glasses out of her hands and set them on the coffee table, then he again took her in his arms and kissed her deeply, sending little shivers running up her spine. Her whole body was reaching towards him, crying out for attention. Mark continued to kiss her but at the same time he was fumbling to take her t-shirt off. She stopped him, stood up, took a swig of wine and then led him to the bedroom. Her head was trying to protest, but her body had waited a long time for this and it wasn't going to be stopped now.

CHAPTER 18

As the first rays of light from the rising sun snaked their way across the Eastern sky Sarah was laid awake in her bed, listening to the sound of breathing next to her. It hadn't been quite as romantic as she had expected. The initial wave of passion had led to a quick fumbling around for contraceptive as Sarah tried to remember where she had scornfully thrown the packet of Durex her mother had conspicuously left on her bedside table one day when she had been looking after the boys. At the time Sarah had questioned Maureen as it was a strange thing to do, but all her mother had mysteriously said was that one day she might need them in a hurry. Then, after finding them deep in the bedside cabinet drawer there was another scare as Sarah tried to establish if they were still in date. They were – just. No it hadn't been quite the romantic love-making she would have liked.

The sex itself was also nothing to write home about. Mark had a fit and lean body, and he was a sensitive lover. He had made her moan and groan in all the right places and her orgasm had been very nice thank you very much, but Sarah had felt there was something missing. What she just didn't know. They again had sex just before dawn, but Sarah still felt the same, and now, without the enhancement of alcohol, Sarah was sure she didn't want to repeat the experience again with Mark.

She got up, wrapped her robe around her, and went into the kitchen to make herself a cup of coffee. Mark found her sat by the bay window, staring out across the sea, watching the early morning weekend sailors manoeuvre their yachts between the Napoleonic forts guarding the harbour entrance. "Hello," she said, smiling at him, "Would you like some coffee?"

He smiled back, "Thank you," he said. He followed her into the kitchen. She made him a cup of coffee and handed it to him. She didn't know what to say.

Mark walked across the living room and stood over by the bay window looking out at the view. "It is really beautiful," he commented, "I was really worried about coming to this island, that there wouldn't be anything to do, but it's a beautiful island." "Well I think so," said Sarah, coming to stand next to him.

Mark looked around the room, then his eyes alighted on the clock on the bookshelf. "Shit, is that the time?" he said, draining his cup, "I didn't realise it's so late. I'm so sorry, I've got to run. I'm supposed to be working in an hour." He handed her the cup.

"Do you need a lift?" asked Sarah.

"No, thanks, I'll be fine. If I go now I can reach the top of the road in time for the bus. No don't worry," he turned and smiled at her, and gave her a swift peck on the cheek, "Thanks for the offer." He looked round to make sure he had all his belongings. "And thank you for a lovely well, night. God, I'm so sorry I've got to run, but can I call you? We'll make arrangements?"

"Yes, yes," agreed Sarah and smiled at him as he waved goodbye and disappeared out of the front door. She watched him run down the steps and out of the front garden, turning to run up the road. He was very nice, she thought, but something was just not there.

CHAPTER 19

A couple of hours later, after Sarah had changed the bed sheets, and had a long shower, Kate rang her. "Well?" she asked, dying to know what had happened after her and Steve had left in the taxi.

"Yes, thank you," said Sarah, deliberately misinterpreting her friend's question.

"What happened after we left you?" asked Kate keenly, "Did Mark come in for a NIGHTCAP?" she said the word 'night cap' slowly, pronouncing every syllable.

"Yes, he did," said Sarah. She was deliberately being awkward. Kate was exasperated. "Well aren't you going to tell me what happened?" she asked, almost shouting it.

"No," said Sarah simply. "Why not? We tell each other everything," said Kate.

"I don't remember you telling me every salacious detail of your affair with Steve," Sarah pointed out, "Actually as I remember you were deadly silent on the subject." "But that was different," said Kate.

Sarah was a bit annoyed at being questioned by her friend. "Well if you really must know, he came in for a drink, we went to bed, he fucked me stupid and then he left early for work this morning," she could almost hear Kate flinch at the harsh tone of her voice, "Satisfied?"

"Oh Sarah, don't be like that. I've only got your best interests at heart. What is the matter? Didn't it go so well?" Kate sounded quite hurt.

"I'm sorry," said Sarah hearing her friends quiet voice, "It was fine, and the sex was good. I guess I'm just tired."

"Do you want to come round?" Kate asked, "Steve has taken the boys to BMX and is going to drop Tom and Alfie back with you later. He could drop them back here."

"No, thank you," said Sarah, "I've got some things to do."

In truth she wanted to be alone. Last night had been a big event for her. She hadn't so much as snogged a bloke in 6 years, if you didn't count that New Year's Eve when she had got completely rat arsed and licked the face off that poor guy in the wheelchair. She wanted to analyse her feelings. The sex had been nice, she couldn't fault that, but she knew she didn't want to repeat it with Mark. It lacked something. Was she hankering for romance? she wondered. An after dinner dalliance wasn't her style. She wanted more than that, but she knew that Mark wasn't the man.

CHAPTER 20

The year moved on, and, crikey, it was April already. Sarah really didn't know where the time was going. She had already organised one visit to the Magistrates Court that had been a huge success, and now she was planning another. Her life had settled down again, and Kate and Maureen had stopped trying to fix her up with dates, especially as their last attempt hadn't been very successful.

Sarah and Mark had gone on another date, this time to a local pub on their own, but, although it had been very pleasant and they had got on well, they both agreed that a relationship wasn't in the running. They liked each other, but that was it. Sarah was after romance, someone to share her life with, and Mark admitted he just wanted a casual relationship, something to dip into from time to time. They were also very different: Mark wanted someone to go rock climbing with; Sarah thought clambering over the large pebbles on Bembridge beach was enough; Mark wanted to stay up all night partying; Sarah couldn't wait to get under the duvet by 9pm. No, they were geometrically opposed and it wouldn't have worked. They remained friends, and after a little while any awkwardness between them disappeared.

March had started and ended in torrents of rain and gale force winds, but now it was April and nearly Easter and it had calmed down into chilly yet sun filled days. Spring filled the air, and the daffodils were blooming.

So now Sarah and the boys were at their first BMX race event of the season. It was taking place through woods in the heart of the island, and Sarah had volunteered to work in the First Aid tent. As she was an Advanced First Aider, these events always gave her chance to practice her knowledge – last year she had sewn her first stitches when a boy had cut his leg on a shard of glass. She had loved it.

The boys had gleefully gone off with their grandparents and Kate and Steve, and their boys, to the track to prep their bikes and get ready for their races. Kate promised to come and watch at the right time, but for the moment she was busy. The dry weather had meant an influx of grazes and cuts where bodies had connected with the hard ground.

As she was clearing up after a particular bloody cut, someone hobbled in, moaning in pain, and plonked themselves down on one of the waiting chairs. "Ow, ow, ow," the man said, and Sarah turned recognising the voice.

"Hello, hello, PC Lewis," she said standing over him, hands on hips and mimicking his words to her, "What is going on here then?" She smiled at her police joke and Ben looked up and smiled weakly. "Oh very funny," he said. He pulled down his sock and peered intently at his leg. It was matted with mud but he could just see bits of blood mixed in. He prodded it gently then yelped.

Kate bent down and studied the leg, also prodding it around the edges of the mud. Ben yelped again. "Oh give over," she said, "It's only a scratch."

"It bloody hurts," said Ben.

"I'll clean it up for you, but I think you will live," said Sarah reaching over to the table and picking up a bottle of distilled water. "I'll wash the mud off and then put some antiseptic on it." She dribbled the distilled water onto some cotton wool and began carefully sponging off the mud. "Ow, owww," moaned Ben.

Ben watched the back of her head as she bent over his leg. He was dying to ask about the man he had seen her with in the restaurant some weeks ago, but he didn't know how to approach the subject.

He began with general chit chat. "Do you come here often?" he asked.

Sarah smiled up at him. "I didn't know you did BMX," she said, "I've not seen you before."

"Oh I've been here before," Ben said, "Only normally I'm more careful than this, but yeah, I come as often as I can." He winced as she started applying antiseptic to the graze.

"Oh yeah this will sting," said Sarah rather belatedly.

"You're enjoying this aren't you?" commented Ben, seeing the glint in her eye.

"Well it does make a change you being on the wrong end," she agreed.

Just then Tom came running into the tent. "Mum, Mum," he called, running up to Sarah, "Come on Alfie is about to start."

"I'm coming Sweetheart," Sarah called back, putting the bottle of water and antiseptic back on the table and throwing away the blood and mud soaked cotton wool. "There," she said, carefully pulling up Ben's sock as far as it would go, "You will live to BMX another day. Now go," she helped him to his feet, "go make me proud."

He laughed and thanked her, and then hesitated. "Can I get you a drink to thank you?" he asked. Sarah laughed. "No thanks," she said, "I'm filled out with tea."

"No I meant take you for a drink, at a pub, in the week, or sometime," Ben gabbled, "Or a meal?" He felt this was his last chance to ask her.

Sarah blushed. She thought quickly. She didn't know what to say. Her heart was doing little jigs in her chest but her head was screaming WHAT THE F?

"Oh, I'm sorry," Ben said quickly, seeing her face, "Of course, you're with someone. In the restaurant. Sorry, I shouldn't have asked you."

"No, no I'm not," said Sarah quietly, "He was my friend's work colleague." She didn't know why she was explaining to him. She looked up at him and took a deep breath. "Oh go on then," she said letting out her breath, "Why not?"

"MUM! COME ON!" called Tom, grabbing Sarah's hand with urgency, "We're going to miss Alfie's race!"

"Sorry, motherhood calls," said Sarah, beaming at Ben, "I'll have to catch you later." She let Tom drag her out of the tent.

Sarah really enjoyed the rest of the event, but she didn't get to see Ben again. She watched her children's races – neither of them won anything, but they didn't mind – and she was busy in the tent with a broken leg from a bystander who had got in the way of a biker coming over a hill. It was a nasty fracture, and Sarah spent the rest of the afternoon looking after the man until the ambulance came to take him to the hospital. Then she helped the other First Aiders to pack up the tent and supplies before her own family collected her and they went home.

She was happy. For the first time in ages she felt peaceful. It was like all the events of the recent past had been building up to that one proposal. She was now excited for Ben to get in touch to make arrangements, and she found herself jumping every time her phone rang, or someone knocked the door.

Eventually, the next day on Sunday evening he called. "Sorry not to have called earlier," he said, "I can't believe I have slept most of today. I was exhausted from yesterday."

"How's the leg?" asked Sarah, "Has it fallen off yet?" She could hear the smile in Ben's voice.

"No it's still hanging on," he said, "But it is sore. I was thinking, about our date...." Sarah's heart did a little flip. Was he now going to say he had changed his mind? "Yes," she said quietly dreading his next words. "Well, I was wondering if we could take your boys ten pin bowling one evening?"

Wow, that came out of the blue. For a moment Sarah didn't know what to say. She considered the idea. It would save having to ask Mum and Dad to babysit yet again, and she knew the boys would love it.

"Oh yes," she said enthusiastically, "But are you sure?"

"Yes, I'd love it," he said, "Are they on Easter holidays soon? We could go then." "Yes," confirmed Sarah, "The Easter holidays start next week."

"Why don't we go on Monday?" suggested Ben, "I don't think it will be so busy then." Sarah agreed and they made arrangements to meet outside the venue on the following Monday. God a whole week to wait, thought Sarah, how would she survive?

CHAPTER 21

Sarah didn't know how she made it to the following Monday. The week was a disaster. Her car was bashed by a hit and run driver, who backed into it in a car park and then sped away, without leaving any details. It wasn't badly damaged, nothing that really needed urgent repair, but the paintwork was scratched and there was a sizeable dent in the bumper.

She thought of reporting it to the police, and that made her smile. How ironic was it that there was never one around when you genuinely needed one?

George had fallen off a ladder whilst hanging a picture which one of the boys wanted up in their bedroom. Sarah had heard an almighty crash and had walked into Alfie's bedroom to find her dad sprawled across the floor, with the ladder on top of him. He had bruised his ribs, and her mother had reprimanded Sarah for allowing George to climb ladders at his age. She knew he had vertigo. Sarah was annoyed at being blamed as she had had no idea what her father had been up to until she heard the crash. She argued with Maureen and they didn't speak to each other for a couple of days.

And then to cap it all she washed her mobile phone in the washing machine. She had forgotten it was in her jeans pocket and she had just gathered up all the washing and in her haste threw it all in the machine, and switched it on. It wasn't until she heard a clanking noise that she saw the dammed thing swishing about in the soapy suds. Shit, shit, shit, she muttered, stopping the cycle and waiting for the safety timer to unlock the door. She quickly took the back off, and removed the battery as her dad had shown her to do, and putting the phone into a bag of rice she popped it into the airing cupboard to dry out. But for the rest of the day she fretted: what if Ben tried to call her? She didn't have his number now because she had torn up his card and threw it away, and Kate had kept the one he had given her when Sarah had been sick, and anyway she didn't have a phone to call him or Kate.

But she needn't have worried because that Monday Ben was outside of the Bowling Alley at the appointed time. He was wearing jeans and a casual sweater, and he again had a slight shadow of stubble that Sarah guessed indicated he had been off work for the last couple of days.

Ben greeted the boys enthusiastically, giving them high fives and then he bent forward and gave Sarah a casual peck on the cheek. Sarah's skin burned where his lips had brushed it, and she blushed slightly.

"Come on," he said, taking her hand and leading them all through the door into the Bowling Alley.

It was great fun. The boys had begged to be allowed to bowl with the other children in the kiddies' club, and they happily squealed and shouted at the lanes at the other end of the alley. Sarah found out that Ben was quite competitive, and Ben found out that Sarah was quite good at 10 pin bowling. It was after a series of strikes that she confessed she had spent much of her teacher training in the Bowling Alley as it had been free and warm and served alcohol, unlike her student digs.

After Ben had let Sarah win, so he said, he took them all to the Alley's café and bought them burgers and chips. The boys were really excited, chatting away to Ben, and telling him how they had won their games. Ben was fantastic with them, asking them questions and oohing and aahing at the right moments.

"You are so good with the boys," Sarah said as they walked along the road back to her flat. "I love kids," admitted Ben, "I always wanted a brood of them, my own football team." Sarah nodded and said wistfully, "Me too."

And then she told him about her husband, how he had left her as soon as she had given birth to Alfie, practically running out of the Maternity Ward in panic, boarding the first plane to his little Thai nymph to find himself.

"He never contacted us again," she said sadly, "I tried to trace him through the British Embassy but they couldn't help much. I found his address book and wrote him letters, sent him pictures of the boys, but I gave up after a couple of years. He left me everything: an empty bank account, a huge credit card bill, unpaid bills and his untaxed, uninsured car."

Ben nodded - he sensed her pain. He remembered Jenny Pudgy-Smith, as Paul had called her. He took Sarah's arm and folded it into his, and as they walked he told her about his life in London.

Their walk took them through the park, and while the boys stopped to play on the slides and swings, Ben and Sarah sat on a bench. By now the sun was setting, and from the bench they could see across The Solent, the last rays of the sun lighting up the boats anchoring for the night. Sarah shivered a little. With the beautiful sunny weather and lighter evenings it was easy to forget that it was still only April. Ben put his arm around her and pulled her closer to him.

A dog walker passing by smiled at the couple kissing on the bench, their two boys playing nearby. "What a beautiful family", she said to herself, "they look so happy together".

CHAPTER 22

It was George's 65th birthday. He hadn't wanted a fuss as he had retired from his Civil Service job some years earlier when they had made redundancies, and they had had a big family celebration then. This time he had planned a weekend to Disney Paris for himself, his wife and his grandsons. He said it would be a good chance to spend time with the boys, and he felt they would enjoy Disney, but everyone knew that really he had wanted to go for himself. He was a big kid at heart and having two small grandsons was the perfect excuse for George to be a child again.

Sarah wasn't able to go. She had another Magistrates Court visit to prepare, and the older children were going to be taking exams soon, and she also had to prepare paperwork for them leaving to go up to the Big School. She had set aside the weekend the boys were away as the perfect opportunity to get some work done.

The boys had left with their Grandparents on the Friday afternoon, sailing to France from Portsmouth, just across the water from her flat. Sarah had watched the large car ferry sail across the Solent from Portsmouth Harbour, and out into the Channel. When the ferry had been at its closest she had stood on the beach in front of her flat and waved and waved, sure that her boys would be waving from the decks. And then they were gone, and she went back into an empty flat.

Kate had asked her round for dinner that evening, but she wasn't really in the mood for company. She felt a bit reflective. The Bowling date had been earlier in the week, and although she had received a couple of casual texts from Ben, they hadn't arranged to meet up again yet.

It was still early evening when Sarah decided to call it a day on her paperwork. She was tired, so she poured herself a glass of wine and went to the window. It was a lovely evening, the setting sun shining red on the water sending rays of light sparkling across it, and she got the urge to go and sit on the sea wall. From that position she could just about watch the sun set in the western end of The Solent.

She took with her the bottle of wine and her glass, and walked to the waters edge. She rested the wine bottle against the sea wall, and kicking off her flip flops she plunged her feet into the freezing seawater. It was cold, but strangely exhilarating, and she kicked her feet about to stop them from going numb.

Then she heard a shout behind her. She turned around and saw Ben propping his bike up against the sea wall and coming over to her. She thought how fit and attractive he looked in his casual sports gear, and he was still sporting that beard, now with a regulation trim of course. She thought it suited him.

He came over to her, and kissed her gently on the cheek. "Hello," he said looking at her questioningly. "Hello," Sarah said and smiled. She raised the wine glass she was still carrying, "I'm just celebrating finishing four hours of paperwork," she explained, "Fancy one?" She motioned to the bottle by the sea wall.

"That would be nice," Ben agreed.

"Make yourself comfortable, I'll fetch a glass," said Sarah, slipping on her flip flops and making her way back to the flat.

By the time she got back with another wine glass, Ben had deposited his bike in her garden and was now sat on the sea wall, bottle of wine by his side. Sarah sat next to him and poured him a glass. They sat and watched the sunset, and darkness make its way from the east. They didn't say anything for a long time, and then Sarah said "Do you fancy a Chinese, assuming you can stay of course?"

Ben smiled. "I was just riding round on the off chance that you were in," he said, "I was going to ask you out for a drink."

"I don't want to go out," said Sarah, "I'm tired and just fancy a night in, if you don't mind." "Sure," said Ben, "that sounds just as nice."

They got up, gathering up the glasses and wine bottle and made their way into the flat.

Sarah fetched the Chinese takeaway menu and they chose a selection of dishes. Whilst Sarah was phoning through the order, Ben was looking at her bookshelf and at her extensive collection of historic novels. He pulled a book out and showed it to her as she came back into the living room.

"Patrick O'Brian," he said showing her the front cover, "Captain Jack Aubrey. I love these books."

"Yes," Sarah agreed, "They're great aren't they? 'Master and Commander' was based on them."

"I love that film too," said Ben, putting the book back into its slot, "And you have Sharpe and Hornblower," he chuckled and pulled out another book, admiring it's cover, "And Flash. Wow! But aren't these, well…."

"Very masculine books for a feminine brain?" Sarah finished his question for him. He shrugged. "I wasn't going to quite put it that way, but yes."

"They're great books. I love the mix of fact and fiction," explained Sarah, "I learnt a lot about the Napoleonic Wars from Sharpe, and of course Captain Jack Aubrey is all about sailing." She took the book from Ben and put it back in its place. "And I did my dissertation on the characters from a woman's perspective."

Ben was puzzled, so Sarah explained. "I suppose as a man you just love the fighting bits, but from a woman's perspective there is a lot of romance in them. Not just because the leading characters are heroic but because they are vulnerable. Well, perhaps not Flash," she laughed, "He's just a scoundrel. But Sharpe," she pulled out a Sharpe book, "he falls in love with every woman he beds, or he believes he's in love with them. Captain Jack is a loving husband at a time when a sailor spent years away and probably had a girl in every port. Hornblower is shy and ungainly around women. He's not very successful at relationships."

She put the book back and crossed over to the TV cabinet and opened a drawer underneath the TV. "Fancy watching Master and Commander?" she asked turning to Ben, "Or Hornblower, or Sharpe?"

Ben laughed and crossed over to the TV and bent down, rifling through the DVDs. "Oh my God," he said joyfully, "I knew you were the right woman for me." He picked up Master and Commander, "Shall we start with this one?" Sarah nodded, "Excellent choice," she agreed.

Sarah laid up the coffee table with plates and place mats and they watched the film whilst munching through the Chinese and drinking wine. And when they had finished the meal they curled up together on the settee and continued watching the film.

As the credits rolled at the end of the film Sarah sat up. "I suppose I'd better clear this mess up," she said, trying to get up, but Ben grabbed her arm and pulled her to him. He gave her a long and deep kiss that melted her insides. She folded into him and let him kiss her neck, sending hundreds of shivers down her spine. He pulled her tee-shirt aside and kissed the exposed skin at the top of her shoulders. Her heart was pounding in her mouth and she couldn't feel her legs anymore. He laid her back on to the settee and gently removed her tee-shirt, then kissed every part of her skin. Sarah didn't think she could stand anymore if he didn't take her there and then. She pulled at his shirt until he removed it and then she kissed him deeply, running her hands over his taut torso, luxuriating in the feel of his skin on hers.

Sarah stopped him. She wanted him more than anything but first practicalities. She ran to the bedroom and frantically searched for the discarded box of condoms. Thank God there were a couple left. She came back into the room, triumphantly holding the box aloft. Ben laughed. She rolled him on to his back and sat astride him. Now it was his turn to experience what she could do for him.

They made love on the settee, slowly and passionately, and once spent they moved to the bedroom, abandoning the left over meal and plates, and curling up into the middle of the bed, their bodies folded around each other. This was how

Sarah had imagined love-making, this was what she had been longing for. Ben shared her interest in books and films, he was a lovely sensitive guy and his love-making was just that. After they had made love again, she fell into a restful and contented sleep wrapped in his arms.

CHAPTER 23

Ben gently extricated himself from the limbs of the sleeping Sarah, and quietly walked into the living room, where he found his clothes. He pulled them on and then went back into the bedroom. He leaned over Sarah and kissed her gently on the forehead. She moved slightly and her eyelids fluttered. "I'm going to find us some breakfast," Ben whispered to her, "I'll be back soon." He kissed her lips and she mumbled "OK" very sleepily, then she turned over and pulled the duvet cover over her shoulders.

Ben got on his bike and shot off down the road as fast as he could. His plan was to get home quickly, shower and have a quick change, grab a jar of his favourite locally made jam and then call in at his favourite bakers for oven fresh croissants to take back. It should take half an hour maximum.

Arriving at his cottage he saw a police van outside and one of his police colleagues pacing up and down. "Everything all right Andy?" Ben asked his colleague as he dismounted from his bike.

"Where the bloody hell have you been?" asked PC Andy Morris, "We got a tsunami in Japan, huge earthquake. There's a Custom cutter coming to pick you and Reg Newton up in," he looked at his watch, "about 10 minutes. Look lively."

Ben immediately sprang into action. He was a highly trained rescuer, part of the UK's contingency squad who went to far flung places to help out in rescue missions. He had been part of the rescue squad who had worked in New Orleans after the hurricane that had caused substantial flooding. It could be harrowing, and hard work, but in a strange way he enjoyed it.

So now he was called on to help out in Japan. He ran up the cottage path, and hastily unlocked the front door, all the time Andy was giving him a running commentary. "The earthquake happened about 6 hours ago, just off the coast line, Magnitude 9. It caused a huge uplift of the sea bed which set off a tsunami. It hit the Japanese coast about 4 hours ago. We don't know much but the Japanese Government is calling for international assistance. It's reporting whole villages swept away."

Ben ran upstairs. His rescue kit bag was constantly packed, even down to spare boxer shorts, so he grabbed that, and a couple of other bits and pieces, and ran out to the police van, locking the door behind him. As soon as he was in the van Andy sped away, to the Pier Head and they arrived just as the Cutter was tying up. A fellow rescuer, Reg Newton, a highly trained paramedic whom Ben had worked with before, was also at the Pier Head, and he grimly acknowledged Ben before tossing his own rescue kit on board the Cutter. Ben was helped aboard, and it quickly set off across the short expanse of water to the mainland.

It was some time later, as they were speeding up the A3 that Ben had chance to think of Sarah. Shit, he thought, she'll be wondering what's happened. He reached into his pocket for his mobile, but it wasn't there. He searched his bags but his mobile was nowhere to be found. Double shit. He reached for his notebook. I'll leave a message to be sent down to her, he thought, and hastily scrawled an apology, which he gave to the driver as he left the van, with instructions on how to get it to Sarah.

And then he was on his way to heaven knows what in Japan.

CHAPTER 24

Sarah slept in quite late, and then woke feeling a small thrill as she remembered the night before. She looked at the clock on the bedside table. It was 10.30am. What? She looked again, sure she had read it wrong, but no, it was clearly saying 10.30. Where was Ben? He had left hours ago, to get some breakfast if she remembered rightly.

She got up and wrapping herself in her robe she went into the living room, expecting to find him in there, perhaps with breakfast waiting for her. But there was no sign of him. And no sign of breakfast. The dirty plates of their Chinese meal seemed to mock her. She quickly cleared them away into the kitchen and squared the settee back up, fluffing up cushions. She picked up her clothes from the night before, and threw them in the linen bin. Even after all that Ben still wasn't back.

She was getting worried. Had he had an accident? She peered outside but couldn't see his bike that had been propped up against the wall under the bay window. There was no trace of him anywhere.

Sarah thought, and then picked up her mobile. She had his number and now she called it, but it went straight to Voicemail. She left a message. "Hello Ben, where are you? I'm waiting for breakfast, haha."

She thought she should go and look for him, especially as she couldn't settle without knowing what had happened to him. She got herself washed and dressed, put on her jacket, and set off. She would walk along the Esplanade. She didn't know where he lived, but she was sure it was somewhere near there.

She ended up walking for miles, hoping to bump into him, or another policeman who she could try and ask if they knew where he lived. But she saw no one who could help. She wondered about going into the Police Station and asking, but what was the likelihood they would tell her, and anyway she didn't know what she would say. "Hello, I'm looking for PC Ben Lewis. Why do I want him? Well we had the most terrific sex and I was looking forward to repeating it tonight." Mmm, sounded kind of lame and needy even to her.

She went back to her house, all the time continuing to call his mobile but it went to Voicemail each time. After a while she gave up.

CHAPTER 25

By the time the children and her parents returned on Monday afternoon Sarah had gone through a range of emotions. She had been worried, and then fretful, imagining every bad thing that could possibly have happened to him. Then she had been angry. Why had he gone without telling her anything? Where was he? How on earth could anyone disappear off the face of the earth like that?

By the time her family returned she was bitter. Yet again a man had promised her everything and then had let her down. He had made love to her and made her feel like she was the only woman in the world for him. She had thought of it as love making, but clearly it hadn't meant anything to him. PC Ben Lewis was the same as any other man. She should've known he would be no different. She was finished with men. Oh yes. That was it. No more. Over. She might even turn lesbian. At least she could borrow her lover's dresses.

But she told no one. Mostly because of her pride, because she didn't want to admit that she had been a sucker. She squared up her shoulders and she welcomed her boys and her parents home as if she had had the best weekend of all time. And no one noticed her grief.

The boys and George were too excited anyway at telling her all the things they'd seen and done, and showing her photos on Granddad's mobile, and their new toys they'd been bought. They had met Mickey Mouse, they said, he had sat with them at breakfast, and they had done lots of other marvellous things. Sarah oo'ed and aa'ed in the appropriate places and plastered a big smile on her face. She was determined to put on a brave face and show men like Ben Lewis that she just didn't care.

Anyway, she had far more pressing things than Ben Lewis's disappearance. Her best friend was getting married in two week's time and she had a Hen Party to get through. Kate didn't know it but most of their mates from school, and a lot of Steve's female colleagues from work were descending on Ryde the following Friday night to party. Sarah had called in a few favours, and she had organised a pub crawl, with all of them dressed as naughty school girls, and she had even hired a male stripper to perform in one of the pubs they would be in. Even if she no longer had the heart for it she couldn't let her best friend down.

CHAPTER 26

That Friday night Sarah carefully got ready, making sure her stockings were torn in the right places, and her black lacy bra peeped out just enough from beneath her tight white shirt. She wanted her friend to have the best night ever, especially as Kate hadn't had a Hen party when she had married her first husband. It had been a hasty wedding as Kate had been pregnant, and they were moving to Sheffield. So Sarah was keen to make it up to her.

The boys were staying with their grandparents again and it was arranged that Sarah would sleep at Kate's, just so that Sarah could look after her if she got too drunk. Steve would be working in Southampton again, and Kate's boys were staying at their grandparents'. George came to pick her up, and they picked up Kate on the way. Kate looked fantastic in her tight gym-slip and torn fishnet stockings. She had added some freckles across her nose that made Sarah giggle.

"Here, I've got my eyebrow pencil," she said to Sarah, delving into her bag, "You can add some too." She balanced the mirror while Sarah attempted to add some dots across her nose, a difficult task with her dad speeding around corners.

Eventually they arrived at the first pub. Kate stood by the door for a second. She was nervous. Sarah grabbed her hand. "Come on old girl," she said encouragingly, "Let's get the party started." And together they both barged through the door to be met by enormous cheers from the twenty-odd gym-slip clad women waiting on the other side.

It was turning into being a great night. Kate had thoroughly enjoyed the evening, especially the stripper, and now in the last pub, which coincidently was the same one the two of them had been thrown out of the summer before, she was now drinking champagne out of her shoes.

Sarah was drunk but not wasted. She knew what she doing but she was in no fit state to drive. She watched her friend down the fizzy liquid in one go, not spilling one drop, and she felt enormously proud of her. There was a woman who had been in a crap marriage but had got on with it. She had never complained, never tried to leave, just accepted her life and tried to make the best of it. And then she had met Steve, her gentle, handsome, fit gym instructor. Sarah thought she had met HER Steve in the shape of Ben Lewis. She sighed and picked up her glass. It was empty. One for the road, she thought making her way over to the bar.

There was a woman at the bar who Sarah did not know, but she was clearly one of the Hens as she was also dressed as a St Trinians school girl, bursting out of a red wine stained tight blouse. "White wine, please," Sarah said giving her order to the barman. She looked questioningly at the woman. "Hello, said the woman, "I'm Sadie. I'm a friend of Steve's." "Hello," said Sarah politely, "I'm Kate's Maid of Honour."

They exchanged pleasantries and some chitchat over Kate and Steve's meeting, and then their conversation changed to men and sex. It was sometime after that Sarah, thinking the conversation through, wondered how it had got there, but there it did.

Sadie was quite forthright in her opinion. "Sex is for enjoyment," she spouted The Gospel According to Sadie, "Yes of course both parties have to enjoy it, but more importantly I have to enjoy it." She laughed and took a big slug of wine.

Sarah realised Sadie was very drunk. "Now my lover knows where we stand," she continued, "Most important that. I told him from the beginning. I don't want marriage, I don't want babies, and don't even give me any of that love shit. We have great sex, we enjoy ourselves. Who wants to be burdened with love and babies?" Sarah nodded in what she hoped looked like a wise nod, but it didn't matter because Sadie was still spouting on.

"Ben is a very considerate lover," she was saying. Sarah's ears pricked up. Ben? No, it couldn't be the same Ben – there must be hundreds of Bens on the island. "You know once I made him do it with his uniform on in the back of his van. He had just come in from work, and was all ruffled and ooh, looking very sexy." She giggled to herself at the memory. "I mean we've done it loads of times with his uniform on but straight in from work and in the van, well that was special." She drained her glass.

"What does he do, this eh Ben?" Sarah asked, hoping there might be a clue as to what kind of uniform he had been in.

"Oh he's a policeman," said Sadie. Sarah blanched, and then recovered herself. There must be hundreds of Bens in the police force.

"He's not really a boyfriend," Sadie continued, not noticing her new friend's pallor, "He's more a shag buddy. I live in Florida now – I'm working on a cruise ship – but he comes over sometimes and we have a lovely shag. He's very good in bed. I do miss him, I suppose. I suppose we are a bit of an item." Sadie stopped talking, and stared into space, a sad expression on her face.

Sarah wanted to know more, to rule out her Ben. Her Ben? Who was she kidding? Anyway she wanted to know more. Noticing Sadie's glass was empty she offered to buy her one. "Oh thank you, that's very kind of you," Sadie said, "I'll have a G&T please," she smiled at the barman and gave him a big wink, "Better make that a double Honey," she said to him.

"So this Ben," encouraged Sarah, "How long have you been, er, shag buddies?" Sadie thought for a moment and counted up some fingers. "Must be .... A couple of years I guess. We got together when he came back from London, was transferred here, and we've been going ever since. He was in diplomatic protection, or something like that"

Something triggered in Sarah's memory. London? Ben had told her he had lived in London before he had come back to the Island. It WAS the same Ben, Sarah was without a doubt now.

"And when was the last time you saw him?" Sarah asked cautiously. She wasn't sure she wanted to know the answer. "I dunno," said Sadie, "I guess couple of weeks ago. It's hard to keep track. No wait, probably a week ago as I've only been back ten days. I'm going back to Florida on Monday."

Sarah tried to do a quick mental calculation. The date crossed with their Bowling date. The bastard. "What does he look like, your Ben?" she asked Sadie, trying to sound as casual as possible.

"He's good looking. Got lovely eyes. He's got a stubbly beard at the moment. Oooh, hang on," said Sadie, drunkenly fumbling in her handbag, and eventually managing to pull out her mobile. "I have a photo of him," she smiled and showed Sarah a photo of a naked man lying on a dishevelled bed, his hands cuffed together in front of him, desperately trying to cover his manhood.

"Whoops," said Sadie giggling, "Wrong photo." But it was too late, Sarah had seen it was Ben Lewis. Sadie quickly whizzed through some more images of Ben in compromising situations, and then the next photo confirmed his identity – a smiling bearded Ben in casual slacks and a Hawaiian shirt sipping cocktails at a bar taken a few weeks before.

Sarah's heart plummeted to the floor, hit it and bounced back. So she really was just one of a batch of suckers who had fallen for his charms. She should've stayed dating Mark, at least she knew where she stood with him.

Sarah felt sick, and was now very, very sober. She wanted to cry but most of all she wanted to go home. She muttered something to Sadie, and went off to find her friend, the bride.

Kate was sat slumped in a corner of the pub. She was crying, gently sobbing to herself. Her eyes were black with smudged mascara. Sarah sat next to her and took her friend in her arms in a caring hug. "What's the matter Love?" she asked her, gently stroking her hair.

"I'm so fucking happy, and I'm so fucking drunk," sobbed Kate, "But more I'm so fucking happy. I mean look at me. I've got fucking fantastic friends, wonderful family, and the best fucking boyfriend in the world. And he wants to marry me, ME. Can you believe it?"

Sarah stopped cuddling Kate and reached into her bag for some tissues. Kate stopped crying and suddenly looked at Sarah, horror on her face. "You don't think he'll change his mind, do you?"

Sarah laughed. "No, Love I don't think that's going to happen," she reassured her friend.

"No, but there's still a week to go. What if he says fuck it, he's been married before, and she was a bitch. I mean what if he decides he doesn't want to take that risk again. I don't know what I'd do," Kate started sobbing again.

Sarah made her spit onto the tissue she was holding in front of Kate's mouth and started wiping the tears and mascara from Kate's face. "I don't think there's any chance of that," she said, "He's besotted with you." She pushed strands of hair away from Kate's face. "Come on, let's call it a night and get you home." She pulled her friend to her feet. As she did so the barman called "TIME!" She picked up Kate's bag and looked around for her own, which she had been sitting on. "Yep, it's time to go," she said, leading Kate to the exit, and calling out "BYE!" to their friends as they went.

CHAPTER 27

Sarah didn't tell anyone about her chat with Sadie but she did play it over and over again in her head, and she just couldn't stop thinking about the image she had seen of Ben tied up during sex. She was shocked. Shocked and furious. Was that photo taken during their last sex session? Sarah wondered. And was this the same time as he had been dating her? Had he gone from snogging her on the park bench straight into Sadie's bed? Sadie probably liked the thought of threesomes, Sarah thought. They probably had a good laugh about her. Sarah was gutted, and felt defiled. He really was a shit, and after she had explained to him how her husband had made her feel.

But for now Sarah had to put that all to one side and get through life, or more specifically, Kate's wedding. The Sunday after the Hen Party the two friends spent the morning lazing around, and then they met Steve, and the children, and both Kate's and Sarah's parents at a local restaurant for a pre-wedding lunch. It was a lovely afternoon but by the time Sarah took the boys home she was exhausted from trying to appear normal.

But life went on, the wedding preparations revved up, and Sarah found herself roped into a few errands. She grew more tired and more fractious and was starting to snap at people. Maureen didn't say anything but she could tell something was troubling her daughter. She'll tell me when she's ready, she thought.

One morning Sarah came out of the kitchen to find a disaster had hit the living room. She had left the boys to watch TV quietly. It was a damp morning and she needed to do some cleaning in their bedrooms, so they had been left in the living room with a few snacks and a couple of DVDs.

She had just finished cleaning the second bedroom when she heard shouting, and knew from experience that the boys were fighting. She walked into the living room to find the settee covered in crisp crumbs, some of it crushed in, and the boys were rolling around on the floor on top of each other with limbs flailing.

"EXCUSE ME!" Sarah said in a loud and stern voice, "WHAT ON EARTH ARE YOU BOYS DOING?" Her sons stopped immediately and Sarah pulled Alfie to his feet. "EXPLAIN," she commanded.

Alfie burst into tears. "It wasn't me," he sobbed, "he hit me first." He pointed to his brother so Sarah could be in no doubt to whom Alfie was referring.

Sarah turned to her eldest son. "EXPLAIN," she commanded again.

"Alfie wouldn't stop turning the channels over," explained Tom with his arms angrily folded across his chest, "I was trying to get the clicker off of him."

Sarah motioned to the crisp crumbs chaos. "And how did this happen?" she asked.

"Dunno," said Tom, looking down to the floor. Sarah tried Alfie. "How did this happen?" she asked him. Alfie also looked at the floor. "Dunno," he replied echoing his brother.

"I have just spent over an hour cleaning your bedrooms," Sarah said through gritted teeth, "Right, you made this mess, you can clean it up. Fetch Henry," she ordered Alfie to fetch the vacuum cleaner from its home in the under stairs closet. "And you can take what's left of the crisp bag back to the kitchen," she told Tom.

Sighing she pulled off all the cushions and seats from the settee and began to shake them out. Alfie wheeled the vacuum cleaner over to her, and Sarah gave Tom the plug to push into the socket. She attached a long pipe to the nozzle, one especially for furniture, switched on the machine and then gave the nozzle to Alfie. "Gone on then," she ordered, "Every single bit of crisp, and don't forget to do down the back and side of the settee." Tom came over and helped Alfie hold the nozzle and between them, working together for once, they sucked up every single piece of crushed crisps.

It was as Sarah was putting the cushions back that she noticed it. A black mobile phone peeping out from down the back of the settee. It had obviously got itself wedged between the seat frame and the back. Sarah pulled it out. She wasn't sure but she guessed it was Ben's. Thinking about it, it would have to be his. She hadn't had any other guest round, only Kate, and she hadn't lost her phone. Sarah tried to switch it on. It was dead.

Well that would explain why his phone had switched to Voicemail every time she had called, she thought, and why she hadn't heard it. But it didn't explain his disappearance, nor why he hadn't called round, or tried to contact her any other way. No it didn't explain it at all. It didn't change a thing.

But it did give her an excuse to go into the Police Station, which she did later that day.

"Hello," said the Officer on the desk as she walked in.

"Hello, please could I see PC Ben Lewis," Sarah asked in her best casual voice.

"Sorry, " said the Officer, "But PC Lewis isn't available. Can I take a message or help you with anything?"

Sarah placed the mobile on the counter. "Er PC Lewis, well, I think this may be his. He came round the other day, well a couple of weeks ago I suppose now, and I've just found this," she motioned to the phone, "I just found this when I was cleaning, stuck down the back of the settee. It must've fallen out when he ….. er …… erm …. sat down on the settee." She felt very tongue tied, and self conscious. Did the Officer guess it must've fallen down there and wedged itself whilst she was exploring Ben's naked body? She blushed.

"Yes, it must be his," she said decisively, "because no one else has been round, except my friend and she hasn't lost her phone."

"Well thank you," said the Officer, picking the phone up. "I'll write you a receipt, and put it in PC Lewis's pigeon hole to pick up when he's next in."

"And when is that?" asked Sarah shyly. The Officer looked at her kindly. "Oh now Miss," he said, "you know I can't tell you that. Would you like me to give PC Lewis a message?"

Sarah hesitated. For a moment she nearly said "Tell the slimy little toe rag I hope his penis withers up and dies," or something as equally venomous, but instead she just said "No, no thank you."

"Can I have your details, Miss, for the receipt," said the Officer, writing the information down as she gave it to him and afterwards handing her a copy of the receipt. "Would you like to leave a contact number for PC Lewis?" he asked. "No," said Sarah, turning away, "He knows where I am."

She came out of the Police Station slightly disappointed. She had geared herself for meeting Ben. She had been rehearsing in her head the things she would like to say to him, but she hadn't even got to see him. And on top of that she was no nearer knowing where he was or what had happened to him. But he was still on the island she knew that much.

She went back to the car parked on the side of the road, with her two boys strapped into their seats in the back. "Right boys," she said, pushing Ben from her mind, "We've wedding suits to hire."

CHAPTER 28

The wedding went well. It was an informal affair, and only family and close friends attended the Registry Office ceremony. Kate wore a beautiful white 50s style dress, short to the knee, with a wide floaty skirt and loads of lace. Think Christian Dior A-line dress with nipped in waist and you'll have a good idea. Now that Kate had lost loads of weight, and kept it off she certainly had the figure to show off a dress like that. And she looked radiant.

A very talented vintage hairdresser had come to the house early and pinned up both girls' hair in a weave of plaits and curls. Sarah was wearing another 50s style dress, also with a nipped in waist, and they both wore little short gloves and carried little bouquets.

All four boys, both Kate's and Sarah's, wore little suits with waistcoats. Only Kate's twelve year old Liam hadn't complained about his suit, admiring himself over and over again in the mirror. Kate whispered to Sarah that Liam had asked if a certain young lady had been invited to the wedding breakfast, the daughter of one of Steve's colleagues. It was only after the other younger boys saw the other men – both granddads, and Steve - dressed the same that they were mollified.

After the ceremony the entourage made their way to the Leisure Centre where Steve worked, and where now was waiting a huge buffet and disco, with all their friends and colleagues. Kate and Steve didn't have much money, so everyone had been tasked with bringing different parts of the buffet, and so well organised was it that the tables were now groaning with sausage rolls, home cooked quiches, vol-auvents, cheese sticks, crisps, plate after plate of tiny sandwiches, and much more. Steve's boss at the nightclub he worked in Southampton had donated crates of Prosecco for the opening drink and toast. Sarah now grabbed two glasses as she walked into the hall, gulping down one as fast as she could. She needed something to take the edge off of her emotions.

Her mother caught her. "Take it easy," she said out of the corner of her mouth as she went passed, "You've got the whole evening to go yet."

"Exactly," said Sarah irritably. She provokingly waved the second glass at Maureen and walked off to the main table to sit down. Her feet were killing her already.

As the evening wore on Sarah drank more and ate less. She wasn't in the mood for eating anyway. She just wanted to get wasted. She wanted to blot out the whole past couple of weeks.

Mark was at the party, and at one point he asked her to dance, but she wasn't in the mood for dancing either, and spent most of what should've been a romantic shuffle leaning on him for support, telling him why he hadn't been right for her. Mark was glad when the song finally ended and he could escape. He didn't ask her again.

The free Prosecco ran out, and Sarah managed to persuade her Dad to fund the next two large white wines. But after the second one Maureen showed up and told George not to buy Sarah any more as she had had enough. Sarah was indignant – she was a grown woman and her mother couldn't tell her what to do. "I can when I'm looking after your children," her mother had replied. "And what's got into you recently? You're like a bear with a sore head." Sarah just waved her away, and defiantly took a large glug of wine. "Go away Mother," she said swaying slightly, "You just don't understand."

"I understand that you're spoiling it for Kate if you carry on drinking," whispered her mother, "Don't be so selfish. Whatever is eating you make it keep until tomorrow." Sarah drained her glass, and ignoring Maureen, tottered off to find someone else to buy her a drink.

By the time it came for Kate and Steve to leave, Sarah was very drunk. The bride and groom had been given an overnight stay in a local luxury hotel as a present from Kate's parents, and were keen to be on their way. Kate kissed her best friend in the cheek. "Thank you for being an absolute star, Sarah," she said, giving her a hug for good measure. Kate turned away to kiss and hug other members of the family.

Steve caught Sarah in his arms as she swayed a bit. "Whoops," he said chuckling, "Got a bit of a speed wobble?"

Sarah flung her arms around his neck. "I've always fancied you," she told him, trying to focus on his face, "I imagine you're a good kisser. Will you do me one thing, and give me a snog?" Steve laughed and tried to pull away.

"Come on, Sarah," he said but Sarah pulled him closer, "Just one, on the lips. Kate won't know, she's not even looking, just one."

Sarah lunged at his face, but he turned his head and she ended up planting a slobbering kiss on his cheek. He was trying to keep it friendly but his face showed that he was slightly freaked out by Sarah's actions.

Kate saw what was happening and came over. She pulled Sarah's arms away from Steve's neck. "Come on Steve, time we were going."

"Nothing was going on," Sarah felt like she had to explain, "It's not what it seems." Kate could see what was going on, and she just laughed. To her eyes she saw a very drunk, and very lonely young woman trying to get it off with her new husband, but she wasn't cross. She felt very, very sad for Sarah and vowed that when everything settled down after the wedding she would do everything she could to get Sarah a man of her own.

She hugged Sarah again, and passed her over to her mother, and then she left with Steve for their wedding night.

Maureen motioned over to George whilst still holding on to Sarah. "Round up the boys and fetch the car. We need to get this lady home," she said.

CHAPTER 29

The boys got up early as they were going fishing with George, and Kate's boys and their Granddad, Brian. George and Brian were old friends, since the families had known each other for many years, and they often went fishing, or to football games, and on occasion took their grandsons out for the day. Maureen had packed them off with flasks of coffee, sandwiches, chocolate bars and even some home made walnut and date cake. They were not going to go hungry.

She left Sarah to sleep in, thinking that the more sleep she got the less of a hangover she would have. There was something upsetting Sarah she was sure of it, as Sarah didn't usually go out of her way to get wasted like she had last night at Kate's wedding. Maureen wondered if Sarah was jealous of her friend: after all it had been a long time since Sarah had been in a relationship.

Now she was coming upstairs to see Sarah, Paracetamol and Alka Seltzer in one hand and a large coffee in the other.

She had expected Sarah to still be fast asleep but she was awake, half propped up on the pillows, and staring into space. "How are you feeling?" asked Maureen, putting the Alka Seltzer and coffee down on the bedside table and handing the Paracetamol to Sarah.

"Oh I'm probably feeling better than I should be," admitted Sarah. She took the tablets and placed them in her mouth, then washed them down with the Alka Seltzer. Maureen winced, she wasn't sure that was how you were supposed to take the hangover remedies.

Maureen sat on the edge of the bed. She squeezed Sarah's hand. "What is it love?" she asked gently, "You know you can tell me anything." She felt Sarah's hand go rigid underneath hers and Sarah stared out of the window, not looking at her Mum, her face stony. Except for two tears sliding down each cheek.

"Whatever it is," Maureen continued, "I can't help you unless you tell me." Sarah made a strangled sob, trying desperately to keep her emotions in check. "You can't help me anyway," she said very quietly.

Maureen squeezed her hand. Horror gripped at her chest. My God what had the girl done? "It's not Steve, is it?" she asked fearfully, "You haven't, you know, him and you haven't?" She wasn't sure she wanted to know the answer.

Sarah shook her head, the tears flowing faster now. "No, no, not Steve," she tried to laugh, "He's a lovely guy, but he's Kate's."

"Oh, only you know you were making a bit of a show of yourself last night," Maureen reminded her.

Sarah hung her head. "Yes I know," she said, "But there is nothing in it. I guess I just wanted some attention." She tried to wipe her tears away with the back of her hand, but she just ended up smearing the wetness across her face. Maureen reached across the small bedroom and grabbed a box of tissues from the dressing table and handed them to Sarah. "Then what is it love?" she asked.

"Oh Mum, I have been such a fool," said Sarah, now sobbing. Maureen reached over and gathered her only daughter into her arms and cuddled her. Sarah buried her face into her mum's shoulder, and wept, crying out all the emotion she had felt over the past couple of weeks. Maureen held her until the tears were spent, and then propped her back against the pillows and handed her the coffee. "Drink this and tell me all about it," she said. She settled herself comfortably onto the bed; she felt this was going to be a long story.

Sarah told her everything, right back from the time she first met the policeman with the lovely eyes. Maureen nodded and asked questions and gradually began to understand the hurt and loneliness that her daughter had felt. It was hard to judge with Sarah. She didn't usually show her feelings – she was always so capable and dependable, someone you would want in a crisis – so it was doubly difficult for Maureen to now see her daughter in so much distress.

"I thought I was falling in love, Mum," Sarah explained, "For the first time since Simon left me I thought I could allow myself to fall in love because I had met someone who felt the same about me. I thought I could trust him. I thought I had met MY Steve." She finished off the last of the coffee and leaned back on the pillows, eyes red rimmed from crying.

"I'm sure there is some reasonable explanation," said Maureen, "It's very difficult for someone to disappear these days."

"It's not that," said Sarah, "Not just that he's disappeared with no trace, no explanation, it's not that. But it's the fact that he's so obviously already got a girlfriend. And one he's so, well, active with. He had the cheek to ask me if I was involved with anyone and yet he so obviously was. He lied to me."

"Well, he didn't lie," pointed out Maureen reasonably, "He just didn't tell you the full story. Seems to me, my girl, the only thing hurt here is your pride. And you'll recover from that. But it's such a shame. You really need to meet someone who you can trust and move on from Simon." She patted Sarah's legs. "Now come on, move yourself, you can't wallow in self pity all day. I'll take you home after a spot of lunch and I'll help you get the kids clothes ready for school tomorrow. Dad can drop the boys back off at your house when they come back and we'll have a takeaway shall we?"

Sarah smiled. "As long as it isn't Chinese," she said.

CHAPTER 30

Ben was on the last leg of his long journey back from Japan. He had already been travelling for over twenty-four hours when he boarded the catamaran at Portsmouth Harbour bound for the Island. He hadn't slept for, well, he guessed since he had left the island, which must be about three weeks ago. And he hadn't shaved or washed for days, water having been in short supply where he'd been. He didn't wonder that no one was sitting near him on the vessel – he must stink to high heaven.

It wasn't the journey that had been bad. He had tried to sleep, and seemed to achieve some state of unconsciousness for most of the journey, but it hadn't really been sleep. Ben wondered if he would be able to sleep again. Every time he closed his eyes he could see the horrors the tsunami had left – bodies of dead children and babies caught up in sluice gates, mangled limbs, devastated buildings, rats. He shuddered despite the warmth of the sun pouring through the catamaran's windows. It was always the same with these rescues. He knew that he would need to have counselling after this trip. He had received counselling after the New Orleans rescue and it had helped.

But now he was looking forward to getting home, and having a hot bath, some sort of rest, and seeing Sarah. That was if she was still talking to him. He didn't know if she had received his hastily scribbled note, or had got any word of his mysterious disappearance.

As he got off the catamaran at Ryde Pier Head he saw his mate Paul waiting for him. It was easy to see him, for Paul was wearing the Police's high visibility jacket and Ben could see parked outside, right up against the concourse ramp, was a police wagon.

"Step this way, if you would, Sir," said Paul loudly and sternly, as he greeted Ben, "And let me take that from you." He pulled Ben's large heavy bag off Ben's shoulders. Passengers were staring at them, curious as to what was happening. "Bloody hell," exclaimed Paul as he balanced himself with the weight of the bag, "It weighs a tonne." Ben smiled and slapped him on the back. "Cheers mate," he said, "I'm done in."

"God and you stink too," said Paul, "I'm going to have to scrub the wagon down after you've been in it," he complained. Ben laughed, it was good to be home.

On the drive back to his cottage, which was all of five minutes, Ben learned that no one at the station had received any note from him about Sarah, or about anything else. Shit, thought Ben. He would have to go round and make sure everything was OK.

Paul dumped Ben and his bag at the cottage and then sped off. He had a hot date that night, and anyway Ben looked exhausted.

Ben let himself into the cottage. He left his bag outside. It would need to be unpacked and properly fumigated, but that could wait until tomorrow. For now Ben needed food and rest. Paul had also left Ben with some groceries, including a chicken curry and rice ready meal, for which Ben was exceedingly grateful.

Ben ran himself a bath, and opened a bottle of beer that had been in the fridge. He relaxed in the hot soapy water and sipped his beer. Thoughts were whirling around in his head. Crying babies mixed in with Sarah's face.

The next thing he was spluttering as he inhaled water. He quickly sat up, limbs flailing until he realised where he was, and that he had fallen asleep in the bath. God that was close. He picked up the beer bottle. Dam he had accidently poured that into the bath. He quickly washed his hair and got out of the bath. Wrapped in a towel he shaved off his scraggy beard at the sink, and gave the bathroom a quick tidy round before changing into clean boxers and wrapping his bathrobe around him. He felt a bit better now.

Luckily his ready meal only took minutes to cook, as Ben was finding it difficult to stay awake. He ate it quickly, and retired to the tiny living room to watch TV. He opened another bottle of beer and put it on the coffee table. He changed channels until he got the Sports News, but within minutes of sitting down he was fast asleep.

Sometime in the middle of the night Ben woke with stiff legs and a crooked neck. He realised he was still on the settee, so he took himself off to bed where he quickly fell asleep again.

He woke to the sound of the front door banging. "BEN!" BEN!" a voice was yelling. Ben recognised the voice of his mother. He got up, still groggy from lack of sleep, and stumbled downstairs to let her in.

"If you hadn't put the chain on the door I could've let myself in, "grumbled his Mother, kissing him on the cheek. She was balancing a large plate in one hand and a bag of goodies in the other. "I've brought you some food," she said going through to the kitchen and setting the plate on the side. "Roast dinner I cooked myself this morning, and a cake."

"Ah thanks mum," Ben said. "Come here son," said Deidre, giving her boy a big cuddle, "Was it really as bad as it looked on the TV?"

"Worse," said Ben, squeezing her back, "It was like New Orleans all over again." "Oh poor you," said Deidre, "Well I can look after you today if you want." She smiled at Ben and let him go. He looked exhausted.

"To tell the truth, Mum," Ben said, "I just want to sleep." "Sure you do," said Deidre, "and you go back to bed. I'll start unpacking your kit bag and sticking in the wash anything I can find. Now go on off with you back to bed. And when you wake up I'll heat up the dinner for you."

Deidre was as true as her word, as when Ben woke up hours later his Mum had unpacked his kit bag, cleaned it all out, fumigated everything and his clothes were now clean as a whistle and hanging on the washing line. She was a gem. She reheated the cooked dinner and watched him as he ate, filling him in with the local gossip. She was better than the local newspaper.

After he had eaten his meal, and drank a glass of beer, Ben sat exhausted on the settee while his mother washed up and tidied around. He couldn't believe he was so tired.

"Go back to bed, love," Deidre said when she saw how washed out he looked. "I'll stay for a bit in case you wake up again and want a bit of tea." Ben went to say she didn't have to, but she waved him away. "Go on with you. Up those stairs.

I'll make myself a nice cup of tea, watch the Corrie Omnibus and maybe have a slice of cake. I've got nothing to rush home for."

This was true. Since her husband, Ben's father, had passed away a few years before from cancer she lived alone, but it was through choice. As an active member of the local British Legion Club, and a looker to boot, she was a popular dancing partner with the men in the club, and she never went lonely. But she joked that she kicked them out before breakfast.

Ben slept all afternoon and into the evening, and when he still hadn't woken up by bedtime, Deidre decided she would stay overnight and sleep in the spare room. She had heard him cry out in his sleep a few times, and when she had gone in to look at him his head felt quite hot. She didn't want to leave him in case he had caught something and deteriorated over night.

By the morning Ben felt fully rested. He had a bit of a fretful sleep early on but then had settled into a dreamless one, and awoke feeling like he had slept for a week.

Downstairs his mother gone already but she had left a note:

Breakfast in the oven. Don't do too much today. Give me a call later. Love Mum xx

He smiled when he read it, and helped himself to the bacon and mushrooms she had left for him warming in the low oven. She had also ironed his uniform and left it on hangers. Good Old Mum, he smiled to himself as he got washed and dressed and ready for work.

CHAPTER 31

Ben's first job was to find his mobile phone, but it wasn't in the cottage, he was sure of that. He looked everywhere and tried to retrace his steps from three weeks ago when he had run in to grab his kit bag. But it was nowhere to be found.

OK, so as he couldn't find his mobile his first job was to report into the Station, his second job was to find his mobile and his third was to find out how Sarah had taken his sudden disappearance. He was not looking forward to his third job as he now guessed that she would be pretty mad with him.

Arriving at the Police Station he was greeted by his colleagues with lots of slaps on the back. He was ordered to report to the Chief Superintendent immediately for a debrief.

Ben entered the Chief's office a little cautiously. It wasn't an area of the station that he normally frequented and it felt a bit like entering the Headmistress's office when he was a kid and was sent there for smoking around the back of the bike sheds. Triggered by the thought of school an image of Sarah flashed through his mind and his heart plummeted wondering what she had been thinking the last few weeks.

Chief Superintendent Noel Parker looked up from his desk when he saw Ben entering the room, and stood up, coming round to the front of his desk with his hand outstretched. "Welcome back, Ben," he said shaking Ben's hand. "Sit down." He walked back to his own side of the desk and sat down.

"I've been hearing great things about you," he continued, referring to a piece of paper on his desk," It says here that you saved a young girl from a crushed house?" He looked at Ben questioningly.

"Yes Sir," said Ben, "She had been buried under the rubble since the tsunami and she was in a few feet of water. She'd been there about five days. We found her because I heard her cry out, very faintly. We dug for twenty-four hours, she was buried that far down."

"It says here that the team were ready to give up, as they didn't think there was any body under there," said the Chief, "But your tenacity kept them going."

"Well," said Ben modestly, "They didn't think there was anyone under there, but I had heard a cry, and I was sure there was. The dog, our sniffer dog, kept reacting every time he combed the area. Not a lot, but he definitely smelled something. They would've moved the rubble eventually anyway, but I convinced them they shouldn't wait, and at the end of the day we could see her hand and it was moving."

"And how are you feeling within yourself?" asked the Chief concerned, "You will be booking yourself into Counselling won't you?"

Ben smiled. "I'm OK," he said, "I've spent the last two days sleeping, and I've not had too many nightmares so far. But, yes, it helped me before so I will contact them."

"Well, don't go doing too much for a few days." The Chief stood up, indicating the interview was over. He leaned across the desk to shake Ben's hand again. "Thank you for popping in," he said, and then as an after thought he added "I shall be recommending you for a Queen's Award for Gallantry."

Ben went to protest but the Chief waved it away. "I know what you're going to say, Ben, but these things are good for police PR. Oh and on that subject I've allowed the County Press to contact you for a report for their paper, with photos, so make sure you look smart."

"Yes Sir, thank you Sir," Ben muttered, although he wasn't sure what he was exactly thanking the Chief for.

CHAPTER 32

"Hey, Ben," called out PC Matt Davies, "Fancy a bite out, mate? You've been hunched over that laptop all morning." It was true, Ben acknowledged. Since giving an interview to the County Press newspaper reporter, and having photos taken, and at almost the same time giving an interview to the local radio station, he had been doing nothing except clearing off emails from his account. He was ready for a bit of fresh air if nothing else.

On the way out of the station Ben passed by his pigeonhole, and there, laying on another batch of reports, was his mobile phone. He picked it up and looked around. He was sure it hadn't been there earlier. Perhaps he'd missed it. He tried to switch it on but it was dead. He looked through the papers in the pigeonhole, looking for something to indicate where it had been, perhaps a note, but there was nothing. Its disappearance and reappearance were mysteries.

Matt Davies drove them both into the town centre, a street running down the hillside, filled on either side with shops and bars. He found a parking space and Ben got stiffly out of the passenger side. Weeks of strenuous activity and now a couple of days of sleeping were making his muscles ache.

He stretched as Matt joined him on the pavement. "Getting old, mate," Matt smiled at him. Ben smiled back, "Feeling it," he said.

They were just about to go into the sandwich bar when there was a scream, and shouting. Both policemen whirled round and ran off in the direction of the commotion, towards a very drunk man standing outside a shop with his trousers round by his feet, and waving his not inconsiderable penis about in his hand.

Ben and Matt looked at each other. "Yours, I think," said Ben, trying not to laugh. Next to the man, an old woman was having palpitations on a bench. "Make him stop," she was screaming hysterically, "Make him put it away."

Ben went over to her while Matt tried to get the man to pull his trousers back up. "Come on my love," said Ben kindly, "Surely you've seen it before?"

"Not his," said the old woman, "and not since my husband died twenty years ago have I seen anything like that." Ben smiled and sat beside her. "Tell me what happened," he coaxed.

"Well he just started waving it about," the old woman explained, "I was minding my own business, and just passing by and he pulled his trousers down without a bye your leave, and started waving it about." Ben patted her hand as the old lady wiped her eyes with a handkerchief she had taken out of her pocket. "Oooh gave me such a fright it did."

"I'm sure it did, love," said Ben, trying very hard not to laugh. He looked over to Matt who was having a hard time coaxing the man to put his tackle away.

Ben took out his notebook, "I'll just get some details," he said, "and then when you're ready you can be on your way." He wrote the lady's name and address and put his notebook away. "Thanks love," he said.

Another younger lady came up to the old woman. "Now what trouble have you got yourself into, Mum?" she addressed the woman, "I only leave you for a moment to nip into the Co-op and the next minute I come back to find you surrounded by the police."

"Nothing to worry about," said Ben, "Your mother's just had a bit of a shock. I think she may need a nice cup of tea." The younger lady took her mother's bag that was by the old lady's side, and helped her up. "Come on Mum," she said, "I think I need a cuppa myself."

Ben turned his attention back to Matt and the drunk, but as he did so out of the corner of his eye he saw Sarah walking towards him up the hill. He was about to call out, when he saw her stop, turn, and then start walking very fast back down the hill.

"Can you finish up here?" he called out to Matt, "there's something …." And he was gone running down the road towards the rapidly retreating figure of Sarah before he had time to finish the sentence.

He saw Sarah's figure turn into a side street, and then dive into the women's public toilets. He caught up with her and without thinking ran inside, and as he did so he heard the bolt of one of the cubicles slide across.

"OK, come out with your hands up," he said sternly, "You're surrounded." He thought Sarah would find his joke funny. But there was no movement. "Come on, stop messing about. You don't want us to get nasty," he banged on the nearest cubicle door.

He heard a little yelp, and then the bolt slid back. The door opened very slowly, and out came a terrified old lady. Her face was nearly as white as her hair, and she came out of the cubicle with her hands up.

"S..S.. Sorry," she said in a tiny voice, "Please don't shoot me." Ben pushed his hands through his hair. Shit, he'd done it now. He was sure he had seen Sarah dive in here.

"No, I'm sorry," he said to the little lady, "I was sure I'd seen a FUGITIVE," he said fugitive in a loud voice, addressing the other cubicle door, "run in here but I must've been mistaken. I'm really sorry."

He heard a snigger and turned round to find Matt standing at the entrance. "What are you doing, mate?" asked Matt, "Taken to arresting innocent ladies now, like we haven't enough to occupy us."

"I thought…," Ben started to explain, "No, you're right. Sorry love, on your way." He escorted the old lady from the premises, and then walked with Matt back to the sandwich bar, casting a few glances backwards towards the toilets but seeing nothing.

Sarah waited for about ten minutes, crunched up with her feet on the seat, so anyone looking under the toilet door would think no one was in there. She waited until her heartbeat reduced to normal.

Then she got off the toilet seat, cautiously opened the cubicle and stuck her head out. The toilets were empty, and there was no one outside either. What was she doing? Why was she running away from him? She didn't know why but it had been instinct to run the second she saw him in the street. She knew she should've faced him, had it out with him, exactly where had he been, and why had he run off like that without a word? Oh loads of questions, but she couldn't trust herself not to become emotional. He had really hurt her.

She had her answer as to where he had been from the car radio on the way home. It had broadcast Ben's interview with the reporter earlier that morning. The report had explained how Ben was part of the Rapid Reaction Force and had spent the last three weeks up to his eyeballs in debris, dead bodies and God knows what else trying to save people and give them at least a part of their life back after the devastating tsunami.

Very noble, thought Sarah, with a flicker of guilt for all the horrible things she had thought about him over the last 3 weeks. But that didn't explain why he hadn't called, especially as the report had said that he had been back on the island since Saturday. He had been home three days and he hadn't attempted to get in touch with her. No, he was as bad as she had thought, she reasoned.

CHAPTER 33

It was an awful day. It was wet, and Sarah was not in a good mood. She had spent the day in the Magistrates Court with another excited group of children, and now, on the way home, the minibus had got a puncture. Shit, shit, shit, she muttered under her breath. It didn't help that every time she turned on the radio she had to listen to Ben Lewis's dulcet tones as he explained how heroic he had been in Japan.

Sarah pulled over into a layby and stopped the minibus. She turned the engine off.

"MISS, MISS, WHAT'S HAPPENING?" called the children. Sarah stood up. "SHUSH, EVERYONE BE QUIET," she called down the bus. "We've got a puncture. Now everyone wait on the bus whilst I give Mr Payne a call." John Payne was the school caretaker, and Sarah was sure he would bring out the other minibus to collect the children and arrange for the tyre to be changed on this one.

"STAY HERE," she called out again above the noise of the chattering children, "Miss Read," she said to the Assistant who was accompanying them, "Please keep the children entertained, and don't let them off the bus." Miss Read nodded, and got up to stand at the front of the bus. "OK children," she said, "We're going to play a game of charades. Who wants to be first?"

Sarah got off the bus, and went to look at the tyre. It was well and truly flat, with a great big nail sticking out of its side. Bugger, said Sarah under her breath, and gave the tyre a kick. She found Mr Payne's number on her phone and called him. She explained their predicament and Mr Payne promised he would bring the other minibus immediately and arrange for a garage to come out. He would be fifteen minutes.

She was stood looking at the tyre, trying to delay the moment she would have to get back on the bus and join in with yet another tiresome game of charades, when she heard a car pull in behind them, and looking up she saw it was a police car. Oh fuck, she thought, really, could the day get any worse?

She stared stony faced at PC Ben Lewis as he walked towards her, trying to keep her emotions in check. Her heart was leaping all over the place and her knees felt weak. She could feel herself shaking. She concentrated on showing no emotion. Really, were there no other policemen on this island?

Ben tried a smile. "Hello," he said. "Hello," said Sarah coldly. She was going to make it hard for him.

"I'm sorry for ...," he started. "No, don't," said Sarah, cutting him off. "I have a minibus full of children, and a flat tyre. I don't have time for your apologies."

He looked shame faced. "I know but I am sorry. I did try to let you know what had happened but I had lost my phone."

"I don't want to know," said Sarah, brushing his apologies away. She was very angry, and trying to keep her voice level as she said "At first I thought something had happened to you, and then I realised you are just like all the other men I've known." She could hear the children shouting and squealing in the minibus as they shouted out film titles in their game.

"But you know where I've been," asked Ben quietly. "Yes, yes I know NOW," said Sarah, her voice wavering. She turned away from him and stared at the tyre, blinking back the tears. Don't you dare cry, she scolded herself.

"Can we start again, please?" begged Ben. "I didn't know we had started," said Sarah tight lipped. She knew she was being hateful but she couldn't help herself. She had been hurt, and now she was pouring that hurt out on Ben.

She walked passed him as she saw Mr Payne turn up with the other minibus. "Now if you'll excuse me, I have to get the children home."

"Mr Payne," she called out to the caretaker as he got out of the second minibus and came to look at the tyre. Mr Payne nodded to Ben. "Thank you PC Lewis, but we, I, don't need you any more," Sarah said dismissively to Ben. He tried to look her in the eye, but she looked away. He nodded at her, and walked back to his car. Her coldness was chilling.

CHAPTER 34

It was a couple of weeks after the puncture that Sarah was in the Staff Room, making herself a coffee before the start of the school day, and chatting with the other teachers. Ben had tried to call her a few times after their confrontation but this week she hadn't heard from him at all. She had ignored his calls, as she had ignored his knock on the door when he had turned up one evening. Perhaps he had finally got the hint. She told herself she felt relieved.

He had pushed a letter through her door on that evening, which turned out to be about the case against the youths who had attacked the old man earlier in the year. As her Case Support Officer, Ben was informing her that the case had already gone to court and as the youths had pleaded guilty there would be no further action. Good, thought Sarah, at least he won't have an excuse to bother me again.

She was now looking at the teacher's rosters posted up on the Notice Board, and noticing how many times she was on Playground Duty over the next couple of weeks, when Mrs Gilmore, the Headmistress walked in and stood in the middle of the room clapping her hands for attention.

"Right everyone, this week's rosters are up on the notice boards," she waved a hand at the Notice Board. "People on playground duty, please make sure you're not smoking round the back of the bike sheds when you should be supervising the children. I know you do it, and I know who you are. I would've thought you had grown out of the habit of sneaking around the back of bike sheds but it appears some of you haven't. Anyway our neighbours can see you and it doesn't look very good. Don't do it." She stared around the room and her gaze alighted on the Teaching Assistant. Miss Read bent her head in shame.

"We have some forecasts for heavy rain mid week so wet weather playtime will be introduced in the Sports Hall," Mrs Gilmore continued. "Mr Payne has kindly said he will make the sports cupboard available. Please remember to put the equipment back afterwards, and keep the bean bags and balls separated. It is very helpful."

"We're having a visit from the Isle of Wight Constabulary on Tuesday afternoon. Don't worry Sarah they are not after you again, this is purely an educational visit." The Headmistress had caught the look of horror on Sarah's face. Everyone else tittered. "We are hosting two officers to talk about road safety and general looking after yourself type stuff. I have a list here of the things they would like set up in the Sports Hall for their session so these will be available tomorrow afternoon. Timetabled PE is cancelled and all pupils will be asked to assemble in the hall at 2.30pm. Sarah, because you seem to be on very good terms with the police at the moment I have detailed you to look after the officers."

Sarah blanched. "Me?" she started to argue, "Headmistress do you really think....?" "Yes," said Mrs Gilmore, cutting across her. "Be at my office at 2pm tomorrow afternoon. All right everyone, onward and upward. Have a good week." And without further ado the headmistress strode out of the office.

Sarah cursed and thought what were the odds it would be him?

The odds were pretty high. Sarah presented herself to the Headmistress's office at 2pm the next day, as requested, and reluctantly knocked on the door. "Come in," she heard a voice call from behind the door. Sarah walked in and there, leaning nonchalantly against a bookshelf, was PC Ben Lewis. Sarah walked into the room, trying very hard not to look at him. "Headmistress," she said stiffly to Mrs Gilmore.

"Sarah," said Mrs Gilmore, "I think you already know PC Lewis." She nodded to Ben as she said this. Ben turned his gaze on Sarah, and there was nothing she could do but say hello. She mumbled a greeting and briefly cast a look in his direction, but avoided his eyes. "And this is PC Tom Watters." She indicated the other policeman sat on a chair in front of her desk. "Hello," said Sarah, more pleasantly to the younger policeman.

"Well, Sarah, if you would like to take these gentlemen through to the Sports Hall I believe Mr Payne has set up everything you need." She stood up, indicating their conversation was over. "And Sarah, the classes will start coming in at twenty past so sit them in rows as for assembly."

"Yes Mrs Gilmore," said Sarah. "Come this way, please," she said to PC Watters.

Sarah led the policemen the short distance to the Sports Hall, and showed them the equipment and furniture they had asked for. She stayed in front of both men, determined not to be caught by Ben in conversation. Stony faced, Ben helped Tom to organise their presentation and carefully ignored Sarah.

At twenty past the hour the excited children started arriving and Sarah was busy organising them into their classes and sitting them in front of the policemen. Once all the children had arrived she indicated to Tom to start, and then she took her seat at the side of the stage as Mrs Gilmore introduced the men, and Tom and Ben started their presentation.

An hour later it was all over. The children had shuffled back to their classrooms and the policemen had packed up the equipment. "I'll show you out," said Sarah walking ahead of them.

Ben caught her up. "Can we talk?" he asked.

"There is nothing to talk about," said Sarah through clenched teeth, mindful that the other officer was following them.

They got to the front door. Tom suggested he went ahead and got the car turned around. He could see that Ben wanted to have a chat with the pretty teacher.

Once Tom had gone to the car Sarah turned to Ben. "There is nothing to talk about," she reiterated.

"Don't I get a fair hearing?" Ben asked. "It can't be just because I left without saying anything."

Sarah shook her head. "No," she said quietly, "it's more than that." Ben looked at her pleadingly, "Well what is it?" he asked. "Can I make amends?"

"I met Sadie," said Sarah. She waited for it to register with Ben, but he looked confused. "She explained your relationship," she continued waiting for the penny to drop. Ben looked even more confused. "But we don't have a relationship," he said puzzled. "She doesn't want a relationship."

"Well, I've seen the photos," said Sarah. Ben stared at her blankly. "The photos seem to suggest you and her are very much in a relationship," Sarah said. Ben's face showed that he now understood which photos Sarah was talking about. "Shit," he muttered and pushed his hand through his hair in desperation.

"Mis-use of police equipment I'd have thought," said Sarah in a haughty tone. "It's not like that," Ben tried to explain. "I think it is," said Sarah. "You see Sadie explained your relationship to me. In explicit detail, with photos to match. I have a very good idea of what it is like." She looked at Ben. "Shag Buddy was the term I think she used."

She turned to go. "Good bye Ben," she said sadly and then disappeared back through the front door.

CHAPTER 35

Paul Dorey ordered two beers and took them over to where Ben was sitting. "Sure you don't want something stronger?" he asked his mate, "You know, for the pain?"

Ben sadly shook his head. "I don't understand women," he stated, "So she accepts I went away for three weeks without a word. That is acceptable. But I can't have a relationship with another woman. It's not even as if I was seeing Sadie at the same time. Sadie had ended it and was in Florida for heavens sake." He shook his head again and took a large glug of his pint.

Paul also shook his head. "Well mate," he concurred, "You're not the only one. I've never understood women either. I'm not sure anyone does. I once had a girlfriend who had this dog. Besotted with it, she was. The dog could do anything it liked. It even slept on the bed. One night we were, you know, in full throes and I felt like I was being watched, and I opened my eyes to find the dog sat on the bed staring at me. Put me right off. She thought it was hilarious. She wouldn't throw it out though. I had to perform with this dog staring at me like it wanted to eat me."

"What happened with the relationship?" asked Ben. "Nothing, I never went back," said Paul.

"But I never got the chance to explain," Ben carried on with his own thoughts. "She just cut me off. Said she didn't want to know. How fair is that?"

"You want my opinion?" Paul asked, "She's a mental bitch," he continued without waiting for Ben to reply. "She's got a screw loose. She didn't even ask you for an explanation. You're better off with Sadie, mate."

"How do you work that one out?" asked Ben.

"Well, stands to reason, doesn't it," said Paul, "Sadie doesn't want any strings. She just wants sex. Straight forward sex." He thought for a moment. "Well not straight forward." He pushed his wrists together as if they were handcuffed and laughed. "You know what I mean." He winked at Ben, and Ben blushed. "Don't tell me you've seen those bloody photos as well."

Paul guffawed. "I don't think there's anyone in the station who hasn't," he said. "What even old Mrs Murray?" asked Ben aghast. Mrs Murray was the station cleaner and must've been well into her seventies.

Paul nodded. "Even Old Mrs Murray Mop," he agreed. Ben rubbed his hand over his face. "God no," he said, "I wondered why she winked at me when I passed her yesterday."

Paul laughed. "I wouldn't worry. You got some good reviews from the WPCs," he said. "I heard PC Alison Harris saying she'd give you one any time you liked." Ben shook his head. "No, no think about it before you dismiss it," cautioned Paul.

"No thanks, done WPCs remember. Ended in disaster," Ben reminded his mate. "So when did you all see these photos?" asked Ben.

"The station BBQ," replied Paul. The annual station BBQ always took place just after Easter, and it was a good chance for everyone to relax and get to know each other and their families. This year it had happened whilst Ben was in Japan.

"I didn't know Sadie had gone," said Ben, "Why should she go without me?" Paul looked a bit sheepish. "Well, it was like this," Paul started to explain, then noticed Ben's glass was empty, "Another mate?" he asked.

"You can get them in after you've explained why Sadie was at the BBQ," said Ben.

"Well, I didn't have anyone to go with, and I didn't fancy going on my own. I'd seen Sadie in town, and just sort of ended up asking her. You know what she's like for a party," explained Paul.

"So she went and got completely rat arsed and showed everyone the photos," Ben finished the story for him. "And did you…?"

"God no way mate," said Paul emphatically, "Talk about dipping your pen in someone else's ink. No way."

Paul got up and fetched two more beers. "And anyway," he continued when he had brought two fresh pints back, "why did you let her take those photos?"

"I didn't LET her," clarified Ben, "You can see I was slightly indisposed at the time." Paul raised an eyebrow. "You certainly were that," he laughed.

"And drunk too," added Ben, "And I didn't actually remember them being taken until she showed them to me weeks later."

"Didn't you ask her to delete them?" Paul asked. "Of course I did," said Ben, "but she didn't want to. She said they were something to remind her of me when I wasn't there. I didn't know she was going to get them out every time she got pissed."

"I think that kinda shit it with Sarah, you know," said Paul returning to the original subject of conversation. "I know," said Ben, "though I still don't understand why."

"I don't think you ever will, mate," said Paul, "Anyway, she is yesterday. We got to get you back in the game. Fancy a pub crawl one Saturday night? We could do the clubs in Soton. The guy in my gym works as a bouncer over there. He says if we flash our I.D. cards we can get in free."

CHAPTER 36

It was a lovely summer evening as Sarah sat on the beach across from the flat. She was sat on the same wall she had been on when Ben had turned up on that fateful evening, she mused. Her and Kate's boys were in front of her, running up and down the beach with a football, shouting and calling to each other. They will sleep well, Sarah thought, they've been running about all day.

Kate came up behind her with an opened bottle of wine and two glasses. She sat down next to Sarah and poured a glass of wine. "Lovely evening," she said, handing the glass to her. "Thanks," muttered Sarah, putting the glass next to her on the wall. "Yes, it is isn't it?" she agreed, "But the year seems to be rushing past now."

It was still only May, and only four weeks since Kate's wedding, but Sarah felt that the time was speeding past. "Only another six weeks and it'll be the summer holidays again," she continued musing, "I can't wait."

Kate smiled. "That is spoken with your teacher's hat on," she said. "I give you two weeks of the holiday and you'll be wishing you were back at work."

Sarah gave a little laugh. "I know," she agreed, "I go through the same emotions every year. I long for the summer holidays, and then can't wait to be back at work." She took a sip of her wine. "Anyway it might be a bit different this year," she said. "Why?" Kate looked at her curiously.

"Well, Mr Jackson, the Deputy Head, has announced his sudden retirement and is leaving at the end of term." Kate nodded. She knew that Mr Jackson had come into some money, and the school gate talk amongst the mothers was that he was planning to go and live in Spain. "Well, I was summoned to Mrs Gilmore's office the other day," Kate nodded again to show she was listening. "She said that she was really pleased with my progress and suggested that I might like to apply for the Deputy Head vacancy."

"Ooh that's good," interjected Kate, really pleased for her friend. Sarah continued: "Of course, Mrs Gilmore was at pains to point out that I might not get the job. It wasn't in her power to decide; that would be up to the Governors but she would certainly recommend me."

"I know, but you are the best teacher they've got," said Kate, "I'm sure the Governors will snap you up."

"If I apply," warned Sarah, "I haven't made up my mind whether to or not yet."

"And why wouldn't you? You're good at what you do, and I know the other teachers like you," encouraged Kate.

"Yes but it's moving away from the actual teaching," explained Sarah, "I don't know if I want to do that. I enjoy teaching, but Mr Jackson seems to spend most of his day walking around with a wodge of files under his arm, and he moans about the amount of paperwork he has to take home."

"I think Donald Jackson makes heavy work of it," said Kate, " Do you remember what he was like when we were at school?" Kate and Sarah had been pupils in Mr Jackson's class when he had first started teaching on the island thirty years before. "He used to wander around with our school books under his arm, and was always moaning about having to mark our homework." Kate laughed, "Do you remember we used to try and persuade him not to set us any, then he wouldn't have to mark it? He used to say it was more than his job was worth!"

Sarah laughed too, remembering a young Mr Jackson walking down the corridors muttering under his breath. "He hasn't changed a bit," she said.

Sarah's mobile starting ringing next to her. Sarah picked it up and squinted at the screen. "God I can't see anything without my reading glasses these days," she said, passing it to Kate, "Who does it say?" she asked.

"Ben," said Kate. She paused, "Shall I answer it?" she asked.

"No," said Sarah, snatching it back, and cancelling the call. Kate looked at her. "You never did tell me what happened between you two," she said.

She proffered Sarah the bottle of wine and offered to refill her glass. Sarah passed her glass over, and looked over to the boys who were now throwing sticks into the sea for her neighbour's dogs. "There is nothing to tell," said Sarah sadly, "It all went horribly wrong. I thought he was the man for me and he wasn't. That's all."

"Is there no way back?" asked Kate, putting her arm around her friend who was looking very dejected. "No," said Sarah definitely, "Anyway he has someone else."

"Already? Wow he didn't waste time," amused Kate.

"No he already had her, it appears," said Sarah, "That's why there's no way back." She sighed, "I always pick the wrong ones."

Kate squeezed her friend's hand. "Then we must find you the right one," she said. "Now drink up, let's get the boys in and get another bottle out."

CHAPTER 37

The car had an oil leak, wouldn't you know it? More expense, Sarah thought as she dropped it off at the garage and started to walk to the nearest bus stop. The garage had estimated around £260 to repair the leak, and Sarah was calculating where she could make savings in order to afford it.

As she approached the bus stop, the advertising hoarding on the back of it caught her eye. It was of a cosy family, a mother and father and two children, advertising how easy it was to foster. Sarah smirked as she recognised the woman in the advert – it was a friend of hers, Jody, who boasted of her part-time modelling career. The ironic thing was that Jody hated children and certainly wouldn't have fostered any herself.

As Sarah got nearer to the bus stop she had to smile even more when she realised someone had defaced the poster. They had added little horns to Jody's head and a moustache. Oh that was funny, thought Sarah, naughty but funny, especially given that it was only Jody's picture that had been defaced.

However, when she got right up to the bus stop she realised that the whole bus stop had been vandalised, and there was glass everywhere. She picked her way carefully through the shattered shards, and picked up a marker pen that had been thrown down under the defaced advert.

A car skidded to a halt next to her and someone jumped out, and then she looked up into the steely eyes of PC Ben Lewis. She stared at him, and he stared back at her, sadness in his eyes.

He looked at the defaced advert and shattered bus stop, and then pointedly at her.

"Ben, you can't possibly think I…." Sarah said, also looking at the defaced advert.

Ben looked at the marker pen she still held in her hand, and then back to her. "Mrs Blake, why is it when there is trouble about you always seem to be in the middle of it?" he asked sternly.

Sarah caught his tone. "PC Lewis, are you the only policeman on this island?" she asked.

Ben took an evidence bag out of his pocket and motioned for her to drop the marker pen into it. "I suppose it was like this when you arrived?" he asked sarcastically.

Sarah nodded, ignoring his tone. "Ben," she tried to placate him, "I'm sorry. About the last time we met, you know at school. I'm sorry I …"

He cut her off. "I don't want to know," he said, throwing her own words back at her. He looked at her coldly. "You had your reasons. Now you can be on your way. I'll report this to the Council." He gave her one last sad look and turned and got into the car.

Paul started the engine. "God I wish you two would get a room," he said, pulling off. Ben looked at him questioningly. "The electricity between you. You've got to get it sorted or you'll burn yourself out."

Ben humphed. "That or give Sadie a call," Paul suggested with a smirk on his face.

CHAPTER 38

It was the week of half term, and the family were having a big BBQ over at Kate's parents, Brian and Ann Wilson's house. The family included Sarah and the boys, and her parents too. Kate's sister, Karen, and Kate's ex-husband, who was now about to be Karen's husband, were also going to be there. Sarah shook her head every time she thought about what Kate had gone through recently, and how she had found love and happiness with Steve and how she had forgiven both her husband and her sister. She knew she would not have been so forgiving herself.

Sarah had made a quiche, and her famous Malibu trifle, but without so much booze just in case the children decided to try it, and she had packed up sausages and burgers, baps and Marmite sandwiches. Alfie was going through the 'not eating anything unless it was Marmite sandwiches' stage. Tom had also been through this but his fad had been mashed potato sandwiches. Sarah had suspected her father had introduced him to that. At least Marmite was more practical for carrying about.

She got the boys seated in the car, before going back in for their games bag, which they had forgotten, and then eventually they set off.

It was a lovely day, one of those May days that are long and warm, and the Sunshine Isle was certainly living up to its name. Sarah felt that it was the first real day of summer, and she had had to dig out her shorts from the back of the drawer, and had hastily shaved the tops of her legs that morning. She hoped she hadn't missed any bits at the back.

She was the last to arrive at the party, so there were hellos and kisses before she was able to get into the kitchen to pour herself a long cool glass of fruit juice. The boys had already run off, delighted at being with their friends, and also the Wilson's old dog, which was also called Wilson. Brian, Kate's Dad, had named him, and Ann, her mother, always joked that it was a good job she hadn't allowed him to name their daughters.

Sarah seated herself at the table where Kate and Karen were sat. Kate got out her mobile phone and started clicking the screen. "So," she said, still clicking away, "Karen has made a very good suggestion in your hunt for romance." She showed Sarah the app on her mobile that she had opened. "Tinder," she said triumphantly. "What?" said Sarah, peering at the mobile.

"Tinder," repeated Kate, "Look, you swipe the photos like this." She swiped her hand across the screen and the photos changed. They were all of men. "These are all the men on this island looking for dates. You click on the one you like." She carried on swiping. More photos came up.

Sarah took the mobile from her, reached down for her bag, got out her reading glasses and peered at the photos, experimentally swiping her finger across the screen to the next page. "No way," she said at last and handed the mobile back. Karen took the mobile and started swiping the photos.

"Why not?" asked Kate, "It's either that or your mother is going to sign you up to internet dating." Sarah glared at Kate in horror. "God she's not is she?" she asked. "Oh yes," confirmed Kate, "and I think she also mentioned the Walking Festival speed date. Just be glad that one was last week."

Karen was studying the photos on the App. One of them caught her interest. "Now he's quite nice," she said, showing Kate and Sarah the photo. Kate burst out laughing. "I've had him," Sarah said.

Karen looked at the photo confused. "You've what?" she asked. "Yeah I've had him," said Sarah. Kate grabbed the mobile, still laughing, and called over to her new husband who was stood around the BBQ with the other men.

"HEY STEVE!" she shouted, "COME AND HAVE A LOOK AT THIS!" She was still laughing when Steve came running over. She showed him the photo. "What's this?" he asked.

"Tinder," said Kate. "Tinder the dating App?" asked Steve. "Yep," confirmed Kate. Steve laughed. "Haha, wait until my mates hear about this," he chuckled. He gave the mobile back to Kate and strolled back to the man camp.

Karen wanted to know what was going on. "What's so funny?" she asked, puzzled. "And what do you mean you've had him?"

"He's Steve's mate from the leisure centre," Kate explained, "And Sarah's dated him."

"But he's quite good looking," said Karen, "What on earth is he doing on this site? I wouldn't have thought he couldn't get dates."

"Oh he can get dates all right," said Kate, "He's a bit of a lady's man." "Which is why I only went out with him once," said Sarah.

"But you, you know," commented Kate, nudging her. Sarah blushed. "Just the once," she said. She saw Kate give her a look. "OK twice but it was the same night so it counts as once in my book."

Karen whistled appreciatively. "Lucky you," she said. Sarah shook her head. "It wasn't all it was cracked up to be," she offered.

"All quantity, no quality," confirmed Karen. Sarah nodded. "I know just what you mean," said Karen, "but he has a fit body."

She looked over to her fiancé, Michael, as she said this and took in his bulging waistline. "Michael's diet's going well then," commented Kate with a little smile. She had been married to Michael for over a decade before their divorce. She knew his love of take aways and dining out. She couldn't help comparing him to Steve's lean body and his well defined legs in his slim shorts, and remembering their passionate love making of the night before, and deep down she thanked her sister.

Maureen and Ann came bustling out of the kitchen. Ann was carrying a baby alarm and Maureen had a laptop. Ann put the alarm on the table and switched it on. They could hear a baby coo-ing to herself as she fell asleep.

"She's gone down," said Ann to Karen, "Took her time, mind, poor little mite with all this activity going on." "Thanks Mum," said Karen, "Hopefully she won't be so fractious when she wakes up." "

"Well she better improve her mood for her birthday party," commented Ann. Karen and Michael's baby was now nearly a year old. Kate often wondered where the time had gone. All the hurt of Karen and Michael's affair was far behind them now, and baby Olivia had helped to mend any rift. As Ann and Brian's first granddaughter they were besotted with her and spoiled her rotten whenever they could see her, but as Karen and Michael lived in Sheffield this wasn't as often as they liked.

Maureen plonked the laptop on the table. She opened it and started clicking on the keyboard. "HOW LONG FOR LUNCH STEVE?" she shouted over to the men's group.

Steve was in his element wielding a pair of tongs over the crackling BBQ pit. "ABOUT HALF AN HOUR UNTIL WE PUT THE MEAT ON," he called back.

"Just enough time then, girls," Maureen said. The girls gathered around the laptop, except Sarah who had a sinking feeling she was not going to like this.

"Right, I've been investigating online dating agencies," announced Maureen, "And I think this one is best." She clicked on a site and showed the girls the screen. "It's a local one, and it's not too expensive, but I liked it because it had a picture of a very nice man on the first page."

Sarah snorted. "You're willing to gamble with my love life just because it has the picture of a nice man on the first page," she said, "Cheers Mum."

"Don't be so soft," said Maureen, "I've also investigated it and it looks good. Very professional, and comes with good reviews." She clicked on the mouse and a form came up. "Now help me fill in this form."

"I'm not having anything to do with this, you know that don't you?" commented Sarah. She was happy for her mother to have a play. Let's be honest, when Maureen had an idea in her head you couldn't stop her, but she didn't have to go along with it. "You play, I'm going to make sure Steve's got some vegetables on the BBQ, or it'll all be meat."

She walked off over to the men's group to supervise the cooking. The other woman gathered around Maureen, and started helping her to complete the form.

Although Sarah wanted nothing to do with Maureen's scheme she couldn't help being curious, especially as every now and again she could hear hoots of laughter.

George came over to her. "You need to look worried if your Mother is mapping out your future," he said giving her a squeeze. "Thanks Dad," Sarah said, "That reassures me no end." She smiled and gave him a hug back.

"Of course I don't have to go along with it," she added. "True," said George, "But you know for all our sakes, just pretend you are for a little while won't you?"

He reached across the BBQ table groaning with meats, fish and different salads and coleslaws and picked up a bottle of wine. "Have a drink," he said, "It will take away the pain."

Sarah laughed. "I'm driving," she said. "You know you can stay at ours," said George, "Or I'll get us all a taxi." Sarah considered it for a few seconds, and then she reached for an empty wine glass. "You're right," she said holding the glass out while her Dad filled it. "It will be less painful."

Over at the girls' table Maureen was calling out the questions on the form. "What is Sarah's idea of a romantic evening?" she asked. "A drive to McDonalds with the boys," said Kate and they all laughed.

"Don't say that," said Maureen, "Wasn't Sarah's date with Ben at the Bowling Alley with the boys in tow?"

"Yes but that was Ben's idea," said Kate, "I think he sussed out how to get into Sarah's good books," she added.

"And her knickers," commented Karen. They all looked at her aghast. She blushed. "Sorry Mo," she said, "Didn't you know?" "I knew," said Maureen, "I just didn't know anyone else did." She looked at Kate questioningly.

"I only mentioned it," said Kate, "I was so pleased that they had finally got together. How was I to know it would all end in disaster?"

"We need some photos of Sarah now," said Maureen. "I've got some on my mobile," said Kate. She picked up her mobile and started clicking through to choose an appropriate one. "What about that one?" she asked showing the others a photo of Sarah taken on the night of the Hen Party in her St Trinians uniform. Ann pulled a face. "Too suggestive," she said.

Kate chose another one, taken with Sarah sat on the wall outside her flat, with a lovely view of The Solent and Portsmouth in the distance behind her. She was laughing and her hair was flying in the wind. She looked happy. Everyone agreed that this was the photo to use on her profile. Kate 'Blue toothed' it across to Maureen, and then showed her how to attach it to the profile. Maureen clicked through to complete and then they all admired the completed profile. "Yes, I like that," said Maureen, satisfied.

"SARAH, WHAT"S YOUR CARD DETAILS?" she called across to Sarah who was helping Steve with the cooking. "WHAT?" said Sarah, coming over to them.

"I need your card details to complete this application," Maureen said. Sarah peered at the page on the laptop. She squinted her eyes and could just make out a photo of herself. "Is this for the dating thing?" she asked. Maureen nodded. "We just need to pay for it now, although you get the second month free."

"Oh no, no, no," said Sarah, "I'm not paying for that. You want to do it, you pay for it," she said turning and heading back to the BBQ pit.

"Well, you would think she would be a bit more grateful than that," said Maureen haughtily, "All that work I've put in to get her a partner."

"Yes," said Kate, giving Karen a secret smile, "You'd think she would, wouldn't you."

She grabbed her mobile again. "Here, what's the bank details? I'll pay for it. You can owe me." She started tapping away, and then it was all done, and Sarah's profile pinged up on the list of dates page. "Now we sit back and wait," said Maureen, satisfied. "In that case," said Ann getting up, "I'd better get some more wine."

CHAPTER 39

Sarah was busy, busy, busy. Mrs Gilmore had helped her to draft her application for Deputy Head teacher. Although Sarah was unsure if she needed the extra responsibility, the increased salary would come in handy, and her colleagues in the staff room were very supportive. So the application was sent to the Governors, and she was told she would be informed of the interview date. Meanwhile, Mrs Gilmore was giving her extra duties to ensure that she had the necessary experience, and even Mr Jackson was passing over some of his work, although Sarah suspected he was only passing over the stuff he didn't want to do.

Sarah also had a report to write for the Governors on the now much praised Crime and Punishment project that the Year 7s had been participating in, including feedback from the Magistrates Court, and Police Station. She thought she would delegate dealings with the Police. That could be the Teaching Assistant, Miss Read's special project.

But there was no getting away from her Mother. Maureen and Kate had paid for two months on the dating site, and they wanted her to get good use out of it. Almost every day Maureen asked her if she had had chance to look at any of the profiles that had come up. Sarah told her she was too busy at the moment, but she knew she couldn't put them off for too long. She would have to have a look.

The boys were in bed, and she had finished all her marking, so she poured herself a glass of white wine and sat on the settee with her laptop balanced on her lap. She opened the dating site and started clicking through the profiles that had been "specially chosen for her by the state of the art dating programme, sympathetically matching her profile to a…." blah blah blah.

Sarah hastily clicked over the ones she didn't like, and then BINGO! Hey, she recognised him. She clicked in the profile.

> *Ade Fuller. 38 years old, maintenance worker and odd job man*
> *Likes dogs, going for long walks, romantic dinners*
> *Widow*

Yes, she knew him. He often did maintenance work for them at school. He was quite cute, but not knock out gorgeous. She would rather go out with someone she knew, however. She had his mobile number, she would give him a call.

Sarah dialled his number, heart thumping. What was she going to say? And then she heard him say "Hello?"

"Hello, eh Ade?" she said, "Hi this is Sarah, Sarah Blake, from the school."

"Hello Sarah," said Ade pleasantly.

"I'm sorry to bother you, but, well, I saw your profile on this dating agency." She heard him give an embarrassed laugh. "And, well, I've been added to the Agency too by my mother, and I'm kinda under pressure to go out with someone," God she was getting this all wrong. "I mean I don't mean, hell, I'm sorry, I'm saying this all wrong."

"It's OK, Sarah," Ade said kindly, "I know just what you mean. My daughter signed me up to the Agency. She's decided it was time I started dating again, but I'm not really sure."

Sarah sighed, relieved she had just met a kinsman. "No I'm not sure either, which is why when I saw your profile, I thought if I have to go out with someone I'd rather go with someone I knew. Oh God I think that sounds awful too."

Ade laughed again. "Look Sarah I understand completely. I haven't actually signed up for any dates. My daughter is telling me her subscription is running out soon so I had better get started."

Sarah laughed too. "That's exactly what my Mum said. Not that I actually asked her to sign me up in the first place."

"Yep, me too," agreed Ade.

"So, well, in that case, how about a drink, then we can appease both parties?" asked Sarah, mustering up all her courage, "I mean, if you want to."

Ade agreed. "That's a good idea," he said, "But how about dinner? If we have to spend the evening together we might as well do something nice." He laughed again, embarrassed, "Oh no now it's my turn. That sounded awful too."

"No, no that's a great idea. Let's go somewhere out of the way of prying eyes," suggested Sarah, "Where are you?"

"Wootton Bridge, so how about the Woodman's Arms?" suggested Ade. "Yes great idea," agreed Sarah, "Is Friday OK as this is the only time this week I can get a babysitter for my boys?"

"Friday is perfect," said Ade, "How about 7.30?"

"Perfect," Sarah agreed and said goodbye. She took a huge gulp of wine, greatly relieved at the outcome. She looked at Ade's photo again. She knew he was a nice guy, she often had a chat with him when he came into the school. She found that she was actually looking forward to Friday. She couldn't wait to tell her Mum and Kate.

CHAPTER 40

Sarah was sat at the dining table marking her school books when her mother came in and plonked the local paper under her nose. She pointed to the front page. *"Arreton Residents in Fracking Fracas,"* Sarah read the headlines, "God, who makes these up?" Maureen tutted and pointed to a photo underneath of PC Ben Lewis receiving a big lusty kiss from his super proud girlfriend Sadie after being told he would be receiving the Queen's Award for Gallantry for his services with the Rapid Response Team. Sarah pushed the paper away and carried on with her marking. "I've got to get these finished before I go out," she said.

Maureen picked up the paper and looked intently at the photo. "Shame," she said with a heavy sigh, "He's got very nice eyes."

"Yes, shame," thought Sarah, "he's got a very nice bum too." She carried on marking and pretended to ignore her mother's comment.

But Maureen wasn't finished. "He could've done so much better with a nice girl like you," she continued, "And we all thought you were getting on so well. I can't understand why you didn't forgive him."

Sarah bit her tongue. Now was not the time to enter into a debate with her mother over Ben Lewis. As far as Sarah was concerned he was history, even if he did keep cropping up in her thoughts and more often than she liked in her dreams. She continued to ignore Maureen, and concentrated on finishing her marking task.

"What time are you going out?" asked Maureen.

"In half an hour," said Sarah, looking at her watch, and piling the books up. She got up. "I'd better start getting ready," she said rising to her feet and putting the books on the sideboard. She went off to shower.

Thirty minutes later she was ready, dressed in cotton slacks and t-shirt with a light summer cardigan over her shoulders, she looked cool and casual. She wore a chunky pendant on a chain to spice up the look and a thick ring on one of her fingers. She picked up her handbag, kissed the boys goodnight and headed off for the pub.

When she arrived at the pub she could see that Ade was already there so she went to the bar to get herself a drink, and then went over to him. "Hello," she said, sitting opposite him and smiling. "Hello," he said smiling back.

It turned into a very pleasant evening. Ade was very easy to talk to, and funny too, and they both laughed as they told each other their stories of how their respective families had put them into the dating database. Ade's wife had died of cancer a couple of years ago, but his fifteen year old daughter felt that he should now be getting back into the dating game, even though he wasn't sure he was ready.

"Do you think she needs a mother figure?" asked Sarah, "She's at that age when she's starting to explore the world. Perhaps she misses that mother figure?"

Ade wasn't so sure. "I don't know," he said, "She has both her grandmothers, and boy do they have an opinion on what she should be doing in her life."

Sarah laughed. "And my mother has an opinion on what I should be doing with my life too. What is it with mothers? I'm sure I won't be like that with my boys."

"I'm sure you will," said Ade.

The rest of the evening was nice, but by 9pm Sarah was yawning. "Gosh I'm so sorry," she said covering her mouth, "It's not you, honestly. I'm just so tired lately. I've got a lot of work on at the moment and I've been staying up late to get it done."

"That's OK," Ade reassured her, "I know just how you feel. We've got a big job on at the moment and I've been going into work early. I've got to get up early tomorrow as we're working all weekend, so if it's OK with you I'll be leaving in a minute."

"Oh no that suits me fine," said Sarah, "I'm ready for bed already."

Ade stood up, and Sarah did too. They both went to the bar and Sarah insisted on paying for her share. "As it's not a real date I can't let you pay for me," she said.

Ade smiled at her. "I really enjoyed the evening," he said, "I was wondering if you would like to do it again?" Sarah smiled back, "Yes I would," she agreed.

"Great but could we go out next Saturday, then I wouldn't have to get back so early?" asked Ade. "OK," said Sarah, "I'll see what I can do baby sitting wise. Can I text or call you?" Ade nodded, and together they left the pub.

CHAPTER 41

Ben twirled the take away chicken curry around his plate. He wasn't really hungry. All around him his colleagues in the Staff Room were chatting and passing poppadums around, but he didn't feel very much like conversation. He had only agreed to the meal because everyone had insisted that he celebrate his Gallantry Award.

PC Alison Harris was sat opposite him, and she noticed Ben's morose mood. "Everything OK?" she asked.

"What?" Ben looked up at his colleague, "Yes, yes thanks," he said.

Paul Dorey leaned over to grab some more rice. "Take no notice of him," he said, "He's just been dumped by his girlfriend, again." He took a big portion of rice and heaped it on his plate.

Alison looked sadly at her colleague. "I'm so sorry to hear that, Ben," she said sympathetically. Ben looked like a little lost puppy and she felt the urge to gather him up in her arms and give him a big cuddle.

"She's gone to play for good with the big boys in Florida," continued Paul, who had about as much sensitivity as a razor blade. Alison caught Paul's eye and shook her head at him to get him to stop, but Paul took no notice. "Got fed up with the brooding type," Paul finished.

She could see Ben had clenched his fork, and she felt the tension in the air. Ben was clearly upset and Paul wasn't making him feel any better. She decided to take Ben outside.

"Coming out for a ciggie?" she asked him. "I don't ..." Ben began, but Alison had stood up and was motioning for him to go with her. She felt that they were good friends, as well as colleagues, and Ben had done a lot of listening to her lately as she went through some of her own trauma, so she thought it was now her turn to help Ben.

Once outside they sat companionably on an old bench. Alison lit a cigarette and inhaled deeply. "What happened?" she asked quietly, "Sadie was only here last week all over you for the photo." Ben stared into space, remembering the events of the weekend.

He laughed harshly. "We had our first, and it seems last, row," he said, "To be honest," he admitted, "I was getting fed up at always being at her beck and call." He went quiet while Alison sat and dragged on her cigarette, waiting for him to talk. He was remembering how the events had panned out.

Sadie had been excitable all week, and wanted some of the fame that the Gallantry Award announcement had brought. She had insisted in being in the photo taken by the local newspaper, even though Ben had not wanted her there, and kept talking about accompanying him to the Presentation Ceremony when it happened, even if she had to fly back from Florida for it.

But the crux had come on Saturday. Ben had been working all Friday night. It had been a long shift, and Ben was exhausted. There had been two rival stag parties on in Ryde, one comprised of locals, and the other visitors from the mainland. It had all kicked off at closing time. The visiting party had followed the local party from pub to pub, taunting them, and when the pubs closed a full scale riot broke out. Fighting, knives, bottles being thrown – it had been carnage. One guy had got knifed and had been taken to hospital, and several had been injured with flying glass and flying fists. It had taken all night to process them all, and by Saturday morning Ben just wanted to crawl into his bed.

He hadn't been in bed long when Sadie phoned and wanted him to go round. He had tried to protest but she was adamant. It might be the last chance they got to see each other as she was flying back to Florida on the Monday, and she was spending the Sunday with her family. He explained that he was tired, and she said they could spend the afternoon snuggled up.

However when he got to her house, snuggling was the last thing on her mind. She had met him dressed in a flimsy dressing robe, which she pulled aside to reveal a red basque and fishnet stockings. Ben's heart plummeted despite stirring in other parts of his body. He couldn't help himself, but he was really too tired to perform anything more than kissing. For once he had resisted her efforts to engage him, and they had ended up arguing.

He had told her she was selfish, and she only called him when she wanted sex, and didn't she just want to snuggle. She said he was boring, he acted like an old man, snuggling was for oldies and you were a long time dead. And anyway if he didn't want it he should leave now as she knew of real men in Florida who would be glad to be getting a bit. If it hadn't been for her, she told him, his tadger would've withered and fallen off now for all the action he'd have got.

He had got his coat and left, slamming the door behind him, and she had not phoned or text so he guessed it was final. But he didn't regret it. He actually felt relieved. It was like a spell was broken at last. He had liked her, hell he could even have loved her if she had let him, but he needed more in his life. He was nearly forty, and he had thought, many years ago, that he would be spending his fortieth birthday surrounded by a beautiful wife and glowing healthy children. That wasn't going to happen. He thought of Sarah, how they had snuggled in the middle of her bed and fell asleep in each other's arms.

Alison put her head on Ben's shoulder, and, lost in his own thoughts, he automatically put his arm around her and pulled her in to him. She said something and Ben looked down at her. As he did so Alison planted her lips on his in a gentle kiss. Ben was taken back, and immediately stood up.

"Sorry, sorry," said Alison, flustered, "Sorry, I didn't mean…" Ben looked confused for a second, and then started apologising, "No, sorry, I was miles away, sorry."

"Sorry, I didn't mean.." Alison started lighting up another cigarette. She was shaking. "God I'm so sorry," she said again, taking a deep drag of the cigarette and blowing the smoke out, aiming it away from Ben. "Phil and I, well, it's not easy, and I miss, well … sorry." Ben knew she was having relationship problems as she had told him snippets when they had been in the station together on their own.

"No, no, I'm sorry too," said Ben, "Look, I'd better go and …"

"Yes, OK, see you," said Alison. She waved the cigarette around. "I'll finish this and …"

"Yes," said Ben and walked inside. He threw the congealed chicken curry in the bin, and grabbed his coat.

"You off mate?" asked Paul, "You don't fancy a quick one on the way?"

"No thanks," said Ben, "I've got some stuff to do at home." He just wanted to get out of the station and get home, even if he didn't really have anything to do at home.

CHAPTER 42

Sarah didn't know how she had made it to the beginning of the summer holidays. It had been a hard term. She had had an interview for the Deputy Head teacher's job a few weeks before, but she was not hopeful. It had been a very difficult interview conducted by three of the Governors. They had asked her probing questions, like what would she do if she thought a child was being abused at home, and how would she react to a drunken teacher?

She had blushed a little at that question, remembering a lunchtime birthday party when she had drunk a glass of wine in the Staff Room in the lunchtime, and in the afternoon a pupil had asked her if she had been drinking kitchen cleaner as her breath smelt. She had been mortified, although she had wondered, briefly, how the child knew what drinking kitchen cleaner would smell like. She didn't want to dwell on that.

She had also stumbled over the question on what were her thoughts on the controversial two-tier education system that the Island Education Authority had brought in a few years before. She had been very vocally against it at the time, even raising a petition, as she thought it was just an excuse to cut budgets. However, which way would the Governors think? She didn't want to alienate them. In the end she had stumbled through an answer that hadn't made any sense. The main interviewer had looked at her as if she'd grown two heads. She knew then she had blown it. When she told Mrs Gilmore the Headmistress had gone quiet and mumbled "oh I expect they thought you did well," but without conviction.

And now it was the last day of term. The teachers were having their traditional end of term party in the Staff Room once the children had departed. They had all brought in wine, beer, gin, lots of gin it seemed, tonic, and party food.

Sarah was really looking forward to letting her hair down. Last year everyone had got absolutely smashed and ended up going down to the beach at Appley and skinny dipping at about midnight. Sarah smiled to herself, trying to remember what had happened. It was hazy but she thought the police had turned up at some point. Not PC Lewis she was sure, God imagine if that had happened.

The school bell rang, trilling like a release alarm, and the children jubilantly poured out of the school gates into the waiting arms of their parents and grandparents. And suddenly all was quiet. Sarah put some things away and tidied up some chairs, but the classroom had been stripped of all of the children's embellishments and now it echoed.

Sarah breathed a deep sigh and gathered up her bag and coat. She always felt this was like New Year's Eve, that moment when you said goodbye to the old year, taking a few minutes to remember the highlights, before continuing with the cycle of life and plunging into the New Year. She hesitated and looked around the classroom, and wondered what would happen to the children who had spent a whole year in this room. Would they remember it in years to come? She sighed again, and said a silent goodbye before hurrying to the staff room.

All the staff were gathered around Mrs Gilmore, who was making a goodbye speech for Mr Jackson. This year's end of term party was a special celebration as he was retiring, so there was champagne on the table as well as the usual wine. The staff had clubbed together and bought flowers for his wife and for him they had bought a special edition toy replica of the Flying Scotsman as they knew Donald Jackson had a huge miniature railway laid out in his attic. He was speechless and his grumpy persona nearly cracked as he fought back the tears. Sarah was the only teacher who had also been one of his pupils when he had first started teaching in the school, and she was given the honour of presenting him with his present and making a little speech.

Everyone clapped, and Mrs Gilmore called for silence. She held a piece of paper in her hand. "Thank you, Sarah, for those fine words in recognition of a long and creditable career. Donald Jackson, you will be sorely missed, but I have some news which you may all be interested in. As you know the Governors have been interviewing for a new Deputy Head, and they have given me permission to reveal to you who has got the position."

Sarah's heart plummeted. It obviously wasn't her, or she would have been advised before now. It was probably another teacher from the mainland, as they usually did, thinking a mainlander had more experience. She braced herself, and told herself not to be too disappointed, and that there would be other opportunities.

Mrs Gilmore took a dramatic pause and then said "The Governors said they were very impressed with this candidate. She had conducted herself well and they unanimously agreed she was by far the best candidate. So next term we will be welcoming Mrs Sarah Blake as our new Deputy Head."

She beamed at Sarah, and everyone starting clapping and congratulating Sarah. She didn't know what to say. Mrs Gilmore called for hush again. "I think it is only fitting that one of Donald's young protégés should take over from him, and I know Sarah, that he is as proud of you as we are." Donald Jackson was nodding, and she was sure she saw a tear roll down his cheek before he hastily wiped it away.

Sarah was gob struck. She couldn't believe it. She had got the job! Her first thought was that she might be able to afford to take the boys on a little holiday now. Her second was that she would have even more work to do.

Donald came over and shook her hand. "I am very proud of you, Sarah," he said, "I always knew you would make it whatever you did."

Mrs Gilmore brought her over a glass of champagne. "I hope you didn't mind me announcing it like that," she said to Sarah, smiling, " I thought that if I had told you separately you might persuade yourself out of taking the job." Sarah smiled. Her headmistress was a good judge of character.

Mrs Gilmore raised her glass and chinked it against Sarah's. "I'm looking forward to working with you," she said. "So am I, Headmistress," said Sarah, taking a sip of the amber nectar.

Sarah couldn't wait to call her parents. "MUM, MUM," she shouted down the phone, "I GOT THE JOB!"

"WHOOOHOO," shouted back Maureen gleefully, "Wait, wait, tell your father," she said and Sarah next heard her father's deep tones. "DAD, DAD, I GOT THE JOB," Sarah yelled into the phone again.

"Well done, my girl," he said and Sarah could imagine him beaming with pride down the line. Then he said, "You go and

enjoy yourself and I'll pick you up at midnight from the beach."
Sarah laughed, "Oh no Dad, not this time," she said, "I don't
think I'm going to stay long. I might walk back about 7 ish."
Her father laughed, "OK, midnight from the beach," he re-
iterated.

Sarah was laid on her towel on the beach, her head whirling
from seemingly gallons of wine and gin and tonics, and she
wondered how they had all got there. She couldn't remember
the evening very well. One minute they were chatting, drinking
and eating in the Staff Room, and the next she seem to be laid
on a towel, with Alan Vorsey, the Music teacher, strumming
tunes on his guitar, and Mr and Mrs Gilmore slow dancing to
them in the sand. It was a beautiful night and as she laid
there she looked up into a sky full of thousands and thousands
of stars. It was heaven!

She chuckled at her own little joke, but this was short lived as
someone shouted "Let's go for a dip!"

Oh no, not again, thought Sarah, but Beatrice Gilmore
grabbed Sarah's hand and dragged her to her feet. "Come
on," she urged her, "The Deputy Head designate has to learn
about leadership." She pulled Sarah down to the water's edge,
and then the Headmistress started stripping off her clothes.
Sarah could see that most of the staff were already in the
water. On her cocktail of alcohol she felt exhilarated, so she
quickly stripped off and plunged into the water. It was
surprisingly warm, and she swam in the shallows and floated
on her back, gazing up at the stars.

And then the police were there, and she could hear a voice
she recognised requesting that the party came back to shore

and disperse. She did a few more strokes, ignoring him. She didn't want the moment to end.

"SARH BLAKE," PC Ben Lewis called out, "COME ON IN, YOUR TIME IS UP!" She swam further into the shallows, but remained under the water, just out of reach. "COME AND GET ME," she called back flirtatiously, and floated on her back. It was dark, but Ben could just make out the whiteness of her breasts on the surface. God, she was sexy.

"I CAN'T COME IN," he called. "I'LL GET MY UNIFORM WET."

"TAKE IT OFF," she answered, "I'VE SEEN YOU NAKED BEFORE!" As she said this, the music stopped and her words echoed over the beach. Her colleagues started cheering and whooping at this announcement.

Ben chuckled, and fetched a towel. "COME ON," he encouraged her, "BEFORE YOU GET COLD." This was how he liked Sarah, playful and flirty, and not how she had been on the last couple of occasions they had met, when she had been hurtful and haughty. He held the towel up as she reluctantly came out of the water, wrapping it around her naked body. She stayed for a moment in his arms, and then giggled and pulled away from him.

Her colleagues were getting dressed and gathering up their stuff, and then they were dispersing, calling out goodbyes, hugging and kissing each other and making promises to see each other over the summer, which they almost never did. "Come on," said Ben, "we'll give you a lift home."

"That's ok," said a voice behind him, and George appeared with Sarah's clothes and bag in his arms. "I'll take her from here."

Back in the police car his colleague Alison asked him "What's the story with Sarah Blake?" "Oh, nothing," he said, "I thought we had something but it didn't work out."

He started the engine, watching George pull away in front of him.

"What's with the skinny dipping?" he asked Alison.

"Happens every year," said Alison, "The last day of term for the last four or five years we've had to go and break up their little party. Always ends up in the sea. And we get the same complaint from the residents opposite. I think they must sit up with their binoculars, waiting for the teachers to kick off their clothes." Ben laughed, thinking of the image of Sarah's naked body picked out in the starlight.

CHAPTER 43

Sarah's hangover did not last as long as a vision of PC Ben Lewis wrapping her naked body in a towel as she came of the water. On first waking she thought she had dreamt it, but then she remembered the party of the night before. Exploring her fractured memory she thought that her dream was of a real memory but she couldn't be sure, and her father, who had picked her up from the beach, was giving nothing away. On the one hand she was embarrassed – that kind of 'oh no did I really do that, head in hands' embarrassment people with hangover get the next day (along with the 'oh I wish I hadn't got that drunk' feeling) but on the other hand she was secretly titillated that it was Ben who had ordered her out of the sea. She still fancied him, she knew it, but she was not sure that she had forgiven him or she was ready to trust him.

The summer holidays were progressing well, and so was her relationship with Ade. OK, they weren't at the kissing stage, or even the holding hands stage, but they had had a few more dates, mostly dinners, and she was enjoying his company. So much so that she had invited him and his two girls to the BMX Summer Event and BBQ the next weekend. Her Mother was excited to meet Sarah's new boyfriend, even though Sarah kept telling her that he was more of a friend than a boyfriend.

The day of the BMX Event was a cloudless one, and all the family, including both sets of grandparents from Sarah and Kate's families were going. The four boys had a few races to ride in but this time Sarah was not doing her usual stint in the First Aid Tent as she wanted to accompany Ade.

Ade arrived at the BBQ a little after the Blakes and Blairs. He had his two daughters in tow – Esme was twelve, in pigtails and fascinated with the bikes the boys were showing her. She knew Kate's son, Liam, as they went to the same school, so the boys took her off to watch the races. Geraldine, on the other hand was fifteen. Fifteen, going on eighteen. Tall, slim, stunningly beautiful and with that haughty look only fifteen year old girls can muster, she grunted hellos to everyone and then looked distinctly bored with everything. She seemed to spend most of her time texting, taking absolutely no interest in the racing.

Until that is the 16-18 year races came on, and she recognised the school heartthrob who was taking part. Clocking there were no other girls her age in the vicinity she positioned herself near the finishing line, and started flirting with him as soon as he finished the race. Watching her, Sarah guessed that would be the last they saw of Geraldine for the duration of the BBQ.

Ade was personable: saying hello to everyone, he chatted easily to Maureen and George, and Steve and Kate and agreed with Ann about the joys of parenting teenage girls, something that Ann could remember from Kate and Karen's teenage years. Watching Geraldine, they agreed that nothing had changed.

The BBQ started after the races, and as she went up for a burger for the boys, Sarah caught sight of Ben Lewis. He hadn't been racing, having only just finished his shift, but he looked relaxed in faded jeans and a casual t-shirt. Sarah blushed when he caught her gaze, and he gave her a knowing smile, which made her blush even more and she turned away from him as she tried to concentrate on putting sauce on the burgers.

He came up behind her and whispered in her ear, "Been swimming lately?" Sarah flinched, and involuntary squeezed the plastic sauce bottle, causing it to completely miss the burger and spill over the table. Shit. She quickly tried to collect herself as she turned around to face him. He was very close, being pressed by the weight of hungry bikers eager to get to the table crushing in behind him. She could smell his aftershave, causing her heart to beat faster as she studied his face.

She had no witty retort so she just smiled mysteriously (at least she hoped it was mysteriously) and pushed herself passed him, trying not to smear burger down his shirt.

The event was being housed under a large tarpaulin strung between the trees. There was an electrical supply for lighting, and a DJ had brought his equipment, and after everyone had eaten he struck up his music. At first the kids danced and messed around, but soon they grew tired and took to the chairs and deckchairs and rugs people had strewn about, playing games, chatting and sleeping.

Sarah felt she was too tired to dance, and spent much of the time hanging about on the edge of the dance area, watching Kate and their mothers strut their stuff. It was hilarious watching them, especially her Mother, who was trying to fit the 80s two-step to the modern music.

The music pace changed to a bit slower, and Steve grabbed Kate and took her on to the dance area, holding her tightly. Sarah felt someone next to her, and turning saw it was Ben. "Shall we?" he asked, holding out his hands to her.

Sarah hesitated for a second or two, and then nodded. She had to give him his due for persistence. He held one of her hands, and put his other arm around her waist, pulling her into him. "I can't dance," Sarah said apologetically. "That's OK, neither can I," Ben said into her ear, his head close to hers, "We'll just shuffle."

They shuffled and swung in time to the music, and Sarah felt herself relax into Ben's body. It seemed right, the smell of his jacket, the warmth of his arms. If she closed her eyes for a second she could almost believe this was how it was meant to be.

Then he spoiled it. "We're over," he said, "Sadie's gone."

At the mention of Sadie, Sarah stiffened. She tried to take a step back, but Ben held her tighter. "We were never really together," Ben continued, "She used me. But she's gone now."

"I don't need to know," said Sarah, trying to extricate herself from Ben's arms, "I don't want to know. I'm ....." She looked over to Ade who was stood at the side of the dance area, laughing at something George was saying. Ben followed her gaze and dropped his hold. "I understand, " he said sadly.

"Thank you for the dance," Sarah said in a monotone, "I need..." She turned and left him on the dance floor wondering where he had gone wrong.

The DJ continued to play slow dances for a little while longer. The party was beginning to break up anyway as families were reunited with their tired children.

Sarah felt that she had been neglecting her guest, so she grabbed Ade and pulled him onto the dance floor. He couldn't dance either, so they shuffled round in each other's arms, laughing at their inept moves. As the music ended Sarah reached up and kissed Ade on the lips. She felt him freeze. And then he gently pulled away from her. "I think we need to talk," he said, and grabbing her hand, he pulled Sarah off the dance area, and led her into the trees into a little private spot.

"I'm sorry," said Sarah confused, "I thought, you know, we've had a few dates. I thought it was going well. You liked me."

"I do like you," confirmed Ade, "But…. How can I put this? … This is so hard…" Sarah looked at him intently in the little light reaching them from the dance area. His face was partly in shadows but she could see it was struggling. Suddenly it dawned on her why he hadn't made a move on her yet. "Oh my God, you're gay," she said.

"Well, the thing is…" Ade said, "I don't really know." He laughed, embarrassed, "Sounds daft, doesn't it? Something as important as my sexuality and I can't decide."

"No," said Sarah, "It doesn't. It's just that, well, you've got two daughters, and I thought, well, you gave the impression you were happily married."

"We were, for a while anyway," he looked into the distance, remembering his marriage, " We were married young and had Geraldine straight away. I never thought about it. But it didn't feel right. I never felt right. I loved my wife, sure but I was never really attracted to her. It's so hard to explain. I've never told anyone this."

Sarah touched his arm in encouragement. She felt he was making a much needed confession. "Gone on," she said.

He laughed, "I'm sorry but I fancy Steve Blair more than I fancy you," he shook his head, "Gosh that sounds hard, but it's the truth."

Sarah laughed too and squeezed his arm. "Don't tell Kate," she said, "But most people fancy Steve."

"You know what you should do," she continued, an idea hitting her, "You should date a man and then you can see if that is really what you want."

In the moonlight she could see a look of horror on his face. "No, seriously," she said, "You've dated me and found out that's not what you want. Now you date a bloke and you can see if that really is what you want."

"I couldn't," Ade said, shaking his head, "What about the girls?"

"They needn't know," said Sarah, "Not at first anyway." She was now getting into the idea. "We could go over to Southampton one evening, you and me, and hit the gay bars. I don't mind coming with you for moral support."

Ade wasn't sure. "But then you'll know," she said. She gave him a big hug and a peck on the cheek. "Come on," she said grabbing his hand, "We need to get our kids home."

Ben had been watching them. He had seen the kiss Sarah had given Ade on the dance floor. It looked gentle, intimate. His heart plunged. He saw Ade lead Sarah off into the trees, and his heart turned over. Sadly he turned away, called out goodbye to his mates, and left the party.

CHAPTER 44

It was another hot day on the Sunshine Isle, and Sarah and Kate were on the beach sat on deckchairs under a huge patio umbrella, surrounded by towels, buckets, spades, balls and other kid-type paraphernalia. This time they were on Appley Beach. Even though it was a huge sandy bay relatively safe from tidal currents, Sarah was keeping a beady eye on the children. She was well aware that it was only a year ago that her boys were swept out to sea.

Kate was also keen to remind her of another shameful incident which happened recently on that beach. "Wasn't it here that you were caught skinny dipping?" she asked Sarah, feigning innocence.

"No, further up the beach," Sarah said, blushing.

"Every year you lot do that, and every year you get caught. One day it's going to reach the papers, and that'll look good," commented Kate. She continued "I mean, would you trust your children with a bunch of reprobates who get drunk and expose themselves."

Sarah glanced at Kate. She was smiling mischievously. Sarah smiled back recognising that she was being teased. "They probably know that already," she said, "But when it is the headmistress who goads you on what can you do?"

"I wouldn't dare do it myself," said Kate. "What, strip off?" said Sarah, "Well it was dark, and I was megally pissed, or no, not something I would usually do." "Only once a year," laughed Kate.

"So it was PC Ben Lewis who fished you out," commented Kate. She adjusted her sunglasses and stood up to see where the boys were. They were not far in front of them, digging for all their worth around a huge sand castle. She sat back down again.

"Oh God do you have to remind me," said Sarah.

"He's seen you in the nuddy before," said Kate matter of factually.

"Yes but not acting so ludicrous, and in public," said Sarah, "That bit I am embarrassed about. I think I was a bit flirty with him." She tried hard not to think about that night a few weeks before. "You know I often wonder if there are actually any other policemen on this island. It always seems to be Ben Lewis who is there just when I don't need him to be."

"There could be a reason for that," said Kate. She held up her glasses so Sarah could see the big wink she gave her. "Oh funny haha," said Sarah sarcastically.

"But anyway, forget Ben," said Kate, "I really want to know about Ade. I saw you two smooching at the BBQ. Anything you want to tell me?" She settled herself more comfortably into her deck chair.

"I've already been given the third degree from my mother on that one," commented Sarah, "and you, Mother, and, I have to admit, me, are barking up the wrong tree with that one. Or should I say batting the wrong wicket or whatever the term is."

Kate looked puzzled. "Batting the wrong wicket?" she asked puzzled. She thought for a moment. "You don't mean he's gay?" she asked incredulously. "But he was married and had two children." Sarah nodded. "And you kissed him," Kate continued. Sarah nodded again.

"Ha but there you have it," she said, "I kissed HIM. He hasn't made any play for me, no copping a feel when I'm not looking, no attempt at kissing, nothing."

"That doesn't make him gay," pointed out Kate, "Perhaps he just doesn't fancy you."

"No, he doesn't fancy me," agreed Sarah, "He fancies Steve."

"What?" gasped Kate, "My Steve?" Sarah nodded. "He told you that?" Kate couldn't believe it. Sarah nodded again. "I don't understand," said Kate, "then why is he on a dating agency?"

"Same reason as I am," Sarah explained, "His daughters applied for him. They don't know. I'm not sure he does either. He said that there was something not right with his marriage, and he fancies Steve more than he fancied me."

Sarah stood up and looked over to where the boys had been playing. Yes, they were still there, and as the tide was now going out, to reveal acres of golden sand, they didn't appear in too much danger of being swept away. She sat back down again. "I said I'd take him to a gay bar over in Southampton," she continued, "Maybe if he went out with a guy on a date it might help him decide."

Kate looked at her incredulously. "You know the gay bars in Southampton?" she asked. "No," admitted Sarah, "but your

Steve does. He can tell me which ones they are. And Alan Vorsey at school is gay – he's sure to know too."

"What about getting Ade a date with Alan Vorsey?" asked Kate. "Because he's got a partner," said Sarah.

Kate wrinkled her nose. "You don't half pick them," she said to Sarah. "I know," said Sarah, "I always choose the wrong guy."

"No chance with Ben then?" asked Kate, "I saw you two dancing as well and he looked pretty into you. And I have to say, Sarah, you didn't look as if you were fighting him off."

Sarah shook her head. "He says he's split up with Sadie." Kate nodded, she had heard this on the grapevine as well. Sarah sighed. "I do like him. I think about him a lot, but I don't think I can trust him. I'd always be wondering if he was with someone at the station, or where he was when he said he was working."

Sarah clocked Kate's face. "I know," she said, "I'm distrustful but I can't help it. After Simon left it became clear he'd been carrying on with his Thai strumpet for some time. What an idiot I was thinking another baby would solve all our problems when all the time he was planning his escape. I don't know if I can ever trust any man again. Ben could do the same to me again. I don't think I could face all that hurt again."

"But have you never thought how Ben feels?" asked Kate, peering at her sideways.

"I don't get what you mean," said Sarah, picking up a crumpled towel, shaking it and folding it over the back of her deckchair.

"Well, he has been through a couple of disastrous relationships so I gather," said Kate, "Didn't he catch one of his girlfriends shagging his boss in the station loos?"

Sarah stared at her. How did Kate know that? "And didn't another one just up and disappear, without a by your leave? He came home to find she'd moved to the other side of the world," Kate continued.

Kate answered Sarah's unspoken question, "Oh his mate told Steve all about it. You know Paul goes to Steve's gym. They often have a beer after."

"Don't you think he might distrust you?" Sarah was still staring at her friend. "I'm just saying," said Kate, "It's not all about you."

Sarah thought about what Kate had said and sighed. Maybe she was right, it wasn't all about her. She plastered a big smile on her face as Alfie came running up to them. "Water," he gasped, pointing down his throat, "Water please Mummy."

Around the corner of the headland, on the next beach, Ben was sitting on a pub bench sipping a cool beer.

"I don't know why you're still pursuing her," Paul was saying, "One minute she's hot with you, then she's cold, then she's hot. You don't know where you are. I wouldn't bother." He picked up his beer and took a long sip. And then he pressed it against his head. It was nice and cool in the heat of the day.

Ben picked his bottle up and took a sip, looking out to sea and thinking about Sarah swimming naked in the dark waters. He had thought about that a lot recently. It was an image he could not forget.

Paul was still talking. "Now that little PC Alison, she's a homely little piece, and I think she's got the hots for you." Ben pulled his thoughts back to the present.

"She's married," Ben said simply.

"Since when did that ever stop anyone?" asked Paul, with a mischievous grin, "I hear her husband is away a lot."

Ben pulled a face. "I'm not into married women," he said, "And have you seen her husband? Built like a brick shit house. I wouldn't want to get on the wrong side of him."

"Keep it in the station, no one will ever know," said Paul. Ben looked at him and Paul winked. "You haven't?" Ben said.

Paul nodded. "With Alison?" Ben asked. Paul shook his head. "Who?" "Not saying, my lips are sealed mate, but I'll tell you those were some of the best months of my life."

Ben looked sad. He had a flashback of entering the men's toilet and hearing groaning from behind a toilet door, and then encountering his girlfriend as she walked out of it, with the Commissioner behind her adjusting his trousers. It still hurt him even after all this time.

Paul caught his look. "Oh sorry mate," he said, "I'd forgot you're a bit sensitive about station affairs." He drained his bottle. "Another?" he asked motioning to Ben's empty bottle. Ben nodded.

It was true that Ben didn't know where he was with Sarah. She blew hot and cold at him, and he didn't know if she really did like him. He didn't really know anything about her. She had told him her husband had left her after the birth of little Alfie, and that he had been having an affair which she hadn't known anything about, but other than that he knew very little about her. If he could perhaps find out a bit more maybe he would understand her better.

Paul brought them out a couple of beers and plonked them on the table. He had been watching his mate while he waited for the beers. He had seen how sad he looked and he knew he was thinking of Sarah.

"You're in love with her aren't you?" he asked him. Ben thought for a moment, and then picked up his beer. "I suppose I am," he said sadly.

CHAPTER 45

The boys were packed away to the grandparents for the weekend, and Sarah was free to dance the night away at the nightclub in Southampton because this was the night that Sarah was taking Ade to find his man. They had decided to make a party of it, and invited Steve and Kate to come along too. They needed Steve for their free entry into his nightclub anyway. It was a bit of a busman's holiday for Steve, but he didn't mind. He was happy to have a night out with his wife for a change and without her children or her parents in tow.

They took the bus to Cowes, and met Ade at the Red Funnel Hydrofoil Passenger Terminal. He was dressed casually, and Sarah thought it was a shame he was gay because she could quite fancy him. Ade was happy and relaxed, and he and Sarah chatted whilst they waited for the Hydrofoil to Southampton.

Steve had fetched the crossing tickets, and as he walked up to them stood in the queue for the Hydrofoil, he was being followed by a group of people.

"Hey, look who I found lurking by the Ticket Office," he said, jerking his thumb at the group behind him. Everyone looked, and Sarah's heart skipped a beat as she realised it was Ben. Steve introduced Paul, Matt and Alison to everyone. Sarah glanced shyly at Ben, but he had joined the men and they were animatedly talking about football. Alison came over to the girls and started talking to Kate.

Ben couldn't believe it when he saw Sarah standing at the head of the Hydrofoil queue and then realised that the Steve he had been introduced to at the Ticket Office was Kate's husband. What were the chances of that? He was trying to get away for the evening and forget Mrs Blake, and here she was now part of their group. His mood plunged and he spent the journey to the nightclub trying to ignore her. He tried to tell himself that he wasn't interested anymore as she was clearly with that bloke, Ade.

It was a pleasant crossing, and the group soon found themselves in Steve's nightclub with the music playing. Although Sarah couldn't do the waltz or anything like that, not even the Mamba or Macarena, she enjoyed shaking her stuff, and she dragged Kate and Ade on to the dance floor. Ade protested, saying he would rather stand at the bar with the men, drinking and talking football, but Sarah insisted that his standing there with the men would not attract anyone to him, so he had to get out on the dance floor and shake his booty.

Ben stood sulkily at the bar and drank as much as quickly as he could. Alison stood with him, very close and tried to flirt with him, but he was trying to ignore her too. Out of the corner of his eye he could see Sarah laughing and dancing, and he watched as the straight loose short glittering dress she wore sparkled and shook as she moved, giving a hint of those curvy breasts underneath.

It was getting late, so Ben went to the toilet. He was tired, drunk and really just wanted to make his way back to the ferry – they had all planned to get the first Redjet back to the Island at 5am. On the way out of the toilet he was grabbed and pinned against the wall. It was Alison. She was also very drunk.

She pressed her body against him. "Hello handsome," she slurred, kissing his neck. She held her face up to him, and as he looked down his lips met hers. He hungrily devoured her, his pent up emotions released in a surge. He put his arms around her and pulled her into his body, pressing his hip against her.

"Ooh, hello," she croaked, feeling his erection against her. She fumbled with his zipper and slipped her hand into his trousers and pants, encircling his erection. Ben moaned, and responded by pushing his hands up her blouse, finding her nipples. He cupped her breast and began roughly massaging her nipple. He was consumed with the passion. Alison moaned, and began pumping his erection.

"Sarah, Sarah," he breathed in to her hair. He kissed her roughly, and was about to undo her bra when a light came on in his head.

And then he stopped. It was like someone had thrown cold water over him. This was not Sarah. This was not what he wanted. He grabbed Alison's hand and pulled it out of his trousers. "NO STOP," he commanded, pushing her away. Alison opened her eyes and looked at him in bewilderment. "What are you doing?" she asked drunkenly, "What's going on? I thought you wanted it."

"No, sorry, no I can't," Ben muttered, doing up his zipper, "You're not..." He was going to say "You're not Sarah," but stopped himself in time. "You're married," he said, "and we're both very drunk."

Alison stood looking at him stupidly. She was stunned, and angry. She brought her hand up and slapped his face, and then fuming, she stormed away. He massaged his slapped cheek. I deserve that, he thought.

He saw Sarah still dancing on the dance floor. God she was beautiful, but she wasn't his, and he had to get away. He walked over to Paul and Steve who were still propping up the bar. He quickly downed the end of his pint, and muttered into Paul's ear that he was leaving and would make his own way back. Paul was watching another woman on the dance floor. He half listened to Ben, slapping him on the back. "OK mate," he said distractedly, "Catch you later."

Ben strode out of the nightclub and made his way back to the ferry port. He would wait in the terminal building for the next available vehicle ferry – he knew that they sometimes had night boats running for the lorries. He would wait in the port for whatever came up. But most of all he just wanted to get away.

Kate was finished dancing. She was exceedingly tired, and her feet ached. She left Sarah and Ade to it. Sarah was really happy as Ade had attracted the attention of another man, and they were all dancing together now. Ade was happily flirting with the guy, who was quite cute, so after a while Sarah left them, and made her way back to the group at the bar.

Alison was sitting slumped on a bar stool, a glass of water in front of her, her lipstick and mascara smudged. Matt had also left them, going off with a group of girls to another party somewhere else. Sarah drunk her wine, the same glass she had had all evening, and looked around for Ben. Paul noticed her looking. "Ben's gone," he said, "Back to the island I think." Sarah nodded. She felt disappointed.

But Paul was staring at the scene in front of him. "I think you may have lost your boyfriend," Paul said, nodding over to Ade now standing in a corner of the nightclub, kissing his new friend. Sarah looked over, and smiled. "He was never my boyfriend," she said lightly.

"Did you know?" Paul asked aghast.

"About his sexuality?" confirmed Sarah, "Yes, that was the whole purpose of this evening. I wanted to get him fixed up." Paul closed his mouth and nodded. He now realised Ben had got completely the wrong end of the stick.

CHAPTER 46

Paul was hanging up his coat in the locker room when Ben walked in on the Monday morning. "Where have you been?" Paul asked him, "I was calling you yesterday."

"Oh," said Ben, taking off his coat, and opening his locker, "I went for a long bike ride. I forgot my phone. I just needed to think."

"About?" queried Paul. "Things," said Ben vaguely.

"Could one of those things be Mrs Sarah Blake?" asked Paul. Ben ignored him and busied himself with putting on his safety jacket and belt ready for patrol.

"You know her boyfriend's gay," said Paul, delivering the news as he walked out of the locker room. Ben quickly followed him. "What?"

"Yep, if you had stayed around instead of doing a disappearing act, you'd have seen him copping off with another bloke. Sarah said she knew. The whole purpose of the evening had been to fix him up." Paul poured himself a coffee from the filtered coffee pot continually on the hot plate in the staff kitchen.

Ben was shocked at this revelation. Yesterday he'd taken himself off on a long bike ride through the isolated countryside of the island deliberately to think about Sarah, and he had come to the conclusion that he would be better off if he just forgot about her and got on with his life. Did this news now put things into a different aspect? His mind was buzzing. Did that mean Sarah was available?

CHAPTER 47

Sarah recovered from her disappointment at Ben's early exit from the club that night. She thought that maybe there had been something between him and the lovely Alison Harris anyway – Alison had been all over him like a rash the whole evening, and she had looked pretty dejected when he had done a runner.

But she didn't have time to dwell on it. There were now only a few weeks of the school holidays left, and Beatrice Gilmour had asked Sarah if she could return to school a week early in order to undertake some training before the term started. She had received her new contract, signed it and sent it back, so she was now officially the new Deputy Head. Wow! Sarah still couldn't quite believe it.

As well as that George had announced later on that week that he was taking them all away for a much needed holiday. He had booked a week on the Kennet and Avon canal, in a long boat, starting at Bath. Sarah was a bit dubious that this was a good idea. Her father had no experience of boating, and with two young boys she was sure one of them would end up falling in.

They had set out early one morning, all five of them squashed into George's Volvo. Sarah had the middle back seat, jammed in between the boys. It was not a comfortable ride, and she was grateful when they finally arrived at the boat yard to collect their boat. It was pouring with rain, but this didn't dampen the boy's enthusiasm, although Sarah and Maureen stood on the canal side huddled under umbrellas as George learned how to manoeuvre the boat, and both wondered what they were doing there.

"Mid life crisis," commented Maureen in answer to Sarah's unspoken question, "Your father missed his chance to be in the Navy and always fancied himself as a sea captain."

Sarah smiled but as she watched her father try and park the boat along the canal side she did wonder if this holiday was going to be as fun as George had said it would be. Sarah winced as the boat scraped the edge.

"We'll have to get him a Captain's hat," she said, "and some bumpers."

"They're called fenders, Mummy," said Alfie. "Wow, Alfie," said Sarah impressed, "How do you know that?"

"I just heard that man shout at Granddad to watch the fenders," said Alfie. Sarah laughed. Maybe it would be fun after all.

At last George's lesson was over, and the owner was confident enough to let George loose on the canal. It was still raining and Sarah was trying very hard to maintain her sense of humour for the sake of the boys, but she was cold, very, very cold.

They all clambered aboard, and the owner ran through the safety procedures, including the use of life jackets, which he firmly recommended should be worn at all times they were on the decks. Sarah saw that there was a double bed in the bedroom, and the rest of the beds were converted seats in the dining room area and the lounge. Great, she thought, guess I will be sleeping with the boys.

She was right, of course, but she bagsied the bed in the lounge and told the boys they were sleeping in the dining room area. As the lounge was at the end of the boat she hoped she would get some privacy.

She was also pleased to see the boat had a little stove, and that it was lit and pumping out some heat. She was frozen. The owner had also given them a breakfast hamper, and there were maps, and a file full of useful information of places to see, how to get through locks and all sorts of things. They were scheduled to spend the week cruising to Pewsey and back, and Sarah was keen to get a look at the map to work out where all the locks were.

It was quite late by the time they had finished settling in, so the owner advised them to just go a little bit out of the boat yard and to moor up for the night. He did not recommend trying to steer at night. Sarah was grateful for his advice as the boys were now tired from all the excitement, and she thought her Dad could do with a good night's sleep. She volunteered to cook them all something from the food her mother had brought with her, just some pasta and Carbonara sauce, and by the time she had done this the boys were just about passed out.

It was at this point that the adults decided it would be better for the boys to have the bedroom, and the adults should all sleep in the communal space, so they wouldn't wake the children when they were still up in the evenings. Whilst Sarah settled the boys into their bed, George opened a bottle of red wine, and got out the Information Pack.

"It seems that the average to travel each day is about 10 miles," he said, tracing the line of the canal on the map, "If we don't reach Pewsey it doesn't matter, as long as we have a good time."

"Eye, eye Captain," chorused Maureen and Sarah together, both of them saluting him.

"Less of your cheek," said George, "or I'll make you walk the gang plank." They all laughed, and Sarah poured herself a glass of wine, and then nudged in next to her dad on the short little bench to look at the maps.

For the rest of the evening they all pored over the maps and worked out the best places to stop and visit, and the places to buy food. Soon the wine was finished, and they decided to turn in, a little earlier than Sarah normally did but she had to admit she was pooped. She slept soundly, by the noise of the water lapping against the boat, and the slight rocking motion.

They all awoke later than George had scheduled, all of them feeling restful, even the boys were calmer than they normally were in the mornings. George fretfully examined his schedule, wondering how the delay would upset his plans. Maureen gave him a coffee and put her arm around his shoulders. "Don't worry, Love," she said consolingly, "As you said last night, it doesn't matter is we don't reach Pewsey. We're here to have a relaxing holiday, not win a boat race."

"I just wanted to get the first locks out of the way before it got busy," George said, sipping his tea.

Sarah looked up from the magazine she was reading. She put it down. "If you like Dad, why don't we cast off now. I'll help you while Mum cooks breakfast and if you show me how to drive I'll take control while you eat."

George beamed thankfully, "Excellent idea," he said, "Come on."

"Granddad, Granddad, can we help?" asked the boys, also clambering to their feet.

"Of course you can," said George enthusiastically, "You two are my Best Mates." The boys beamed back proudly.

The driving and even the locks weren't as bad as any of them expected, and after a few hours they were all experts. The boys were sent to the front of the boat to act as look-outs, calling back to their Granddad any hazards they saw. Sarah and Maureen packed up a large picnic basket of food and by the time lunchtime came, George was tying them up at a lovely spot beside the canal for a picnic and a spot of running around for the boys.

It was a lovely day, and Sarah laid back on the picnic blanket, listening to the low rumble of her Mum and Dad talking, and the excited squeals of her children chasing butterflies. Within minutes she was fast asleep.

She woke to someone calling her name. For a moment she thought it was Ben, but it was her father. "Come on Sleepy Head," he was saying, "Time to cast off. Another 5 miles to do before sunset."

Sarah shook herself, trying to get rid of the groggy feeling. Why had she thought of Ben? She wondered to herself, and then she remembered she had been dreaming about him. He had been in her thoughts quite a lot, and she had been thinking about what Kate had said about him being hurt by previous relationships. She had been selfish, thinking she had been the only person ever hurt by a failed relationship.

Her Dad was calling her to untie the rope, and jump aboard, but as she did so the boat swung away from the canal side, and instantly there was a bigger gap than Sarah had judged for. She totally missed the boat as she jumped across the expanse, and fell straight into the canal, feet first.

The small crowd of other boaters cheered as she stood up. The canal wasn't deep, and she wasn't hurt, but she was wet. She looked around. Wasn't it at this point that Ben usually turned up? But he wasn't there, and she thought this was something she would have to tell him. He would laugh about it.

She clambered aboard, laughing hysterically, to find all her family rolling about in fits of the giggles. "Wait, wait," gasped her mother, "I've got to get a photo of this." Sarah stood dripping on the deck whilst her mother grabbed her phone and took the obligatory photo. She knew that would be posted on to social media as soon as they reached a Wi-Fi point.

The rest of the holiday was incident free, and Sarah marvelled that she was the only one who ended up getting wet, as she could've put bets on it that one of the boys would've ended up in the canal. The days were long and sunny, and the family pottered first up and then down the canal, calling into the sights as they went by, and stopping for lunches, picnics, and even a posh meal at a canal side gastro pub one evening. They never did make Pewsey but it didn't matter because they had a fantastic time, and returned home tanned and healthy, and certainly relaxed.

And Sarah needed to be relaxed because the job she was about to start was going to be very busy.

CHAPTER 48

Kate had decided that, as part of the new start to the new academic year, and as she was now the new Deputy Head of the school, Sarah should get fit.

"But I am fit," protested Sarah, puffing behind Kate up the steep hill in Appley Park, as they followed Wilson through the trees of the little wood.

"No you're not," said Kate, "Hark at you puffing like an old boiler. You need to get fit. It'll help you in the long run. You'll be able to cope with your new job more effectively if you're fit."

Behind her, Sarah blobbed out her tongue at her friend. "If we weren't best friends I could really hate you," she said as Kate stopped to wait for her to catch up.

"Anyway, the leisure centre need more members," explained Kate, "and every member of staff has been given the task of signing up new people, and I figured if Steve signed you up, Mo, my Mum and some of their WI friends, then he should get his bonus," she smiled sweetly at Sarah, "And you know how much we need that bonus. So if you really are my best friend you will sign up without complaining."

"If I sign up do I have to actually go?" asked Sarah hopefully.

"Of course you do," said Kate, "Anyway it's fun, and…." She nudged Sarah, "there are some hunks in that gym."

"Other than Steve I hope," said Sarah, "and ones who are single….and not Mark."

"There are loads," Kate enthused. She saw Sarah's incredulous look. "OK not loads but a few," she amended.

Sarah was still not convinced, and was doubly unsure when she arrived at the gym the next evening. She peered through the gym doors but couldn't see any men, let alone any single hunks.

"Looking for someone?" asked a voice behind her, and she turned to find a beautiful young thin slip of a thing dressed in training gear standing behind her.

"Steve Blair," she said, "I've, er, got a meeting with him."

The young girl looked her up and down. "Ah, yes Mrs Blake is it?" she asked. Sarah nodded. "Steve's running a bit late. He's asked me to start your Induction session."

Disappointment must've shown on Sarah's face because The Slip said "I know, they all want Sexy Steve to do the Induction, but I'm afraid you've got me."

"Oh no, I don't mind," Sarah said flustered. God she didn't want The Slip to think she fancied him. It was like incestuous. "He's my best mate's husband. He's like a brother, sort of," she babbled. The Slip just looked at her, waited until she finished and then opened the door to the gym for her. "This way," she said.

Inside the gym The Slip showed Sarah how to use various items of torture, demonstrating the method to elicit the most amount of pain. By the time Steve arrived to take over, Sarah thought she was dying.

Steve looked at her perspiring brow and red face and smiled slightly. "Thank you Bee," he said, nodding at The Slip, "I can take over now." Sarah was on the running machine at this point. The Slip had programmed her into a fifteen minute run, on a slight hill at a medium pace. Sarah just waved vaguely at Steve. She was concentrating hard on trying to stay alive and on the machine.

"You OK?" asked Steve. Sarah nodded. She couldn't say anything, she needed every breath she could breathe.

"Good, you're doing really well," he told her encouragingly, "Only another five minutes. I'll go and set up the rower." In her head Sarah was screaming *another five minutes? SHIIIIITTTTT!*

In the mirror in front of her she saw Steve's reflection wander over to the rowing machines on the far side of the gym. She saw him go up to a man on one of the machines and greet him, shaking his hand. Sarah looked at the reflection. Double shit. It was Ben. At that moment she had a very strange feeling that she had been set up by her friends. How long had Ben been there? Had he been watching her? She thought he had because now both men were looking over in her direction and talking. SHIT!

At that moment she lost concentration and her foot hit the edge of the machine, missing the moving conveyor belt. She lost her balance, and fell on to the moving belt, head first. Although she was wearing the dead man's rip cord, the movement of the belt sent her careering off the end of the belt, on her face and on to the floor.

She lay there, horrified at what had happened. She thought for a moment she should feign something serious, like a heart attack, or sudden coma, anything so it hadn't looked like she had missed her footing and fallen off. Slowly she moved her limbs. They seemed to be all there and in one piece.

Steve and Ben came running over. Concern on Steve's face quickly turned to a big smile as he said "Are you OK? Sorry, I can't help it." He started to laugh. Sarah stared at him, her face red with exertion and embarrassment.

Ben helped her up. "Are you OK?" he asked her seriously, giving Steve a look, "Nothing broken?"

Sarah brushed herself down. "No I think I'm OK," she said, tears in her eyes. She was mortified, and it didn't help that Steve was now holding his tummy in laughter.

"Do you always laugh when your clients fall off the machines?" she asked him tartly.

Steve calmed himself down, and put his arm around her in a brotherly hug. "Sorry Sarah," he said, "But you came off there so inelegantly, I couldn't help it." She glared at him and crossly shrugged his arm off her shoulders.

"Are you OK?" he rubbed her arm in an affectionate gesture. She picked up her towel from the floor where it had fallen, and rubbed it over her face, wiping away the tears of humiliation.

"I think I'm done here," she said, collecting her water bottle from the holder on the running machine and walking out.

Ben followed her, "Are you sure you're OK?" he asked concerned, "You did come off there at a speed."

Sarah nodded. "I think I hurt my pride more than anything else," she said giving him a small smile, "But it's not the most embarrassing thing I've done."

Ben grinned, remembering the skinny dipping. "No it isn't," he agreed.

She looked at him, and suddenly all her anger over Sadie went out of her. She smiled and Ben smiled too, and Sarah could feel the atmosphere between them lift. "I'd better go," she said, looking up at the clock on the wall, "Mum's with the boys." Ben nodded. He gently touched her arm, and disappeared back into the gym.

CHAPTER 49

It was September. The nights were drawing in now, and there was a chill in the air. Sarah was exhausted. It was Friday evening, and as usual the boys were staying at their grandparents' house overnight. Sarah was supposed to be meeting the girls in Ryde for a night out, but she didn't know if she had the energy for it. It had been a tough few weeks as she settled into her new role as Deputy Head. She was on a huge learning curve, and some days she really didn't think she was cut out for this role. As Deputy Head she didn't have her own class but filled in for other absent teachers. As well as lots of paperwork she was now covering for a teacher who had had to have an emergency appendectomy and would be out of school for at least two weeks. Sarah didn't think she could last that long.

She tidied up some papers from the coffee table and put them in a neat pile on the sideboard. She also picked up some of the toys the boys had left strewn over the floor and put them in their respective bedrooms. As she was coming out of Alfie's room into the hallway her doorbell rang.

She chuckled to herself. It must be Kate calling in to make sure she was going out. Kate sometimes did that if Sarah hadn't sounded keen on the phone about a night out.

As she walked towards the communal front door she saw the shape of a man through the stippled glass panel. She wasn't expecting anyone, so she opened the door cautiously. The light from the hallway shone on a man. Sarah peered at him. The man was medium height, honey blond hair, and well tanned. He looked vaguely familiar.

"Sarah," said the man. And then Sarah recognised him. It was Simon. Her husband. "Simon," she gasped, "What the..?" She clung on to the door, her heart beating loudly in her chest.

"Aren't you going to ask me in?" said Simon, coming up to the top step and standing in front of her. Sarah stuttered "I don't know," she finally said but didn't open the door for him to come in.

Simon tried to push the door open "Come on, let me in," he said. A door creaked below them and Simon looked down the steps to see Mrs Nosey Parker standing by her front door peering up at them. He gave a little laugh. "We don't want to be this evening's entertainment for the neighbours do we?" he asked.

Sarah thought for a minute. She was cautious. Their marriage hadn't been particularly happy, and she was wondering what he wanted. She didn't really want to let him in to her little flat. "Come on," he persuaded, and tried to walk passed her.

Conscious of Mrs Nosey below them, Sarah reluctantly opened the door wide enough to allow him in and he stood in the hallway, motioning to the open door into the flat. "Yours?" he asked. Sarah nodded.

Simon wasn't a big man but he seemed to dominate the living room. "Got a beer?" he asked plonking himself down in the middle of the settee. Sarah obliged by getting him one out of the fridge and opening it for him.

"Where's your boyfriend?" he asked her as she handed him the beer and he took a long drink. "I don't have one," Sarah said quietly.

"Sure you do," said Simon, "Don't tell me lies. How would you be able to afford this place?"

"I work," said Sarah simply. She could feel the hairs on her arms stand up, like a cat. Simon wasn't being pleasant and she was on high alert.

"So no boyfriend then?" he asked again. Sarah shook her head and perched on the edge of the other settee at right angles to him.

She took in a deep breath and found her voice. "What are you doing here?" she asked outright. Simon smiled. "Well I'm here to do us both a favour," he said. "I want a divorce."

"You didn't need to come back for that," said Sarah, "You could've just got a solicitor to write to me." He nodded. "True," he said, taking another sip of beer, "but there is a condition."

Sarah was on high alert now. "Money?" she asked.

Simon nodded. "I want what's rightfully mine," he said looking around.

"There's nothing here of yours," said Sarah, "You left me with nothing. Every thing here is what I've earned myself."

"Well I think that's where you're wrong," said Simon downing the beer and getting up from the settee to help himself to another beer from the fridge. "I didn't take everything with me when I left, and there was money in the account. I want what's mine."

She stood up and followed him into the kitchen. "You left me with an empty bank account, thousands of pounds on our joint credit card, mostly your air tickets and hotels bills for you and your strumpet in Thailand, which I had to pay off, so if there was anything of …."

Sarah didn't see the slap coming. Simon's hand hit her face hard. She could feel the sting. "Don't talk to me like that," he said.

She staggered away from him, shocked, and put her hand to her face. She could feel the heat from the slap burning her cheek. "You bastard," she said, "Is this how you get by in Thailand?"

Suddenly cautiousness was replaced by anger. "GET OUT OF HERE!" she screamed at him, "GET OUT OF MY HOUSE!"

Downstairs Doris Grange didn't need to strain her ears to know what was going on. She could hear the shouting, and now there was the sound of china smashing and furniture being moved. She was frightened. Sarah was such a lovely girl, no trouble at all. What was going on? Who was this man?

Without hesitation Doris picked up the phone and called 999.

Ben was just about to settle himself to a Big Mac he had picked up for his tea. It was quiet in the station, and as he was on evening shift, on a Friday night, he knew that he wouldn't get time for much eating later on when the drunks started being kicked out of the pubs.

Alison Harris, who was the policewoman manning reception that night, put her head around the staff room door. "Ben," she called out, "Domestic in Seaview. I think you might like to take it." Ben looked reluctantly at her, and then at his burger. "Where abouts?" he asked. "Springdale Road," said Alison.

Ben immediately jumped up and grabbed his jacket, abandoning his Big Mac. "I'm on my way," he said picking up his hat. He recognised the address.

By the time he got to the flat the commotion had stopped and it was all quiet. He knocked on the front door of Sarah's flat and Doris came to answer it. "You had better come in," she said, leading him into Sarah's flat.

Sarah was sat on the edge of the settee, her head in her hands, and she was sobbing. Ben crouched in front of her, and tried to pull her hands away from her face but she held them tightly over it. "What happened?" he asked, looking up at Doris.

"I'm not sure," said Doris, "There was a man, they started shouting, and then I could hear furniture being knocked over, plates smashed. And then he ran out, off down the road, and I came in and found Mrs Blake like this."

"What happened, Sarah?" asked Ben, trying to cuddle her from his crouched position, but she was rocking back and forth. "Do you need an ambulance?" he asked as he noticed blood seeping through her fingers.

She shook her head. "No, no," she said thickly through her hands.

"Please, let me look at you," coaxed Ben. He put his hands on her knees and she stopped rocking, then he gently pulled one hand away from her face. It was blood stained, and he could see her lip was split. "Tell me what happened," he said gently.

He turned to Doris. "Mrs Nose.. erm, sorry what's your name?"

"Doris Grange," Doris replied.

"Doris, do you think you could run out to my car and fetch the First Aid kit from under the passenger seat, please. It's unlocked. Let's get you cleaned up, my Love," he said, turning to Sarah.

Doris obliged and soon Ben could see the extent of the damage – a bruised cheek and a split lip. "Tell me what happened," he said in clipped tones. He was angry, very angry. He hated domestic abuse at any time, especially if it was physical violence by the man, but he was furious at seeing Sarah like this. He wanted to get hold of the bastard and punch his lights out.

Sarah looked at Doris, and Ben realised she didn't want to say anything in front of the village gossip, even if she had helped her. "Doris, do you think you could make us all a nice cup of tea, please? Put some sugar in Sarah's for the shock."

Doris was happy to make herself useful, and while she was busy in the kitchen, Sarah told Ben in whispered tones who the man was and what had happened.

"Was he always like this?" asked Ben, shocked. Sarah shook her head. "No he never hit me," she said, "He got aggressive sometimes, shouted, thumped furniture, but he never laid a finger on me."

"You'll press charges?" asked Ben. Sarah shook her head. "No," she said, "I've got to think of the boys."

"Why did he hit you?" asked Ben. Sarah shrugged. "I dunno," she said, "I guess he got angry because I refused to let him have an easy divorce."

She stopped talking as Doris came into the room bringing them their tea. "Thank you," said Ben, "You've been most helpful." He turned to Sarah. "Do you want me to call anyone?" he asked.

"No," said Sarah. "I think I'll go to my mum's for tonight. I don't want to stay here on my own." Ben nodded. "I think that will be best," he agreed. "Drink up your tea, and I'll give you a lift."

Doris hovered. "Would you like me to help you clear up, dear?" she asked Sarah, looking around at the broken ornaments strewn across the floor. "No, that's fine, thank you," said Sarah, "I'll come home tomorrow and do it."

She stood up. "I'll just get my things from the bedroom," she said.

Ben thanked Doris once again, and once Sarah had everything she needed and had drunk her tea, he escorted her to his car. Sarah gave Doris a hug as she locked up the flat.

"Thank you Mrs Grange. I'm sorry to have troubled you tonight."

"Oh Lovey," said Doris, "You look after yourself and don't worry. If you need any help in the morning just let me know."

Ben drove Sarah to her parents' house in Ryde. During the journey Sarah explained a bit more about the incident. "You know I haven't heard from Simon for years, since he left. So I was shocked when he turned up like that. He just waltzed in and demanded he wanted his share. HIS SHARE? I tell you, Ben, everything in that flat is mine. I worked hard for it." She could feel tears seeping out of her eyes, and she fumbled for a handkerchief from her bag. "He's not having a penny. Then he started saying if I fought him he would take the boys. He had already slapped me at that point, but I saw red. There is no way he's having the boys. I would kill him first. So he hit me again and I guess that's when he split my lip." She tried to smile ruefully but winced with the pain. "Guess he won't be getting that easy divorce now. I will fight him every inch of the way."

Ben pulled over outside Sarah's parents' house and stopped the engine. "Why now?" he asked.

"Seems like he is going to kicked out of the country as an illegal immigrant. He needs to marry his floozy, but he can't do that because he's already married," Sarah explained, "And he needs money for the wedding and the Residence visa."

She gave a little sob, and the tears flowed again. "You know, if he had got the solicitors to write to me and ask me for a divorce I'd have just gone through with it, but now I'm going to fight him. He's not getting a single penny."

Ben accompanied Sarah to the front door. Maureen opened it and stood there in shock for a few seconds. Then she said "Oh my God, what the hell has happened to you?" She pulled her daughter into the house, calling out "GEORGE, GEORGE, COME HERE!" George emerged from the kitchen, wiping his hands on a towel. He dropped the towel when he saw Sarah being brought into the house, followed by a police officer.

Maureen took Sarah into the living room and sat her down on the settee. Ben came into the room too, and stood waiting. "Well, what happened?" asked Maureen again.

"Where are the boys?" asked Sarah.

"They're upstairs in bed, asleep," said Maureen. Sarah started crying again. "Simon came to the flat," she said quietly.

"Simon?" repeated Maureen confused. "Who, you mean Simon your husband?" Sarah nodded. "Simon did this?" asked Maureen. Sarah nodded again.

"I'll bloody kill him," said George, clenching his fist. Ben put his hand out warningly. "Please don't take action into you own hands, Sir," he said, "We may be charging him with assault."

"No," said Sarah adamantly, "I'm not going to press charges."

"For heavens sake, why not?" asked Maureen, "He can't just turn up after six years and knock you about."

"He wants a divorce," said Sarah, "He says he wants his share. He says he will take the boys if I don't give him his share." Maureen made a snorting noise. "I don't think any court in the land will give him the boys after what he's done to you, so don't you worry on that respect."

George got his mobile phone out of his pocket. "What are you doing, George?" asked Maureen as George started taking photos of Sarah. "I'm taking photos," he said, "Look at what he's done. If he wants to go to court then we'll go, and we'll show them what kind of man he is."

He turned to Ben. "And Sarah will make a statement, but could it wait until the morning?" he asked him. Ben nodded. "I'll file a report when I get back to the station and I'll come back in the morning and take a statement. You should get a doctor to look at her face too. If it does go to court their evidence will help." George nodded. He understood what Ben was saying.

Ben turned to go. "I'll come back in the morning. Try and have a good night sleep," he said to Sarah, and to George he said "Don't do anything rash. I know you're angry, but it will make the situation worse." George shook his hand. "Thank you for your help," he said.

Ben drove back to the station but the whole journey he was looking for lone males walking down the road. The mood he was in it was a good job he didn't see anyone, he thought. He was likely to have knocked six bells out of any man he saw. He hated domestic violence, and the fact that it was Sarah that had been hit just made it worse. He really wanted to meet this Simon Blake on a dark night. He'd give him his share then.

CHAPTER 50

It was late at night a couple of nights later and Ben was in Ryde High Street, investigating an alarm that was continually ringing. He had managed to get hold of the owner of the shop the alarm was coming from, and together they had investigated it, but it turned out to be just an electrical fault, and now the owner had disabled it, and was locking up.

Ben looked down the road. It was quiet, nobody was around except for one man walking up the hill. Ben looked at the man, he seemed familiar, and when the man passed under a light Ben realised it was the same face as the one on the Police report he had read earlier that day – the face of Simon Blake. Ben and Paul had been running checks on Simon Blake, and had found a host of police reports citing him for assault from more than six years ago, but all of the charges had been dropped after the cases had been turned over to the MOD police, as Simon had been in the Navy at the time of the charges.

Ben quickly looked around. The owner of the shop had finished locking up and had casually waved goodbye. Ben was aware of the CCTV cameras in the street, but he knew where the blind spots were.

He casually walked up to Simon Blake. "Good evening Sir," he said, "Out late tonight aren't you?" Simon looked up into the face of PC Ben Lewis. "What's it to do with you?" he said aggressively.

"Have you been drinking?" asked Ben. "Like I said Officer," said Simon, "What's it to do with you?" He made to go around Ben, but Ben put out his arm and stopped him. "Just come over here, Sir." He said, guiding Simon over to the corner of an alleyway where he knew the cameras wouldn't see anything.

"What is this?" demanded Simon, "You can't stop me. I'm not doing anything." "No need to get agitated, Sir," said Ben, pushing him against the wall, "Just stay calm, just a couple of questions to ask you."

Simon went to push him back, and then stopped. "Hey I recognise you," he said, "I know you. You're that Ben guy who's been fucking my wife."

"No need for language like that," said Ben, pushing him back against the wall again.

Simon saw red. He pushed Ben. "You've been fucking my wife," he shouted at Ben, pushing him again, "Can't you get your own tart you have to use my wife?" Ben pushed him back. "Come on then," said Simon, coming forward and squaring up to Ben.

Ben pushed him back again. "So you ready to take a man on now are you?" he asked Simon, "Had enough beating women have you? Ready for a real man?" Simon took a swing, but before he could have another go, Ben punched him hard on the nose. There was a crack, and blood spurted out everywhere, all over Ben's hand and shirt. Simon put his hands to his face.

"YOU BASTARD!" he shouted at Ben through the blood. Ben punched him again in the stomach, and then stepped back. He quickly turned around and walked off, not looking back. He could hear Simon shouting at him. "YOU BASTARD! I'LL FUCKING HAVE YOU!"

Ben walked quickly back to the Police Station. He was aware that he was covered in blood, and that his hand was throbbing where it had hit Simon. Shit, shit, why had he done that? He thought to himself. Fucking hell, he was going to be in big trouble.

Walking into the Station the first person he encountered was his mate Paul. "Fucking hell, Ben," said Paul, "What the hell have you been doing?"

"I fucking hit that bastard Simon Blake," admitted Ben.

"You've done what?" asked Paul, not sure he had heard him right.

"God, I fucking hit him. I think I've busted his nose," Ben was trying to get the blood off of his hands. Paul looked at his shirt. "I'll get you a clean shirt, mate," he said, "Come into the locker room."

"He assaulted you, right?" asked Paul. Ben shook his head as he buttoned up the clean shirt. "No."

"What, you just went up to him and fucking lumped him one?" asked Paul.

"More or less," said Ben. "God you weren't seen were you?" asked Paul. "No," said Ben, "I made sure it was out of view."

He tucked the shirt into his trousers and winced. His hand hurt. "That's going to bruise," commented Paul, looking at it.

Ben flexed it a couple of times. "It was worth it," he said grinning at Paul. Paul grinned back and slapped his mate on the back. "Let's hope it was," he said.

CHAPTER 51

The next morning, Simon Blake came charging into the Police Station like a mini tornado. He thumped his fists on the Reception Desk and demanded to speak to the Police Superintendent, or whoever was in charge.

PC Alison Harris was manning the desk. "Calm down, Sir," she said, "and tell me what the problem is."

"I'll tell you what the problem is," shouted Simon, "See this?" He pointed to his sore and still bloodied nose, "That is the problem. One of your officers, Ben Lewis, fucking hit me and I want to make a complaint. Now run along, darling, and fetch me the fucking boss."

"Language please Sir," said Alison, pulling herself up to her full height of 5 feet 4 inches, "I can take your complaint here and it will be investigated."

"I don't want a fucking investigation," Simon thumped the desk again, "I want that bastard Ben Lewis struck off. I want to see him charged with assault. The police think they can do what they fucking well like." He thumped the desk again.

Alison remained calm. His shouting didn't scare her, but she did wish he would stop thumping the desk. She had a hangover from hell and his thumping wasn't making it any better.

"I'll just take some details from you Sir," she said, poised with her pen.

Simon was pacing the floor, clearly agitated. "Take my details, take my details, darling? GET ME THE BOSS, NOW!" he shouted into her face, "GET ME THE FUCKING BOSS!"

The door behind Reception opened and PC Paul Dorey appeared. "Everything alright, PC Davies?" he asked Alison. She nodded. "This gentleman is a little overwrought," she explained to Paul, "He alleges he has been assaulted by PC Ben Lewis."

"By PC Ben Lewis," Paul echoed. He stroked his face thoughtfully. "When did this alleged assault take place, Sir?"

"Last night," shouted Simon, "Now what are you going to fucking do about it?" he asked, leaning over the desk to Paul.

"Well we'll take your details, Sir," said Paul, "But are you sure it was PC Ben Lewis?" he asked Simon again.

"Of course I'm sure," said Simon, "He's been shagging my wife too." Paul looked at him in feigned amazement. Of course he knew who he was referring to. "And who might that be?" he asked, pretending he didn't know.

"Sarah Blake," said Simon, "I've seen him in the house with her. He's around there every fucking night." Studying the damage Ben had inflicted on Simon's face, Paul felt proud of his mate.

"PC Ben Lewis?" Paul repeated, continuing the feigned amazement, "With your wife?"

"YES WITH MY FUCKING WIFE," Simon shouted his frustration at Paul, "What's the matter with the police here. Don't you bloody well understand English?"

"Oh I understand English alright, Sir," said Paul very calmly. "It's just that I don't understand how you can be making these accusations against No Balls Ben." Alison gave a little snort of laughter and turned her back to Simon, pretending to shuffle some papers on the desk behind them.

Simon looked at Paul confused. "What? No Balls Ben? What the fuck are you going on about?" he demanded.

"Yes, he's known as No Balls Ben in the Station," Paul shook his head, "Sad case really, for an officer so young. Working in the Met when he encountered an armed robbery. He blundered right into the middle of it. They fired one shot, went right through his balls." Paul winced, "They managed to save one of the balls, but firing blanks it is." He shook his head again, "If it fires at all." He held up his little finger and crooked it. "Sad, really sad."

"WHAT THE FUCK YOU GOING ON ABOUT?" Simon shouted. Paul shook his head again. "I'm just saying, Sir, that any accusations that PC Ben Lewis is having an affair with your wife can be refuted as he can't get it up. Nope, not at all. Sad, really sad."

Behind the desk Alison shuffled papers harder. She could not turn round, as she was trying to control her laughter. Simon was clearly shocked and confused. He shook himself.

"He hit me," he said more calmly, the fight clearly gone out of him as he started to wonder if he had got the right bloke.

"Are you sure?" asked Paul again. He leaned over the desk to Simon and asked very quietly "Are you really sure, Sir? I'm asking because if you make this charge there will be an investigation, and I understand there was an incident a few nights ago at the flat of Mrs Blake, which resulted in an assault on Mrs Blake, and she suffered more than a bleeding nose."

He stopped talking and let Simon think about that for a moment. He came round to Simon's side of the Reception area and conspiringly put an arm around his shoulders. And whispered in his ear, "I'll just remind you, Sir, that PC Ben Lewis is a hero. He's just been awarded a Queen's Award for Gallantry. For saving people's lives. It'll be hard to make a charge like that stick on someone so highly thought of. It could all get very nasty, and take a long, long time, and that means you'll have to stick around for the case. And the cost. Phew, loads. It'll cost loads."

Simon went to say something but Paul held up his finger to shush him. "Long drawn out cases these accusations against Police Officers, especially heroic ones. They'll go right through your Police and MOD record going back years and years. And I know you have one. We checked it after Mrs Blake's incident. Every little misdemeanour, every little misunderstanding, every little hospital visit will be investigated. Takes ages. And who is going to believe someone with a history of assaults over someone who has been honoured by Her Majesty. Do you understand what I'm saying, Sir?" He stepped away from Simon.

Simon thought for a few minutes, clearly mulling over what Paul had said. Paul returned to the other side of the desk.

Simon backed out. "On second thoughts," he said, "I don't want to make a complaint."

Paul nodded. "Good decision Sir," he said, "These investigations can get really nasty, and if you're not sure who it was who hit you it can drag on for ages."

Simon backed towards the door, "Yeah, not sure," he echoed vaguely, and turning he opened the door and left.

Alison stood gobsmacked for a few seconds and then burst into laughter. "No Balls Ben?" she asked, shaking, "God he is so going to kill you Paul," she said.

"No he won't," said Paul confidently, "I've just saved his career."

"You think he did it then?" asked Alison amazed because Ben really wasn't like that. She thought he was one of the nicest cops she had known who never abused their position or were overly aggressive. "I know he did it," said Paul, "I was in the Station when he came back."

Alison couldn't believe it. Paul looked at her. "Fucking little scumbag deserved it," he said, "I did a search on him. He has a long record of assault but each time no charges because the MOD plod took over the case. Nasty piece. And I know he beat up Sarah Blake." He shuffled some papers too in agitation. "Ben didn't hit him hard enough. I wish I'd have been there."

CHAPTER 52

Ben knew nothing of what had happened in the Police Station until later in the day when he came on duty for his evening shift. Paul was on the opposite duty, and so was Alison and so he wasn't aware of the confrontation in the Reception.

Ben was putting on his safety vest and equipment belt ready to go out on patrol in the main street in Ryde – it was always busy on a summer's evening, when Matt stuck his head around the staff room door.

"Hang on, Ben," he said, "Chief wants to see you before you go out." Ben was surprised, but then felt foreboding. God, had the little shit complained? He hadn't heard anything when he came on duty. If he had complained the whole station would have known about it, and someone would have said something when he walked in.

He quickly walked to the Chief Superintendent's office. If he was going to be reprimanded he might as well get it over and done with. He knocked on the open door, and Chief Noel Parker called out 'Come in!"

"Ah Ben," he said pleasantly as Ben entered the room, "Sit down." Ben sat down. Although the Chief was pleasant enough Ben could sense an under current to his tone. And then the Chief smiled at him. That was not good.

"Ben, I shall get this over and done with as quick as I can," he said, "I heard a disturbing report of an incident in the night involving you and a certain gentleman in the High Street. Now, I know you've been under a lot of strain since you returned from Japan, and personally I feel you came back to work too soon. Have you received counselling yet?"

Ben shook his head. "No Sir," he said, "I haven't got around to contacting them yet. You know how it is."

"Indeed," said the Chief kindly, "And there is enough for you to do here. But it is important to get some 'me' time, so for that reason I am giving you some recuperation leave. With immediate effect. Go home and get some rest. Two weeks should do it, and hopefully you'll be feeling much better, if you get my drift."

Ben nodded, but inside he was furious. The little shit. He was effectively being suspended for two weeks while they waited to see if the scumbag pressed charges. It would be like waiting for the death sentence.

"You are a very well respected Constable," continued the Chief, "And we all recognise your bravery and unselfish heroism in being part of the Rapid Deployment Team, but go home, go away, get counselling, whatever it takes Ben. I don't know what is happening and I don't want to know, but you need to get whatever it is sorted. It would be a shame to blot your immaculate record."

Ben nodded again. "Thank you, Sir," he said quietly. He stood up and saluted and went back to the staff room to remove his uniform.

Ben was walking down the road back to his cottage, deep in thought. What was he going to do with himself for two weeks, especially wondering when and if the shit was going to hit the fan. He did think of phoning Sadie in Florida, but after their last encounter that would be plain stupid. And then he remembered that his Mum had been going on at him to finish off her bathroom refurbishment for her for ages. She had had new plumbing and a suite put in but she was waiting for Ben to tile the room for her. This was the perfect opportunity to get any jobs she wanted finished.

CHAPTER 53

A few days later Ben was walking back from his mother's, tired and covered in tile dust. He didn't notice walking past the man with the dog until the man spoke to him.

"Ben Lewis," he said, stopping and turning to Ben. Surprised, Ben looked up at the man. "Hello," he said automatically, and then realised that the man was George Dryer, Sarah's Dad.

He smiled and shook his hand, and then looked questioningly at the dog. "Hello boy," he said bending down to pat the dog, "I didn't know you had a dog."

"Oh, I don't," said George, "This is our friend's dog. We're just looking after him while they're away. He's called Wilson." Ben stroked the dog's head. "Hello Wilson," he said again.

"Do you fancy a quick beer?" asked George, motioning to the pub across the road, "I'd like to have a quick chat about a little shitbag we both know." Intrigued Ben nodded. Now he thought about it he was feeling pretty dry.

Inside the pub Ben looked after Wilson while George brought the beers over. Sitting down he said "I want to shake your hand. I saw what you did to Blake."

Ben looked at him warily. "What did I do?" he asked cautiously. George leaned forward. "I saw the damage," he said quietly. "But..." said Ben, still wary.

"Sarah doesn't know this," continued George, "But Blake came around the house. Sarah was out with her mother and the boys," George gave a chuckle, "You did a pretty good job," he said, "Busted nose, bruised ribs. You saved me a job, though I probably would have killed him."

He took a sip of beer before carrying on. "I've been keeping a look out for you, to tell you, but I haven't seen you." He looked questioningly at Ben.

Ben shook his head. "The Chief calls it Recuperation Leave, after my ops in Japan. He reckons I need a proper rest. Suspension I call it. Two weeks. I've been redecorating my Mum's flat."

George nodded, understanding the real reason for the leave. "You needn't worry," he said, "That shit's gone. For good this time."

"How do you know?" asked Ben.

"Because I paid him off," said George. Now it was Ben's turn to look at George questioningly.

"Yeah I paid him off," confirmed George, "He came round, ranting and raving like a lunatic. He claimed Sarah's boyfriend had beat him up. I laughed and said Sarah didn't have a boyfriend, but he named you. Said he'd been to the Police Station to press charges but the bloke on duty hadn't wanted to take down the details. He claimed he had threatened him. It seems our friend had a bit of a reputation in the Navy for throwing his weight around and has a record as long as your arm." Ben nodded, he knew this from the checks he and Paul had done. So it was Paul who had saved his neck. He owed him a beer.

George continued. "So we had a little chat, Blake and me. Seems that he is in a bit of trouble with some gambling chums in Thailand, friends of his potential father-in-law. Owes a fair bit. Also the Immigration Authorities are after him. He needs to marry and fast. He thought coming here he could persuade Sarah it was in her interests to pay him off, and then he'd divorce her. He had this vision of her desperate to get divorced so she could marry her boyfriend. He didn't reckon she would still be single. Then when he saw she had her own flat and a nice little job he thought he could get half of it and not only would he pay off his debts but he'd have a bit for himself too."

Ben took a gulp of beer. Well, well, well, Blake was worse than he thought. It was lucky he had left Sarah when he did. Although Sarah had struggled she had done well for herself. How different her life would have been had he hung around.

George hadn't finished. "He's gone. He won't be causing any more trouble," he said, "I paid him off and he's gone."

"How...?" Ben started to ask, and then stopped. It wasn't any of his business.

"How much?" George completed for him, "Fifteen grand. A bargain. He wanted twenty thousand but I got him down. I just mentioned Sarah's injuries and he suddenly wanted to reduce his price." He laughed at himself. "I've never bartered in my life. Didn't know I could be so good at it."

"He won't be pressing any charges. The condition was that he left right away, and that he wasn't to say anything to Sarah. I don't want her to know I paid him off."

Ben nodded. He understood. He didn't really want Sarah to know that he had lumped Simon one either. He drained the rest of the beer in his glass, and motioned to George. "Another?" he asked. George nodded, "Thanks," he said.

They spent another hour in the pub, chatting about football, Sarah, the boys, the island. When it was time to go an emotional (and quite tipsy) George shook Ben's hand and slapped him on the back. "I hope my daughter sees sense soon," he said, tears welling up, "I'd like you as a son in law." Ben shook his hand back and laughed. "I hope she does too, Sir," he said.

CHAPTER 54

Sarah stormed into the Police Station and was met by Paul Dorey just on his way out. "I want to see Ben," she demanded. Paul blocked her path. "Ben's not here," he said, shielding her from the Reception Desk, "He's on leave."

"Oh run off to Florida and her, has he, or is he snuck in the back with that police woman?" asked Sarah vehemenously. Paul turned around and caught the eye of the Sergeant behind the desk. He pointed to the Interview Room. "OK if I...?" he asked. The Sergeant nodded. Paul gently pushed Sarah into the room and closed the door behind them.

"It's no good protecting him," Sarah said angrily, raising her voice, "I know what he did, and because of him my dad has had to fork out money he can ill afford. Who did Ben think he was, thumping Simon one? Did he really think that would help?"

"Sit down," Paul ordered. Sarah hesitated, and then saw the steely look in Paul's eye, "Sit down and listen," he said. She sat.

"That guy has put his career on the line for you," he said, leaning over the desk to her, "and all you can do is be sarcastic. Your husband is a dirty little shitbag, and he deserves everything he got. He was lucky to have encountered Ben that night, because I'm sure if it had been your father, Simon Blake would have received a whole lot worse than a broken nose and some bruised ribs."

"I didn't ask him to beat up Simon," Sarah countered, "I don't know why he thought it was his fight. He's just caused more problems. My father had to pay him off. He gave him £15,000. He can't afford that money. It's his savings. Now I'm going to have to pay him back every penny. Why did Ben think it was his fight?"

Paul rubbed his hands over his face. "For God's sake woman, wake up and smell the coffee," he said despairingly, "Can't you see what's right in front of you? He's in love with you. Has been since he first clapped eyes on you on that beach."

Sarah looked at him amazed. She didn't believe Paul. "He's got a funny way of showing it," she said, "What about Sadie? I've seen the photos."

"I don't think there is anyone who hasn't seen the photos," said Paul with a hint of amusement in his voice, "But what do you think he was going to do? Become a monk on the off chance you might fancy him? Sadie's been in the shadows for a couple of years, but she used him. Turned up when she liked, crooked her little finger and he went running. But Ben's not really like that. He got fed up with it. They're over, have been for a while."

"And what about Alison Harris?" asked Sarah, "They were all over each other like a rash that night we went clubbing."

"Ah Alison," said Paul, "Ben was never into her, he's not into anyone else. Because he's only into you. Can't you see it? He loves you."

Sarah sat still for a while, her emotions in turmoil. Tears began to run down her face. What a mess. What a big ugly mess it all was. Yet again she had chosen the wrong guy. Well not so much chosen the wrong one, but had discarded the right one.

CHAPTER 55

Deidre Lewis was organising a huge party for her son. They had been up to London and Ben had received his Gallantry Medal from HRH The Prince of Wales. Deidre had been a little disappointed that old Queeny hadn't presented the medal herself, but it had been explained that nowadays the other members of the Royal Family did much more of her jobs, and it had been such a lovely day out, she couldn't complain too much.

They had both had their photograph featured in the local and national papers, stood outside Buckingham Palace, with Ben looking very distinguished in his immaculate uniform (she had spent most of the night pressing it to perfection), proudly holding aloft his medal, and he was now officially PC Ben Lewis QGM. Deidre was exceedingly proud of him, and had shed a few tears both during the ceremony, and on the way home on the train, when she had tried to explain to Ben how proud his Dad would have been. Ben hadn't said anything, he had just grabbed her hand and squeezed it tightly, himself too choked to speak.

And now she had organised a big party in the Royal British Legion, and had invited all his police colleagues, old school colleagues, his BMX biker mates and anyone else she could think of. Ben had sent an invite to George Dryer and his family, hoping that George would understand that he was hinting that he should bring Sarah and the boys too.

Alfie was excited to be going to the party. He had mentioned Ben several times over the summer, since he had seen his photo in the local paper when it had first been announced he had got his award. Alfie wanted to see 'that policeman', as he called him, and touch his medal, because he thought he might like to be a policeman when he grew up and do brave things like that policeman who had taken them bowling.

Ben was dressed in his uniform again, and was having lots of photos taken with different friends and family when Sarah and the family entered the hall. Ben was busy, and didn't notice them, so Sarah was able to spend a few minutes watching him. He looked relaxed, and was happily posing with people, flirting with Deidre's old Legion girls and listening intently to the old veterans' stories as they came up and shook his hand. A woman went up to him with a toddler in her arms. Ben gave her a peck on the cheek, and then took the toddler from her and rested the baby on his hip. He was talking to him, and the baby was laughing. Sarah's heart was doing somersaults – that powerful aphrodisiac of a handsome man in a uniform with a cute baby in his arms. She felt like going up to him and just shouting "TAKE ME NOW!" Get a grip, girl, she admonished herself. Put those hormones away. But she couldn't take her eyes off of him as she followed her father to get a drink.

Ben first noticed her as she was turning from the bar, with a drink in her hand. His face lit up in delight as he came up to her, and she got the impression that he was genuinely pleased to see her.

"Hello," he said, quite shyly. "Hello," she replied, equally shyly. George came up behind her, and shook Ben's hand. "Very well done, my Son," he said warmly, "Now the boys were wondering if you would show them your medal."

"Of course I will," said Ben, bending down to Alfie's height, and pulling a box out of his pocket. He opened it and the boys oohed with delight. Tom put his hand out to touch the medal. "NO!" said Sarah, sharply. Tom quickly pulled his hand back.

"That's OK," said Ben, pulling the medal out of it's box, "Hold your hand out, Tom," he said, placing the medal in the boy's outstretched hand.

"Wow," said Tom in awe. "Me, me," said Alfie stretching out his hand. Ben took the medal from Tom and carefully put it into Alfie's tiny hand, but supporting it for him. Sarah couldn't help noticing how natural Ben was with the boys. He would make someone a good father, she thought.

Ben was called away to talk to some other guests who had arrived, so Sarah, George and Maureen found a table to sit at, and the boys came over to announce that they had found some of their school friends to play with over in the other corner of the hall, so they went off with them. Not long after they had sat down, Deidre banged on a glass and asked for silence. The Chief Superintendent wanted to make a speech. Ben was led onto the tiny stage where bands normally played. He looked embarrassed. Noel Parker, also dressed in his full dress uniform, came up and coughed.

"PC Ben Lewis came to us from the Met Police with a very respectful record, having assisted in a number of high profile cases in London. I also knew that he was a fully trained Rapid Response Rescuer, and he had bravely volunteered to be part of the rescue mission to New Orleans after Hurricane Katrina. That was a particularly dangerous mission as not only did he have to contend with extensive flooding, structural damage, and loss of life, there were also reports of violence against rescuers, particularly those attached to the law enforcement services, but nevertheless Ben was unphased. He has undertaken several other rescue missions around the world, and in the UK, including floods, hurricanes and mostly recently the earthquake and tsunami in Japan. I mentioned the word 'volunteered' and it should be remembered that although Ben is highly trained for these missions, he has volunteered to be a rescuer. He can take himself off the list anytime he likes, but he still keeps going. And now he has been recognised by Her Majesty herself for his efforts. I am deeply honoured and proud to have an officer like Ben in our little force." He slapped Ben on the back, and shook his hand, with tears in his eyes.

Everyone clapped and some cheered. From behind, Deidre prodded her son forward. Several people called out "SPEECH! SPEECH!" Shyly Ben took out a large roll of paper from his inside pocket, and opening it up said "I wasn't prepared for his." He let the roll unravel, falling to the floor. "I've only prepared a few words," he said indicating the long roll of paper. Everyone laughed and clapped again and some cheered. He screwed up the paper, and threw it behind him. "No, seriously," he began, "I don't know what to say. It is a really big honour to have been awarded this gong. I thought the Chief was joking when he told me my nomination had been accepted. I don't do this for any reward. I do it because it's my job. But I'd like to thank my lovely Mum for her continued support, and for washing my kit out when I come back from missions." Everyone laughed again. "And also thanks to my Dad. He's been gone a couple of years and I miss him. I wish he was here now, because I know he would be saying 'Come on son, shut up, and let's eat.'" Ben looked over to his Mum, who was dabbing her eyes with a handkerchief. She nodded at him. "So come on everyone, tuck in and let's get some music on."

As he finished speaking some of Deidre's friends were uncovering a huge buffet to one side of the stage, and behind Ben a curtain was pulled back to reveal a disco.

George got up straight away. "I'll just get some food for the boys," he said, which caused Maureen and Sarah to give each other a secret smile as they both knew George was really going up for himself.

The party was in full swing now, and Sarah and Maureen had been up dancing for some time. They hadn't seen much of Ben; he had been busy talking to all his guests, and then he had disappeared to get changed into more casual clothes.

The music changed tempo, the DJ slowing it down to some smoochy songs. Ben came up to Sarah and asked her if she would like to have a shuffle around the dance floor with him. She agreed. She put her arms loosely around his neck, and he encircled her waist, equally loosely. They rocked back and forth in time to the music.

Even though there was space between their bodies, Sarah's skin burned on her hips under Ben's light touch. She could smell his slightly musky aftershave, and she had a flashback to her bed a few months ago. Her body ached to be touched by him again, and she desperately wanted him to pull her into his arms tightly. It took all her will power to remain calm, and to gently and casually rock in time to the music.

"I was wondering," he started saying, looking at her intently. Sarah held her breath in anticipation. "I was wondering if we could start again?"

"Start again?" Sarah echoed questioningly.

"Yes, you know, start again. Meet each other again," he tried to explain but the words didn't seem to want to come out in a sensible order.

Sarah laughed. "I'm not being arrested for shoplifting again," she said. Ben laughed. "Or being thrown out of the pub for projectile vomiting."

"No, no, we don't have to go back that far," Ben said. He looked at her with a cheeky glint in his eye, "Perhaps as far back as that kiss on the bench?" he suggested.

Sarah smiled, and then considered it. OH YES! Her heart and body were screaming, but her mind was resisting. Yes and look where that led to before, it was saying. He will hurt you all over again. Ben sensed her hesitation. "We'll take it slowly," he said reassuringly, "At your pace, no pressure." He searched her face, hoping for a positive answer.

Sarah looked back at his handsome features and into his lovely eyes, which were now shining with hope. "OK," she said decisively, "But I don't want intensity. I just want a light friendship, nothing heavy, just friends. OK?"

Ben looked at her with a slight smile playing in his lips. He nodded. "A light friendship," he agreed. He stopped dancing and held out his hand for her to shake it. "Let's shake on it," he said. Laughing Sarah took his hand and shook it. As she shook his hand she knew that this deal would not be in place for long. She knew she was falling in love.

CHAPTER 56

Sarah was right. Her determination just to remain in a light friendship with Ben didn't last very long. Their dates began innocently enough – Ben invited her and the boys on another bowling date, which the boys loved, and then he took them all to the cinema to watch some action hero films, which the boys also loved (although Sarah was a bit bored with all the car chases). He also took the boys to their BMX-ing event when it coincided with his day off; in fact Sarah thought he was spending more time with the boys than he was with her.

But when he kissed her, which he didn't do as frequently as she would have liked, her body yearned for more. He was playing with her, and she knew it, but she couldn't help herself.

And the boys loved him. They constantly asked when was Ben coming round? When was Ben taking them bowling, or BMX-ing? Alfie waved to police cars, thinking that every policeman was Ben.

One day Sarah said to Ben "I think you're trying to get to me through the boys. They adore you." Ben had just smiled at her, a cheeky glint in his eye.

And finally she let him back into her bed. She hadn't meant to, but her body had let her down. They had been out for a long walk with Kate and Steve and their boys, and Wilson, Kate's parents' dog who they had borrowed for the day. They had walked along one of the many trails across the island, taking in Downs, marshes, viewpoints across the island, finally reaching the beach. It had been a long walk, punctuated by a baguette lunch in a lovely café, and they had all arrived back at the Seaview flat exhausted.

After the others had left, Sarah had asked Ben if he wanted to stay for supper. She could order Chinese, and they could watch a film – all the time there was the unspoken memory of a similar evening eating Chinese and watching a film.

The boys were in bed, exhausted, not long after the Chinese had arrived. Sarah opened a bottle of wine, and curled up on the settee with Ben, watching a film of his choosing – it was a Sharpe episode, based on the books that they both had confessed to enjoy.

They didn't watch much of the episode. Within minutes their cuddling turned to kissing, and their kissing to exploring, and very soon Sarah was leading Ben into her bedroom.

When she awoke the next morning Ben was still there beside her. Well that was a relief! She lay in the insipid light from the breaking dawn, listening to his regular breathing, and cursing her wanton body. She had given in to her lust, and she felt betrayed by her own needs. But then Ben turned over, and the covers fell away revealing his taut stomach muscles, and she knew she was going to betray herself again very soon.

Ben didn't quite move in, but he stayed over the nights when he wasn't working. They slipped into an easy routine, and the boys loved having Ben around. He bought them an old Subbuteo game from a car boot sale, setting it up on Tom's bedroom floor, and then spending the afternoon showing them how to flick the little men. The boys loved it, and Sarah suspected that Ben was having the most fun.

At night Sarah lay in his arms in the middle of her bed, their limbs entwined after their love-making, and he told her that he loved her. He told her how much she meant to him, how he loved the boys and how he had always dreamed of having a family. She told him she couldn't have any more children – Alfie's pregnancy had been difficult and she had had complications, resulting in the Doctor recommending she did not attempt another pregnancy. Ben had squeezed her tightly and said he understood. It didn't matter to him. The boys were everything he could have wished for.

But Sarah couldn't tell him she loved him. She skirted around the subject whenever it came up. When he told her that he loved her she replied with "I know you do." She could see that he wanted the response back but she couldn't give it. She couldn't give him that reassurance, she couldn't commit to him. Deep down she still feared that he would leave her, walk out one day and never return, and she couldn't give her heart totally while she feared that. She knew she was being unfair and selfish but there was nothing she could do. She couldn't give Ben that commitment, and she knew she hurt him.

CHAPTER 57

It had been a lovely Christmas. Ben had been working Christmas Eve and he had spent the night at his Mum's but he had arrived before lunch on Christmas Day armed with presents. He had bought Alfie a bike – his first real bike, with stabilizers, although within hours of cycling up and down the road outside Alfie had demanded these to be taken off because he wanted to ride the bike like his brother Tom. Ben had given Tom his first real Smartphone. Sarah had admonished him for spending so much money on the boys, but Ben had just shrugged at her. He gave her a bracelet with little tiny charms. It was beautiful and she treasured it. After the present giving they had had lunch around at Maureen and George's, and had relaxed in the afternoon playing silly games. Yes, it had been one of the best Christmases.

Sarah was back at work after the Christmas holidays, and the January days stretched long and dull, with nothing to look forward to except cold, bad weather and dark days and nights. It was difficult to keep the children at school motivated and entertained during the insufferable wet playtimes and Sarah was beginning to despair that it would never stop raining.

Sarah opened the front door one evening and the boys ran into the flat, making muddy footprints across the wooden floor. Sarah tutted. "Boys take off your boots!" she commanded as they disappeared into their bedrooms. But it was too late. She now had mud to scrape off the carpet.

She went inside, dragging bags of shopping, and her school work in with her and trying to kick her shoes off at the same time. The boys were running in and out of their bedrooms, and Sarah wished she had half as much energy as they had.

She unpacked the shopping, and attempted to remove the mud from the carpet, and wiped down the hall floor, before hanging up all their wet coats in the flats' communal hallway to dry. She then started the dinner. Although she was cooking the meal now, only the boys would eat as Ben was coming home later and she would eat with him.

The food was ready and the children ate quickly. She cleared the dirty plates away and washed up. The boys always did their homework after dinner, and she found it useful to sit with them and start her own work.

She was just settling the boys down with their homework, and opening her bag to dig out her list of tasks she had to complete when there was a knock on the front door.

As Sarah got up and walked to the front door she caught sight of a police car parked outside the flat. At first she thought maybe Ben had dropped in on his way somewhere, perhaps to tell her he would be late and had forgotten his keys, but seeing two black shapes through the pimpled glass of the communal front door, she automatically slowed. A feeling of dread came over her, and it took all her effort to walk to the door and open it.

Stood on the doorstep were PC Alison Harris and PC Matt Davis. Alison's face was white as a sheet and Matt looked grave. They all stared at each other for a second, whilst Sarah's heart thudded to the base of her stomach. She felt sick. It wasn't going to be good news.

"Can we come in?" Alison asked, motioning to the open door. It had stopped raining now, but it was still windy and cold.

Sarah opened the door wider, letting the two police colleagues walk into the flat in front of her. She indicated the living room and they entered it. The boys looked up from their homework.

"Hello," Tom said, "Ben isn't here." "We know," said Alison, "We've come to see your mum."

Matt went over to the boys and peered at their books. "What are you doing there?" he asked pleasantly. "Homework," said Tom, proudly showing him his drawings. "Wow," said Matt, "You're quite an artist." Matt looked up at Alison and she nodded to him.

"Hey, Tom isn't it?" Matt asked, "Ben has told me all about a Subbuteo game he gave you? Do you want to show it to me, so your Mum and Alison can have a chat? Is it in your bedroom?"

Tom looked at his mother, suspicious. Sarah was looking as white as Alison. She tried to smile at her son, to give him reassurance, but she didn't feel it. "You show Matt the Subbuteo, Tom," she said, "And Alfie, you go too."

Once the boys had gone Sarah turned to Alison in panic. "Something's happened to Ben, hasn't it?" she said, "He's dead isn't he?"

"He's not dead," said Alison, "But he is very poorly."

Sarah caught her breath, and her eyes filled up with tears. "What happened?" she whispered.

"We had a call come in this afternoon about a farmer taking shots at ramblers on his land," Alison explained, consulting her notepad, "We've had trouble with this farmer before, threatening ramblers. He's got a bit of a screw loose, and gets himself into a drunken rage. Usually he's all mouth and no action but this afternoon he decided to take some pot shots. Ben and Paul were out in the patrol car. I don't think they were even supposed to be in the area – I'm not even sure they really were in the area – but when the call came through Ben came back and said they would respond. I think they had had dealings with him before." Alison paused, waiting for Sarah to say something. Sarah nodded and sunk down onto the settee.

Alison sat too, and continued. "We didn't hear any more for about twenty minutes, and then Paul came on the radio asking for armed response and an ambulance. He didn't sound good, and we could hear shots. We scrambled an armed team and got there as quickly as we could, but it was too late. Ben and Paul had both been shot."

Sarah cried out "NO!" Alison reached over and squeezed her hand. It was distressing her just telling the story.

"They found Paul with a wound to his head. A bullet had grazed his skin. He was in pain, and bleeding heavily but he was relatively OK. Ben on the other hand wasn't so lucky. A bullet had entered his chest. He was knocked to the floor and was bleeding heavily. Paul managed to drag him behind the police car, using it as a shield between him and the farmer. That's when he called us."

Sarah started rocking backwards and forwards in anguish. She couldn't believe what Alison was saying. She had never thought that Ben was in any danger on their little island. Nothing like this ever happened here. If they had been somewhere like London, then she might have been a bit more cautious about him being a policeman. But on the island? Never.

Alison wiped a tear from her cheek. "Ben's been rushed to hospital. He's in a critical condition."

Sarah stood up. "I have to go to him," she said automatically, and then stopped, "The children…" She thought for a moment, and then reached into her handbag for her telephone. She dialled a number. Alison watched her, waiting.

"Mum, mum oh Ben's been shot," Sarah wailed into her mobile, "I need to go to the hospital now." Alison saw Sarah nod, and switch off the phone. "I need to ask downstairs if she can have the boys until Mum gets here."

Alison stood up. "I'll go and ask her, you get yourself ready," and Alison fled outside.

Sarah went into Tom's room. Matt and the boys were playing Subbuteo. Sarah bent down and gave Alfie a cuddle. "Now boys," she said, kneeling down to Alfie's height, "I need to go to the hospital as Ben isn't feeling very well. Nanny's coming over but I have to go now, so Alison is just checking if Mrs Grange can sit with you for a while. But I need you to be very good for me."

Alfie nodded and rubbed his tired eyes. Sarah could see that he was ready for bed anyway, and wouldn't be too much trouble. But Tom was another kettle of fish. He looked at her and immediately started asking questions.

"Where's Ben? What's happened? Is he ill? When's he coming home? Why do you have to go now? I don't want Mrs Grange to look after us."

"Look lovey, I need to go and see Ben now, and you need to be a very big boy for me and look after Alfie until Nanny gets here."

Sarah saw Tom put on a mutinous face and she sighed. "I don't need this right now," she snapped at him, "I have to get my things." She got up and walked out of the room.

She heard Tom throw the Subbuteo everywhere in his tantrum, but she didn't have time to reprimand him. Alfie wailed that Tom had broken some of the pieces. Sarah ignored them and picked up her bag.

Doris Grange came into the flat. Sarah heard her stop off in Tom's room. "Goodness me my lovies," she said, "What is this noise going on?" Tom tried to slam his door shut but Doris caught it before it hit her in the face. "Now, now, Tom," she said, "I thought you were a big brave boy." Tom stuck his tongue out at her. Doris chuckled and walked away.

She went up to Sarah. "Go on my child," she said squeezing her arm, "Go and sort your man out. And send him my best regards when he wakes up."

"Thank you, I'm very grateful to you," said Sarah, and she really meant it, "But I'm sorry.." She motioned to Tom who they could hear was now throwing things around his room. Both Matt and Alfie had retreated into the living room.

"Don't you worry about him," said Doris kindly, "I can sort him out. I had boys of my own. He's just frightened, he doesn't understand what's going on. He'll be OK once you've left. Now just go, go on, you're wasting time." Sarah gave her a weak smile, kissed Alfie, grabbed her bag and went out with Alison and Matt.

They rode on blue lights to the hospital, with Matt driving as quickly as he was allowed. He pulled up right outside the hospital. "Go on you two," he said, "I'll park up and catch you up."

Alison and Sarah jumped out and ran into the hospital. Alison ran up to the Information Desk. "Up the stairs," indicated the lady on the desk without Alison having to ask.

They ran to the area the lady had indicated, and were stopped by Chief Noel Parker. He was comforting Deirdre, who was sat in a chair looking very worried. Deidre looked up, relieved to see Sarah. Sarah went up to her and hugged her.

A Doctor came out of a room. "Who are you?" he addressed Sarah. "This is Sarah," said Deidre.

"Ben will be glad you are here," said the Doctor, kindly, "He was asking for you before he went into the op."

"What's happening?" Sarah wanted to know. The Doctor motioned for Sarah to sit down beside Deidre and then he too sat down. "The bullet has gone into Ben's chest very near to his heart. He is extremely lucky that it missed the heart, but he has lost a lot of blood and it is still a bit too close for our liking. He has been in surgery, what…" he consulted his wrist watch, "two hours. I would expect him to come out soon. They are trying to remove the bullet and stem the blood. He will be unconscious for a while when he comes out, and he will be in Intensive Care."

"Will he be OK?" asked Sarah very quietly. The Doctor half shrugged. "Well we hope so. If it has only done the damage that we can see, then we would expect a good recovery, but we really need to see what the surgeon has to say."

They waited another half an hour, grouped together, not saying very much. Noel got Sarah and Deidre a cup of tea each, and Alison and Matt were sent back to the Station and told to report on news of the farmer. He had been arrested but as he had been ranting and foaming at the mouth at the time of the incident he had been referred to a Doctor. Noel suspected he had flipped and he would be Sectioned under the Mental Health Act.

Eventually the door opened and the Surgeon emerged. He was taking off his scrub clothes as he came across to them. Everyone stood up, expectantly.

"Ben is out of surgery," the Surgeon said, "And I am quietly confident that the operation has gone well. We got the bullet out, and have stemmed the blood flow. There is some damage to the heart wall on the outside, but it's not going to affect him much, and it should heal pretty quickly," he nodded, "I would say he is out of danger now."

Noel Parker breathed a huge sigh of relief. "Thank you, Doctor," he said, "We very much appreciate the work that you have done. He's one of my best officers."

Deidre smiled too. "That is such good news," she said, "When can we see him?"

"I doubt very much he will wake up before the morning," the Surgeon said, "So you can go home now." He looked kindly at Deidre, "Go home and get some rest. Come and see him in the morning."

"I'd like to stay if I may," Sarah said, "I want to be here in case he wakes up. You go home Deidre and I'll call you as soon as he wakes up, or if anything changes."

Deidre nodded. She was exhausted and she was grateful to Sarah for taking the night watch. "I'll be back first thing in the morning," she said.

"I'll give you a lift home," offered Noel Parker, helping Deidre into her coat. "That's very kind, thank you," said Deidre. She kissed Sarah on the cheek and squeezed her hand. "I'll be back in the morning," she re-iterated.

Once Deidre and Noel had left, the Doctor showed Sarah in to the Intensive Care Unit. Ben was over in a quiet corner, wires everywhere sticking in and out of him. There was a monitor next to him recording his heart rate and beeping regularly. Sarah found it a re-assuring sound. The Doctor called a nurse over and explained to her who Sarah was. The nurse smiled at Sarah kindly, and got her a chair. "It's not very comfortable, I'm afraid," she said. Sarah smiled at her. "Thank you," she replied.

The Doctor said he had to go, but he would be around later to check on Ben. Sarah sat down, and held Ben's hand. It was cold. She took it in both of her hands and tried to warm it. The nurse came back. "I'm making us a cup of tea. Would you like one?" she asked. Sarah nodded. "Thank you," she said again.

"You look done in, Love," said the kindly nurse when she brought Sarah some tea.

Sarah smiled. "I'd just got back from work," she explained, "God, I haven't even had my dinner yet! Not that I could eat anything now."

"I'll get you some toast," said the nurse, "Or I'll have a scout around for some sandwiches. If you hear any beeps or bells don't worry. He seems pretty stable now."

The nurse bustled off and Sarah looked over at Ben. He looked like he was sleeping peacefully, though his skin was ashen.

Her phone rang, and she guiltily answered it, getting up and walking out of the ward as she did so. She had seen a big sign that said NO MOBILE PHONES.

"Hello?" she asked.

"How's Ben?" asked her Mum. "He's stable," said Sarah, "He's been shot in the chest, but it missed his heart." Sarah explained what she had found out from Alison Harris and the Doctors.

"My word," said Maureen, "Sounds like he's been lucky. Are you sure you want to date a policeman?"

Sarah gave a sort of laugh. "I didn't think the island was so dangerous." She moved the phone to the other ear and walked over to the corner of the corridor, conscious that her voice sounded loud in the quiet hospital. "Anyway how are the boys?"

"Well Tom has stopped tantruming now," said Maureen, "He's broken a few of the Subbuteo pieces, and Alfie is really upset with him, but Dad is here and is reading him a story. I hope you don't mind but Doris is still here and we've opened the Christmas sherry to calm our nerves." Sarah smiled to herself. She always bought a bottle of sherry at Christmas that never got drunk, but was always referred to as the Christmas sherry. She could just imagine her mother making inroads into it now.

"No that's fine," she said, "I think I could do with a drink myself."

"Dad also ate the dinner you left." Sarah smiled again at her Dad and his stomach. "Well, he had missed his tea with us rushing over," Maureen continued, "And we didn't think you would want it whatever time you got back."

"Yes that's fine too. Thanks Mum," Sarah said. Through the ward door, Sarah saw the nurse motion to her, and raise up a plate of toast to show her. "The nurse had just brought me some toast," she said, "I'd better go."

"OK, my love, and ring us if you need anything or anything happens," said Maureen.

Back in the Unit, Sarah nibbled the toast, and drank the tea. She wasn't really hungry, and she was getting very tired. But she daren't leave Ben's side.

However, after a few of hours sitting there, in the early hours of the morning, the call of nature became too much, and she got up to go to the toilet.

As she sat in the toilets she heard an alarm go off and running feet, but she didn't think too much about it as the nurse had said not to worry about any alarms or bleeps.

However, on re-entering the Intensive Care Unit she realised that there were a lot of people gathered around Ben's bed, working on him. A nurse saw her and came over. Sarah had frozen where she was.

"Just come outside for a moment," said the nurse ushering Sarah back out of the ward. "What's going on?" asked Sarah, looking over to Ben's bed, her heart in her mouth.

"We've just got to help Ben out a bit," said the nurse, pushing her out the door, "Best if you're not there just now."

Sarah looked at her worried. "Is he going to be alright?" she asked. "We'll know more in a minute," said the nurse. Another nurse came to the door, and nodded at the first nurse. "Just sit here for a bit," she instructed Sarah, "I'll be able to tell you more in a moment."

Sarah sat down as instructed. She gazed through the small glass slits in the door, but she couldn't see Ben's bed from there. She was deeply worried. What had happened? Was Ben OK? Oh how she wished her Mum was here with her now. Tears started falling down her face. Please let him be OK, she prayed. Please don't let Ben die. She repeated the mantra over and over again with her hands clasped together.

After about ten long worrying minutes the nurse came back out to her. "He's OK. You can go in now," she said matter of factually, opening the door for Sarah.

"What happened?" asked Sarah. "Oh nothing to worry about," said the nurse calmly, "Just some pressure building up in the chest triggered an alarm, but he's OK now." She smiled as she led Sarah back to the bed, "This is why he is in Intensive Care after all."

Sarah hastily wiped her tear stained face as the nurse smoothed down Ben's bed sheets. "Talk to him," she advised, "We don't know how much he can hear while he's unconscious. Sometimes the sound of a familiar voice can help them wake up."

Ben still looked like he was sleeping peacefully. Even the intervention by the medical staff hadn't changed his tranquil expression. Sarah sat beside his bed, and held his hand again. Her heart was thumping, and she had a splitting headache. She didn't know how much more of this nightmare she could take.

Tears started to fall again down her face as she thought how near to death he could've been. She had never told him she loved him. She had never told him how much happiness he had brought into her life. Maybe she should tell him now, maybe it was time to trust someone again.

It was difficult for her to begin. She felt daft talking to an unconscious person. She started hesitantly, but when she realised no one was around to hear her she became more confident.

"You know it is hard for me to say this," she began, "because you know how much Simon hurt me. I thought he was my world, and that Alfie was made in love, but he was already knocking off his Thai slut when we conceived him. I was so hurt and humiliated. What an idiot I had been. I vowed I would never be sucked in like that again. You seemed too good to be true. I thought you were going to hurt me. I convinced myself that you were just going to use me, and throw me away like he did. "

She looked up at him. He was still peaceful. "When we first met I thought you were really annoying, always turning up like that when I was embarrassing myself. Every one kept telling me you had nice eyes, and I could see it but I stopped myself from becoming interested. I couldn't trust you. You know, I've always chosen the wrong person, and I couldn't believe that you might be the right person."

She looked at his hand and stroked it. "I love you Ben Lewis. There I said it. I love you with every being of my body. Just make the most of it, because I'm not sure I have the guts to say it when you're awake." She felt a faint squeeze of her hand, and she looked up in surprise. Ben's eyes were slightly open and he was looking at her with a bemused look on his face.

"I know you do," he croaked very quietly. Sarah froze. He was awake. "Oh my God," she said, "You're awake." Ben nodded and then winced in pain. "Don't move my love," said Sarah, "Shall I get the nurse?"

"No," croaked Ben, "Just tell me again how much you love me."

Sarah smiled and leaned over the bed to him. "So you got yourself shot deliberately to get me to say that, did you?" she asked teasingly. She was so relieved to see him awake it was as if all her prayers had been answered. She wiped his hair out of his face and then kissed him. "I love you," she whispered again.

CHAPTER 58

Deidre arrived at Ben's bedside at 6am. "I haven't slept a wink," she told Sarah, "I've been beside myself with worry but I knew that you would phone if there was anything wrong." She patted Sarah's arm. "You look done in, Love," she said, "Why don't you go home and get some rest, and I'll sit with him."

Sarah nodded. She was exhausted, and now Ben was truly sleeping and out of danger. She called her Dad and asked if he could pick her up. Of course he was happy to oblige and said he would be there in half an hour.

Whilst she waited for her father, Sarah sat with Deidre and drank the tea that the nurse brought them. The nurse said it was likely Ben would be kept in the Intensive Care for another day or so, but then he would probably be moved into the General Ward for a week or so, depending on how well he healed.

Sarah got a text from George to say that he was waiting for her outside the hospital. She said her goodbyes to Deidre and gave Ben a kiss on the forehead but he didn't wake up.

On her way out, she smiled at the policeman on duty by the Information Desk. The Chief had set up a guard just in case anything happened. The policeman smiled back, and discreetly called her over.

"Is he, Ben, is he, you know? Is he OK?" he asked. "He's out of danger," said Sarah. The policeman looked relieved. "We were worried," he said. "I know," said Sarah, "I think we all were."

The policeman nodded over to a man in an anorak with a camera around his neck. "Be careful of him," he told Sarah, "he's a journalist. There's been quite a few reporters around. This has made the BBC News." Sarah nodded back, and walked away before the journalist could spot her talking to the policeman.

The policeman wasn't wrong. Outside the hospital there were quite a few men and women sat around talking and smoking, cameras around their necks, and Sarah noticed a small film crew. Crikey, she thought. They all looked at her as she walked out of the main doors, but as she didn't look to be anyone in particular they quickly lost interest. George was waving to her, he was parked up in the car park.

"It's been on the BBC news," he said proudly as she got into the car. "Really," said Sarah, "I wouldn't have thought this wouldn't have been of any interest to anyone."

"Are you kidding?" asked George, "This is the biggest thing to have hit the island for a long time." And as they drove back to Seaview, George told Sarah the whole story that had emerged.

The farmer that had shot Ben and Paul had turned out to be a criminal from a notorious gang in the 1970's. The gang had staged a number of armed robberies across the country. The farmer had turned Queen's evidence on the rest of the gang when they had been caught. There had been extensive press coverage of the case in the 70's and to protect the farmer he had been given a new identity when he was released, and had made his home in the middle of the island in complete anonymity, burying himself in his isolated sheep farm. No one knew who he was, or of his past, not even the local police. He had married and had children, and it appeared even his wife and family hadn't known about his past, so carefully had it been hidden. Now his wife had died, and his family moved away, and the farmer's mental health had degenerated and he had become convinced his past was catching up with him. He believed that the innocent ramblers crossing his land on the public footpaths were assassins hired by other gang members, and that's why he had been trying to scare people away.

"I remember the case in the 70s," George said, "I was in my teens at the time and it seemed really exciting. The gang were all sent to prison for quite a long time I seem to recall, and then of course it all died down and everyone lost interest. I didn't know he had come to live here." George seemed quite excited by the whole incident, but all Sarah wanted to do was to forget about it, and most of all, sleep.

Back at her flat, Maureen was watching the TV News whilst getting the boys their breakfast and ready for school. The main news was about some political faux pas the Prime Minister had made on a recent foreign visit, but Ben's incident was about number four in the list and watching it whilst eating breakfast, Sarah was surprised to catch a glimpse of herself leaving the hospital behind the news reporter's back as he did a piece to camera.

Sarah was exhausted. All the stress and worry of the night before, as well as being awake for a full twenty-four hours was now taking its toll, and she was finding it difficult to stay awake as she ate her breakfast.

"Go to bed, Sweetheart," said Maureen, taking her empty plate from her, "Go and get some rest and you can visit Ben later."

"But I have to go to work," protested Sarah, trying to get up from her chair. "Don't be daft," said Maureen, "No one is expecting you to go to work today. Now go and get a few hours kip. I'll phone Beatrice Gilmour. I know what'll she'll say."

Just before he left for school, Alfie came up to give Sarah a hug and kiss. "Tom broke our Subbuteo players. Do you think Ben will mind?" he asked, his face sad. "No I think he won't mind," she reassured him, smoothing his unruly blond hair from his face.

"And Tom said Ben had a hole in his chest, and when he drinks water it will all come pouring out of the hole," he looked at her with big eyes.

"Well, technically I suppose he did have a hole," said Sarah, "but it is all gone now. The Surgeon mended it, and water won't come out of it. By the time he comes home you won't be able to see anything."

She looked over to Tom who was stood peering around the door. He was obviously feeling ashamed of his outburst the night before, but Sarah could also feel he was still in his rebellious mood. She called over to him. "Tom, come and give me a hug goodbye. I'm going to see Ben this afternoon. Do you want me to say anything from you?"

Tom shrugged and turned his back on her. George called the boys from the front door, ready to take them to school. Tom didn't say anything but walked off after his granddad. Alfie put his little arms around her neck and gave her a big cuddle. "Tell

Ben I can't wait to go to the Bowling Alley again," he said before he also followed his granddad.

CHAPTER 59

Although Maureen had left Sarah to sleep, Sarah had not slept very well. She had been haunted by weird dreams, the main one being of Ben complaining of chest pains, and pulling back his shirt to reveal a gaping hole over his heart. Sarah had screamed, and awoke with a start, sweat pouring from her. She knew that she had actually screamed out in her sleep. She lay on the bed, waiting for her heart rate to slow down. It was Tom's bloody fault, telling Alfie stories of gaping holes.

After a while she got up and made herself some coffee. She was still tired but she knew she couldn't sleep any more. She was just thinking about taking a shower to refresh herself when her mobile rang. For a moment she froze, not recognising the number and wondering if it was the hospital calling her. Had Ben deteriorated? Was she needed?

"Hello," she said cautiously on answering the call. "Mrs Blake?" asked a clipped haughty voice.

"Yes," confirmed Sarah, still cautiously.

"Mrs Blake, this is Miss Forsyth, the Deputy Head at Tom's school. I'm afraid I need you to come and collect him straight away," said the voice.

Sarah raised her eyebrows too herself. She knew from the mood he had been in over night that it wasn't going to be because Tom had given her a bunch of flowers. "May I ask why, Miss Forsyth?" asked Sarah, although she had a feeling she knew what was coming.

"He has been fighting, Mrs Blake, and we really cannot stand for that kind of behaviour," said Miss Forsyth. "But…," Sarah tried to interject with a defence, but the Deputy Head was having none of it.

"I know you are going to say he is upset with what is going on with YOUR BOYFRIEND, Mrs Blake. It is all over the news," Miss Forsyth said YOUR BOYFRIEND with as much disdain as she could muster, "But whatever is going on in his life, Tom is twelve years old, and at Big School now, and really must learn to cope with life's ups and downs."

"But …." Sarah tried again, but Miss Forsyth interrupted her. "Shall I expect you in twenty minutes?" she asked. Sarah looked at her watch. Twenty minutes? It would take that long for her to have a shower.

"It'll have to be forty-five," she told the Deputy Head, "As you will understand I have been at the hospital all night waiting to see if MY BOYFRIEND was going to live or die. I'm sure you can keep Tom out of trouble a little longer for me."

Without waiting for an answer she terminated the call. God, it doesn't rain, it pours, she thought. She quickly phoned Maureen. "I've got to go and fetch Tom from school," she explained, "He's been fighting and apparently is such a risk to the school they need me to collect him straight away."

"Do you want me or your father to fetch him? Dad could give him a bit of a man to man chat on the way back?" asked Maureen.

"No, it's OK," said Sarah, "I think I need to do this. Anyway I'm going to give Miss Forsyth a piece of my mind while I'm there.

She's picked the wrong day to be snotty with me." Sarah said goodbye and quickly showered and got herself ready.

On entering the Reception of Tom's school, Sarah was asked to wait outside Miss Forsyth's office as Miss Forsyth was having a break. A break? Bloody cheek, thought Sarah. I've had no supper, no lunch and some measly cereal for breakfast and she's sat in there munching biscuits and making me wait?

Tom was also sat outside, and on seeing his mother he looked at her terrified. Sarah smiled at him, and went and gave him a cuddle. "It's OK, Tom," she said kindly, "We all do silly things when we're upset."

"It wasn't me," said Tom, "I didn't start it, honestly Mum." He looked at her with big round eyes, pleading with her to believe him. "Nigel was really rude about Ben. He said rude names about him being a policeman. That's why I thumped him."

Secretly Sarah was rather proud of her big boy, but she didn't tell him this. Instead she said "Well, we've talked about this before, haven't we, that fighting isn't the way to settle things. And sticks and stones and all that."

"Yes but Mum he was really rude, and with Ben having been shot…" Tom continued to protest his innocence. Sarah gave him a kiss on the head. "Anyway," she said, "Let's go and sort out Miss Forsyth. I haven't got time to wait until she's finished her biscuits." And she barged through the Deputy Head's door without knocking.

"I'm sorry to barge in, Miss Forsyth, but I'm afraid I'm a little short of time," she crossed the room, and sat in a chair opposite the woman without waiting to be asked. "I have to be back for my other son and then I have to get back to the hospital for MY BOYFRIEND." She emphasised the words just as Miss Forsyth had done. "Tom has told me what happened," she continued, "I certainly don't condone his thumping someone, we have discussed his reactions to certain types of incident before, but I would like to know what punishment has been given to the boy who started this fight? Where is he now? Have his parents collected him already?" She waited for the Deputy Head to speak.

"Well…," Miss Forsyth stuttered, her biscuit midway to her mouth. She put it down. "Well, no action has been taken at the moment."

"And why not?" asked Sarah bluntly, "I'm afraid, Miss Forsyth, that I find mental bullying as serious as physical fighting, perhaps even more so. You are allowing a boy to mentally abuse my son at a time when he is most vulnerable, and when he lashes out, and as I said I don't condone his reaction, but when he does lash out you uphold him as the criminal, when in fact he is struggling mentally with a very distressing situation, a very distressing situation for even a TWELVE year old," Sarah emphasised TWELVE, reflecting Miss Forsyth's comment on Tom's age.

Tom was stood by the door, watching his mother intently. Sarah turned around, "Tom come and sit down," she motioned to the chair next to her. She continued before Miss Forsyth had time to reply. "What happened yesterday was deeply distressing for all of us, but even more so as PC Lewis is the first man we have allowed to come into our lives since my husband left us six years ago. We all care very much for him, and last night his life hung in the balance. I understand that this Nigel boy was being deeply unsympathetic about the situation and very rude about someone Tom cares about, and who is still in a critical situation. Now, I am taking Tom home, and he is not coming back for the rest of the week, and certainly not until you have confirmed to me that you have dealt with the other boy," Sarah stood up, "Come on Tom," she said.

Miss Forsyth collected herself, and also stood up. "May I remind you there are penalties for unauthorised absences from school," said Miss Forsyth frostily.

"It's not unauthorised," said Sarah, equally frostily, "I am authorising it, in respect of Tom's mental health. And if you want to take it any further I'll be more than happy to." She grabbed Tom's hand and together they marched out of the Deputy Head's Office.

In the car Sarah let out of sigh of relief. "You was brilliant," said Tom, beaming proudly, "I've never seen Miss Forsyth at a loss for words. Thanks Mum."

"Well, I know Tom, but it doesn't forgive you for hitting Nigel," said Sarah, starting the engine and driving off.

"Nigel calls her Miss Foresk..." Tom stopped, realising what he was going to say to his Mum. Sarah bit her lip so she didn't laugh. He knew what Tom was going to say. Good Old Nigel, eh, Miss Foreskin. That was funny.

"So you and Nigel are normally friends?" she asked.

"Normally but he got me on the wrong day," said Tom. Sarah smirked. "Well Miss Forsyth got me on the wrong day too."

CHAPTER 60

Tom's mood changed once he got home. Sarah made him some of his favourite hot chocolate, with marshmallows and a drizzle of chocolate powder over the top, and then they sat cuddled on the settee talking about Ben and the shooting. Tom told her how much he liked Ben, and that if he was to have a Daddy he would like Ben to be it. Sarah's heart melted as she realised how much Tom had missed having a father figure in his life. It must've been very hard for him when all the other children had their fathers at the BMX events or at school plays, and she knew that he had been bullied in the past over it. She had never mentioned his real father. The subject was closed and the boys never asked. She hadn't told them that Simon had made a fleeting appearance. The boys hadn't met him and she had passed her injuries sustained from the beating off as from falling down the steps to their flat, and the boys had accepted the story without question. But she was acutely aware that now that Tom was growing up he needed a strong father figure in his life.

Alfie came home full of beans. He had been the centre of attention after he had told everyone about Ben's shooting. Of course everyone had seen the News, and were eager to ask him questions. He said that his favourite girl in the school, Alexi Goodall, had given him her heart shaped erasure. He reached into his pocket and proudly showed it to his Mum and brother. Tom snorted dismissively, but Sarah admired it and gave him a cuddle.

Maureen and George came around after tea, and Sarah was able to get back to the hospital. In the dropping off area just outside the main entrance there was a journalist scrum, and Sarah realised they were gathered around Chief

Superintendent Noel Parker, and PC Paul Dorey. Paul looked very pale, and his head was covered in a huge bandage, but Sarah could just see a black eye forming. Sarah caught his eye, and gave a little thumbs up questioningly. Paul gave her a slow wink and a little smile to show that he was OK.

On entering the Intensive Care Unit she was surprised, and a little worried, to see Ben had gone. She spun around, and then saw a nurse coming towards her. "No need to worry," said the nurse, smiling kindly, "Given his celebrity status we've moved him to a more private room. He's just giving an interview to the local paper." She pointed out where Ben's room was. Through the glass window Sarah could see him sat up and talking to a very pretty journalist. The journalist was leaning right over the bed, her blouse stretched tightly across her ample chest. No wonder Ben was grinning from ear to ear. But he still looked very pale, and very tired.

"How has he been?" Sarah asked the nurse. "Oh he has been fine, "said the nurse, "Really good. We've not had another episode. His mother has been here most of the day, in fact she's not long since gone, and he's had a really good sleep. He's also eaten a little. I would say we are very pleased with his progress." She patted Sarah's arm. "You can stop worrying now," she said.

Sarah watched Ben through the window. He really did seem to be enjoying the attention the reporter was giving him, may be a little too much in Sarah's view.

She confidently strode into the little room, and went straight over to Ben and kissed him on the lips. "Hello," she said, "How have you been?" She turned to the startled journalist. "I'm

Sarah Blake, Ben's girlfriend," she said, leaning over the bed with her hand out stretched.

"Oh, hello," said the reporter recovering herself, "I'm Tanya Wooston, reporter from the County Press. Pleased to meet you." She shook Sarah's outstretched hand.

Sarah pulled a chair up on the opposite side of the bed to Tanya. "Don't let me stop you," she said, indicating that they should continue the interview. Tanya put her notebook away. "No I'm about finished here," she said, putting it back into her bag. She pulled out a camera. "Do you mind a few shots?" she asked Ben, "The readers like a hospital shot with tubes and things," she smiled at Ben, and he smiled back, shaking his head. "Go ahead," he said quietly.

Tanya took a few photos of Ben, but deliberately ignored Sarah, as if Sarah wanted to be in any of them any way. Then she thanked Ben and left, muttering a bye to Sarah.

Ben watched the pretty journalist leave, and Sarah watched him watch her, for the first time jealous that he should be looking at anyone else. She deliberately sat in his eye line.

"You must be exhausted," she said, "How long was that reporter here?"

"I dunno," Ben said quietly, "Not long I guess." He looked at her, smiling and grabbed her hand, "But I'm glad you're here now. I've missed you."

"I've only been gone a few hours, and you've had your Mum here," she reminded him. He looked at her blankly. "Have I?" he said, "I thought that was yesterday."

"No, yesterday you got shot," said Sarah. Ben looked confused. "I don't know what it day is," he said. Sarah sat on the bed in front of him, and pulled his sheets up over his chest. She kissed him on his nose. "Don't worry about it," she said, "You'll be back with it soon."

She sat back down on the chair and then realised that Ben had gone to sleep. His face was ashen and he looked exhausted. She tiptoed out of the room to find herself some tea.

CHAPTER 61

Luckily Ben was a fit man, so he made astonishing progress over the next few weeks. Within days he was transferred to a General Ward, and within a couple of weeks the Doctors were happy that the wound was healing, and that there were no complications from the gun shot, and he was allowed to go home. He went to stay with his Mum, at her insistence, because she said Sarah had enough to do with the boys and work, but Sarah visited on her way home from work every afternoon, and at the weekend the boys were allowed to see him for a couple of hours.

By six weeks Ben was chomping at the bit to be allowed back to work, and into Sarah's bed. He tried to persuade Sarah that the only thing that would help him now was a romp between the sheets, and it took all Sarah's will power to persuade him to wait another couple of weeks. She thought that over exertion might do some damage, or set him back, and she was worried about the red angry scar that he still had on his chest.

It was coming up to Easter again, and Sarah couldn't believe that it was only a year ago that she and Ben had had their first date. To celebrate Ben decided that they should go away together, just the two of them. He found them a delightfully romantic B&B in the Bronte village of Haworth in West Yorkshire, knowing how much Sarah had enjoyed the Bronte sisters' books.

They arrived late at night, having travelled all day with Sarah driving. She was exhausted but the little B&B, called the Old Registry having been where couples were married back in the day, was perfect. It had a log fire, still burning brightly, and each bedroom had its own character. Ben had chosen one with a four-poster bed, fireplace and ensuite, and Sarah thought it was beautiful. Despite her tiredness she was enchanted.

The owner of the hotel welcomed them, and brought them up a collection of breads, biscuits, cheeses and chutneys, apologising profusely that the kitchen was closed that night, and included in the supper was a bottle of Prosecco. Sarah didn't mind. There was nothing better than eating the spread on the New England quilt on a four-poster bed, and drinking fizzy wine with Ben.

She laid in a luxuriously hot bath with loads of bubbles and another glass of Prosecco, but by the time she got out Ben was fast asleep. She snuggled up to him, for the first time since the shooting incident breathing in his scent and falling instantly asleep.

She was woken in the night by soft gentle kisses which became more intense when Ben realised she was awake. He began to explore her body, as if he was discovering it again, and she moaned as he touched the exciting places. Their love making was intense, and they both came together, and then laid in each other's arms afterwards, and Sarah realised with a start that throughout it all not once had she thought about Ben's injury.

The breakfast taken in the small dining room was divine – home grown tomatoes, local bacon, black pudding and eggs, freshly baked bread washed down with gallons of Yorkshire tea. Sarah thought they would both go back pounds heavier.

They spent the days exploring the Yorkshire landscape, visiting all the well known places – Skipton, Ilkley Moor, the locks at Bingley, Saltaire and of course Haworth village and the Bronte's Museum. They ate a couple of times in the B&B for supper, which was heavenly food, but they also explored the local eateries, including sampling a deep fried onion in a local pub which they had never had before. Sarah tried searching the Internet to see how it was cooked.

And at night they talked and made love, lost in their own little world behind the curtains of the four-poster. They talked of their pasts, and of their future. Sarah told Ben of her marriage to Simon, how she had met him at a Nurses Ball one day, and how she had been swept off her feet by the handsome sailor. Ben told her more details of his relationships with PC Donna and her bid for promotion, and of Jennifer Pattison Smythe and how hurt he had been when she had just upped and left. He even talked of Sadie and Sarah realised how wrong she had been about Ben. She told him she was sorry for not trusting him at the time, and he kissed her and told her it didn't matter any more. Nothing mattered any more because she was with him now.

The short holiday came to an end all too quickly, but not first before they had decided a few things. Ben would move in with Sarah and the boys. Life was too short and fragile to worry about what people thought, or whether it was the right time. Ben loved the boys and would look after all of them, and that was what mattered. He would sell his cottage, or rent it out, whichever was the best for the moment, and when Sarah's divorce came through they would get married. Whenever that was.

Sarah didn't say anything to Ben but the divorce was dragging. At first she had prevaricated in signing the paperwork. It wasn't that she wanted to remain married to Simon, it was just that she was so angry with him for taking money from her father. She wanted to make him suffer, as he had made her suffer, so making him wait was her vengeance. She had received strongly worded letters from his solicitors, until in the end her own solicitor had persuaded her it was in her best interest to sign the papers.

Then Simon's solicitor had started demanding details of her income, and her investments, like she had any, and what relationship was Ben to her? She told them to mind their own business. They reminded her that Simon could apply for joint custody of the boys. Luckily her solicitor had replied to them on that one, counter reminding them of Simon's desertion and his subsequent assault on Sarah. They also refused to divulge her financial details, claiming that George's payment to Simon had been a full and final payment. It was all getting nasty, and Sarah suspected it was fuelled by the solicitors to get more money from the two of them. Eventually she took matters into her own hands and telephoned Simon in Thailand. She told him in no uncertain terms to tell his solicitors to get on with the divorce. He wasn't getting any more money, and he certainly wasn't getting the boys and surely didn't he want a quick divorce so he could sort out his immigration status? He reluctantly agreed, and Sarah finally received the paperwork for the decree nisi.

But for some reason she didn't tell Ben.

CHAPTER 62

The Honeymoon period didn't last very long. Sarah, if asked, would probably have said as long as it took for Ben to move his stuff in to what now appeared to her to be a very small flat. With herself and the two boys, Sarah had described her flat as spacious, but with another adult, and all his stuff, including surf board, bicycle, and Rapid Rescue Kit, she felt it was now very small.

He had to move some of his things to his Mum's spare room as Sarah flatly refused to have any more crammed into the flat, and she also had to ask Mrs Grange if she wouldn't mind if they used the shed in the communal back garden. Ben asked if they could use his double bed and sell hers. His was slightly bigger, and a beautifully turned Edwardian bed his mother had inherited. Sarah reluctantly agreed. She supposed she would let him have something, but his encroachment niggled her.

She nagged him: Don't put your cup on the table, use a coaster; Please hang your clothes up when you take them off; Please put your dirty clothes in the laundry bin and not leave them on the floor; Are you ever going to help out with the cooking, I've been on my feet all day; You're playing your music too loud, don't forget we have neighbours. And on it went. Sarah knew she was sounding like a nag but she couldn't help herself. How could she expect two boys to obey the rules if an adult didn't?

Ben was getting fed up with the constant barrage of instructions and moans. He felt penned in, allowed just a tiny space for his clothes and personal effects and that was it.

Even his toothbrush was fighting for space on the bathroom sink. He wished he hadn't been so keen to sell his cottage.

When they had returned from Yorkshire, Ben had put his cottage up for sale straight away and it had been immediately snapped up. He had got a good price for it, way more than he paid for it in the first place, so he didn't think he had sold it too cheap. It was a beautiful cottage, so old and of local interest. The purchaser was a local historian who had immediately fallen in love with it. The sale had gone through extraordinarily quickly.

But now Ben was having second thoughts. Maybe they had rushed into things. Perhaps they should've got to know each other a little better beforehand. It even crossed his mind that he could understand why Simon had run off. He immediately retracted that thought. That wasn't fair. Sarah just needed some time to adjust. It must be difficult for her to suddenly be sharing her life again after it being just her and the boys for so long.

Ben loved the boys, he really did. But whilst Alfie was cute and fluffy and like a little kitten, Tom was a handful. And he seemed to like nothing better than testing Ben.

Ben had been upset that Tom had broken the Subbuteo during his tantrum, but he did understand that Tom hadn't meant it. Sarah had made Tom help Ben glue the pieces back together, and for a while harmony had been restored. But one day Ben discovered that Tom had got a knife and had slashed the tyres on Ben's bicycle.

He didn't tell Sarah. He decided he would confront Tom himself. If he was to be the father figure he had to stop hiding behind Sarah's skirts, and Tom had to learn that Ben was the Boss too.

He got Tom alone that afternoon when he returned from school. Sarah was having to stay late at her school for a staff meeting, and Ben was tasked with preparing the boys' tea.

Ben waited until Alfie had gone into his room to play, and then had confronted Tom. "Know how my tyres got slashed?" he asked Tom, sitting across from him at the dining table, and looking straight at him. Tom stopped, forkful of chips poised halfway to his mouth. He looked down, and shook his head.

"Really?" asked Ben, "Because the tyres were OK this morning when I went to work at 6am, and then when I came home they were slashed."

His bicycle was temporarily parked in the communal hallway until a more permanent home was found. He knew it was Tom who had slashed his tyres because he had seen Tom playing with a Swiss Army knife in the communal hall the day before. Tom had hidden the knife as soon as he saw Ben coming.

"Where did you get the knife from?" he asked Tom. Tom slowly finished chewing his chips and swallowed. "What knife?" he asked, trying to act innocent.

"Tom, I'm a police officer," reminded Ben, "I'm trained to notice things. Yesterday I saw you with a Swiss Army knife. Where did you get it from?"

Tom shrugged, and carried on forking chips into his mouth. He looked mutinous, which was difficult to look with a mouth full of chips.

"So the evidence is that I saw you with a knife yesterday, and today my tyres are slashed. Strong evidence that it was you," Ben said. "Why?"

Tom shrugged again. "That's fine," said Ben, "For punishment you will not go BMXing for a month." He got up from the table.

Tom protested. "Hey you can't do that," he wailed, "I'm going to tell my Mum." "Tell her you slashed my tyres and have been playing with a knife?" Ben said.

"It wasn't me," said Tom. "Who was it then? The fairies?" Ben was sarcastic in his reply, "Don't kid me, I know it was you. I just don't understand why."

Tom was furious. "You can't stop me going BMXing," he yelled at Ben, "It's not up to you. You're not my Dad." He stood up suddenly, sending his chair crashing to the floor, and ran into his bedroom, slamming the door shut with as much force as he could.

That went well, Ben thought, picking up the chair and taking Tom's plate into the kitchen to wash up. He felt terrible, and Tom's remark about him not being his dad hurt deeply. He washed and tidied around, hoping that Sarah would be returning in a good mood.

But she didn't. She returned tired and fractious. Her day hadn't gone well, and seeing Ben's bike blocking the communal hallway didn't help her mood. She didn't notice the slashed tyres, only that she had to squeeze passed it.

On entering the flat she could hear Tom throwing things around in his room. Oh no, he is in a bad mood, she thought, I wonder what has upset him.

She poked his head around his door. "Hello Lovey," she said, "Everything OK?" Tom looked at her sulkily. "Ben won't let me go BMXing any more," he said angrily throwing his teddy bears off the bed.

"Why not?" asked Sarah. "I dunno," said Tom, "But I hate him. I wish he had never come to live with us."

Sarah breathed in a big breath. Obviously Tom had done something to upset Ben. She wasn't in the mood for this. There just seemed to be nothing but problems at the moment.

Ben was sitting on the settee moodily flicking through the TV channels. Sarah came in and gave him a peck on the cheek. "What's wrong with Tom?" she asked him, automatically tidying up the newspaper left on the coffee table, and taking his coffee cup out into the kitchen.

On the hob Ben had made a chilli for them, and Sarah went over to it, and stirred it, and then started putting away the draining cups and plates. Ben followed her into the kitchen.

"Did you know he's been playing with a Swiss Army knife and he slashed my bike tyres with it?" he rhetorically asked her.

Sarah turned to look at him in surprise. This was not like Tom. "No," she said automatically, "How do you know it was Tom? Where would he have got a knife from?"

"I think he may have got it from that Nigel friend of his," Ben said.

"But how do you know it was Tom who slashed the tyres?" Sarah asked suspiciously.

"Well who else could it have been?" asked Ben, "I saw Tom with the knife yesterday and he hid it from me as soon as he saw me looking."

"But that still doesn't mean he slashed your tyres," replied Sarah defensively.

"Who else did it?" asked Ben, his voice rising slightly as he was getting annoyed, "Do you think upstairs did it?"

"Well, your bike has been parked there for quite a while," said Sarah, "He might find it annoying."

"So he slashed my tyres?" asked Ben incredulously, "Do you really think a grown man would slash my tyres rather than ask me to move it?" He pushed his hand through his hair in frustration. He had thought he would get no support from Sarah. "I knew you wouldn't support me against your son," he said.

"It's not that I don't support you," said Sarah, "it's just that you are doing the typical police thing of blaming people without any real evidence. I shall deal with the knife issue but I'm sure he didn't deliberately slash your tyres, that's' not the sort of thing Tom would do."

"No, no of course not," said Ben exasperated by Sarah's reluctance to believe her son could have done such a thing. "Not precious Tom," he muttered.

"What's that supposed to mean?" asked Sarah, her voice rising.

"It means you never believe your precious boys could do anything wrong," said Ben, his voice rising too in his frustration, "Every time one of them does something wrong you defend them against me. I might as well not be in this house. It's always you and the boys."

"Well if you don't like it you know what you can do," said Sarah.

Ben walked into the hallway and grabbed his coat. "OK I will," he said as he put his coat on.

"Oh that's right," shouted Sarah, "First sign of trouble and you're off! Just like my husband, run away, give up and go! I knew it, I knew I couldn't trust you! You're just the same! Go on, go, get out of here!"

Ben stood in the living room door way and looked at Sarah in surprise at her venomous outburst. Christ where did that come from, he wondered. He motioned to the door. "I thought I'd just go down the pub for a couple of hours to get out of your way," he said quietly, "Until you've calmed down."

He looked at her sadly, "But if you want me to leave you just have to say."

Sarah looked at him. She was suddenly very tired. She didn't want to fight, but she just felt everything was getting on top of her. "No I don't want you to go," she said, exhaustion in her voice. "You go to the pub, I'll deal with Tom while you're out."

Ben nodded at her and turned and left.

Sarah opened Tom's door. He was laid on his bed reading a comic. "OK," she said in her 'don't mess with me' tone, "Suppose you explain to me what's going on."

Tom looked up, a little frightened. His mum's tone was sharp. He shrugged. "OK, just give me the knife," Sarah said, holding out her hand.

"I don't have a knife," Tom tried to defend himself. "DON'T LIE TO ME!" Sarah shouted at him, her patience just about finished. She took in a large breath and calmed herself down.

"Give me the knife and tell me what's going on," she said more calmly, sitting on the edge of Tom's bed. With tears in his eyes, Tom took the knife out from under his pillow and gave it to Sarah. It was an old rusty thing. "Nigel gave it to me," he said hesitantly, "I didn't really want it, but he found it on the road, he said, and I just took it. I don't know why." He was trying not to cry.

"And why did you slash Ben's tyres?" Sarah asked him.

Tom started crying. Sarah gathered him into her arms. Although he was twelve he was still a little confused boy. "I don't know," Tom said, "I was in the hallway and the bike was there, and I just wanted to see if the knife could cut anything, so I just tried a little bit. And then Ben saw me with the knife, and I don't know, I just cut the tyres. I'm so sorry, Mummy, I didn't mean it."

"Oh Tom, what are we going to do with you?" Sarah asked stroking his hair, "Don't you like Ben?"

Tom sobbed and nodded his head, cuddling into his Mum's embrace. "You don't like Ben?" she asked him again, misinterpreting his nod. "No, no I like Ben," said Tom through his tears, "I wish he was really our daddy."

Sarah brushed back Tom's hair. "Maybe he will be one day, but he won't want to be if you keep being naughty. That wasn't a very nice thing to do to Ben," Tom shook his head and gave a little hiccup.

"Ben is right," continued Sarah, "I don't think you deserve to go BMX-ing for a month, and I also think you need to say sorry to Ben, and I think you should contribute to the cost of the new tyres. What do you think Tom?" she asked him.

Tom nodded. "Sorry Mummy," he said.

CHAPTER 63

Sarah panicked the next morning when she woke up. She had been extremely tired, and after eating the chilli that Ben had made, or at least some of it – her appetite wasn't very good at the moment – she had given herself a relaxing bath and gone to bed, and she had fallen instantly asleep.

On waking Ben wasn't beside her, and his side of the bed was undisturbed. He hadn't come home. She knew it. She knew he would leave her as soon as they had an argument. She wanted to cry.

Instead she told herself not to be so stupid. She got up and looked in the wardrobe. His clothes were still there, except his uniform. Of course he will have gone to work already – he was on earlies.

Sarah walked into the living room, and there on the dining room table was a tatty garage forecourt bunch of flowers, with a hastily scrawled note. It read "I didn't want to wake you so I slept on the settee. I would never leave you. I love you too much xx".

Tears welled up in her eyes. Oh you daft bitch, she thought. She really had to get over this feeling that he was going to walk out on her every time they had an argument or he left the flat. She didn't know what was wrong with her.

Her mother had a good idea. "It's stress," she said, "With all that's happened in the last six or so months, you're stressed out. You need to take some time out."

Sarah laughed. "But when?" she complained, "I'm really busy at work, I've got the boys to look after, and now I've got Ben on shifts to cook and clean for. When am I ever going to get any time?"

"I don't think he expects you to cook and clean for him," said Maureen, "I've heard that he's a good cook, and he gets time in between his shifts."

"I know," agreed Sarah, "But I don't feel like I'm looking after him properly if I leave him jobs to do. It's like I'm palming off my work on to him. I don't know why but I feel guilty. This is my flat after all."

Maureen looked at her. "And that's the real problem," she said pointedly, "It's your flat. It's not Ben's."

She suddenly had an idea. "Why don't you and Kate go out at the weekend, like you used to. Go out and have a few drinks. Me and Dad will have the boys. We've not had them for the weekend for a while. We miss them. Go and just de-stress for an evening."

Sarah was about to say she couldn't because Ben would be home when her mobile phone rang. It was Ben. "I'm really sorry," he said, "I hope you don't mind, but I'll only be home later to pick some things up. Some of us are being sent over to Southampton for the weekend. They've got a huge festival on, and a big home game at the same time. I'll be back on Sunday."

"No, it's OK I understand," said Sarah.

"It is overtime," Ben continued, "I'd be daft not to take it."

"No, no I completely understand," said Sarah. She put the phone away and looked at her mother. "Looks like we're sorted," she said giving her mother a high five.

Kate was up for it too, and suggested they both booked themselves into the local Beauty Salon for a massage and pedicure. She knew that Sarah was stressed out with Ben living with her in the flat, and she had missed her best friend, who always seemed too busy now.

"You've been on your own for a long time," Kate told her, as they were laid on the benches side by side, waiting for the cucumber eye patches to have an effect. "You can't expect someone to move into your life and everything to be rosy."

Sarah thought about it, and then reluctantly agreed. "I suppose you're right," she said, "I just didn't realise what an effect he would have on our lives."

"And he must be feeling it too," said Kate, "If you look at it he has also gone from living on his own, to suddenly having a family to look after. AND he's sold his cottage and moved all his stuff into YOUR flat."

"Well, not ALL his stuff," said Sarah. Kate 'mmm'ed'. "Not ALL his stuff," she said, "he must be feeling like he is the lodger."

"Oh don't," admonished Sarah, "You make me feel awful now."

Kate smiled at Sarah. She knew that she was the only one who could say this to her best friend. Sarah smiled back acknowledging the friendship.

"I know you're right," she agreed, "God I've been such a grumpy bear since he moved in, and he's been so good."

"Why don't you move?" suggested Kate, "Find a place that's yours, both of yours. New start."

Sarah pulled a face. "I know you love your flat," continued Kate, "but it is YOUR flat. It is a lovely flat but it's served its purpose. You could get a lovely house in the village."

Sarah considered her friend's suggestion. She knew it made sense. "In fact, I might know just the place," Kate took the cucumbers from her eyes and ate them, "I went to deliver a 75th birthday cake the other day to one of those Victorian houses up the hill." Kate ran her own cake making business in Ryde which was highly successful. "The birthday girl told me she was having to sell the house as she was moving into sheltered accommodation. She wanted to sell it to a family who would love it. I think the house had been in her family for years, and it has loads of original features. I thought of you and Ben."

Sarah took a sip of the champagne they had been given, and also ate her cucumber eye patches. "OK, sounds good," she said, interested.

"Shall I give her a call and you can go round?" asked Kate. "Sounds like a plan," agreed Sarah.

EPILOGUE

Sarah was watching Ben struggling to fill up the black dustbin with ice and beers from the fridge. She paid particular attention to his backside, marvelling at how good it still looked for a forty year old.

The garden was buzzing with friends, family and neighbours, both new and old for Ben's fortieth birthday party. George had erected a couple of gazebos in case it rained, but so far the day had been sunny and hot.

Sarah had raced around to the house Kate had pointed out in Seaview, and it had been perfect. It still had some original features, such as cornicing in the hallway, the original Victorian tiled hall floor, and terracotta flooring in the kitchen. The old lady who owned the property was charming. She said her grandfather had bought the house when it was first built in the 1880s and her family had lived in it ever since, but her sons didn't want it – they had modern streamline apartments in New York and Singapore, and she had decided to sell it so she could move into sheltered accommodation, but it had to be to the right family. The lady had taken an immediate shine to Sarah and Ben and the boys, and had not only sold them the house at a very reasonable price, but had also left them some of the beautiful Victorian and Edwardian furniture that she had inherited.

Sarah loved it, and so far they had been deliriously happy, even though they had only been in the property a couple of months. Her fears of Ben leaving her receded as he ploughed more money and attention into making the house their family home.

Paul came into the kitchen. "Where's the beers, mate?" he said.

"Well if you grab hold of this they will be quicker," said Ben, indicating the other handle of the bin. Sarah watched them lug the heavy bin brimming with beers and ice out into the garden.

Ben reappeared wiping sweat from his brow, and went to open the fridge door, ready to start reloading it with more beer from the crates piled up in the corner of the hallway.

Sarah grabbed his arm, and pulled him into the hallway. "Come here for a sec," she said, "I want to give you your birthday present."

Ben put his arms around her waist and pulled her to him. He nuzzled his head into her neck and started biting her earlobes. "I thought you had given me that this morning," he whispered huskily.

She laughed and gave him a light push away. "No this is your real present. At least I hope you think it is," she said, thrusting a large envelope at him. She bit her lip and looked at him worriedly as he looked at it confused.

"What's this?" he asked. "Well open it," she said.

He ripped open the end and pulled out the papers. "Decree Absolute," he read out, "The marriage between Sarah Louisa Blake nee Dryer and Simon Robert Blake …"

"Yes, yes, I know what it says," said Sarah frustrated at his lack of excitement. It took him a minute to take in what the paper was saying.

"You're divorced?" he said looking at her, a smile appearing slowly. Sarah nodded.

"Hang on a minute," Ben said, thrusting the envelope and papers back at her. He ran up the stairs two at a time, and she could hear him rummaging around in his bedside table. He reappeared instantly with a small box.

He got down on one knee in front of her. "Sarah Louisa Blake nee Dryer," he said very solemnly, "will you marry me?" He opened the box to display a delicate white gold, diamond and ruby engagement ring.

Sarah laughed, a bit embarrassed by his display, a bit in excitement. "Oh yes please Ben," she said. Ben stood up and placed the ring on her finger. It was a perfect fit. "I had the jeweller copy one of your rings," he explained.

They kissed, long and deep, and then she broke away from him again, and gave him back the paperwork. "There's more," she said, "If you want it."

He looked at the other pieces of paper. They were adoption forms. He looked at her questioningly.

"Tom told me he wished you were his real dad," explained Sarah, "and I heard Alfie telling the other children at school that his daddy was a policeman, so I asked them how they would feel if you really were their dad, and they said they would love it."

She looked at him worriedly. "But it is your decision," she said, "I haven't promised them anything."

"But Simon?" asked Ben.

"I wrote to his solicitors asking if there would be any problem, and they confirmed that Simon wouldn't raise any objections." Sarah continued. "I also spoke to that very nice Social Worker, Yasmine something, and she said that although we have to go through the process of getting a social report done she couldn't see any problems because you have a exemplary police record, and the boys clearly love you and Simon has never been a part of their life." She smiled at him hopefully.

Ben stared at her, trying to take it all in, and then tears welled up in his eyes, and he brushed them away, feeling foolish. "Whenever I imagined myself at forty I always imagined I would have a gorgeous wife and lovely family, but as time went by I never thought it would happen."

He picked her and up twirled her around, then kissed her. "It is the best birthday present ever," he said, and kissed her deeply again.

"Hey can't you two save that for the bedroom," said a voice behind them. They laughed and turned round. It was Paul. "I'm after more Coke for the rum," he said. Ben pointed behind him to the pile of crates. "There's some in there," he said. "Hurry up, we've got an announcement to make."

He grabbed Sarah's hand and rushed out into the garden. He grabbed a glass and tinkled it. Sarah stood shyly to one side as he called for hush. She called out for the boys to come and stand by her, putting her arms around them.

"Unaccustomed as I am to public speaking," said Ben, making out to reach into his shirt breast pocket…" Everyone groaned, remembering his Gallantry Award party when he had pulled out a long piece of paper.

"No seriously this will be short as there is some serious drinking to do, but I just wanted to say that I am the happiest man today, on my fortieth birthday." Paul shouted "GET ON WITH IT!" and some of his other colleagues whistled and made cat calls.

Ben raised his hand for hush again. "I have two announcements to make," he said. He put his arm out for Sarah to join him. "Sarah received her divorce absolute, and has now agreed to marry me." Paul shouted out again "ABOUT TIME TOO!" and a few people cheered. Ben kissed Sarah, amid more whistles, and Sarah blushed.

Then he motioned for the boys to come over to him. He put an arm around each of them. "And I have received Adoption forms to make these two officially mine. Do you fancy being a Lewis?" he asked them. Alfie looked at him confused. "What does that mean?" he asked Ben seriously.

"It means, young Alfie, that if you want me to, I will be your real daddy," explained Ben. "Oh yes please," said Alfie, putting his little arms around him in a big hug. Tom beamed at him too.

Later that night, after everyone had gone home, and Ben was in the kitchen loading up the dishwasher, Sarah stood in the garden looking up at the night sky. Suddenly she saw a shooting star light up the sky and as rapidly fizzle out. She looked over to the kitchen window where she could see Ben tidying up.

And she knew, without any hesitation, that she had chosen the right man, at long last.

THE END

Printed in Poland
by Amazon Fulfillment
Poland Sp. z o.o., Wrocław